GREY AREA

WILL SELF is the author of many novels and books of non-fiction, including *How the Dead Live*, which was shortlisted for the Whitbread Novel of the Year 2002, *The Butt*, winner of the Bollinger Everyman Wodehouse Prize for Comic Fiction 2008, and, with Ralph Steadman, *Psychogeography* and *Psycho Too*. He lives in South London.

GREY AREA
AND OTHER STORIES

WILL SELF

BLOOMSBURY

LONDON · BERLIN · NEW YORK · SYDNEY

This selection first published in Great Britain 1994
This paperback edition published 2011

Copyright © 1993, 1994 by Will Self

The moral right of the author has been asserted

See Author's Note for further details on selection

Bloomsbury Publishing Plc, 50 Bedford Square, London WC1B 3DP

A CIP catalogue record for this book is available from the British Library

ISBN 9781408827994

10 9 8 7 6 5 4 3 2 1

Typeset by Hewer Text UK Ltd, Edinburgh
Printed in Great Britain by Clays Ltd, St Ives plc

www.will-self.com
www.bloomsbury.com/willself

Author's Note

I T IS A RARE thing nowadays to be commissioned to write any short fiction at all, so my thanks go to Tony Peake who asked me to write 'Incubus', for the Serpent's Tail anthology *Seduction*, and who arranged the commissioning of 'The Indian Mutiny' for the Constable anthology *Winter's Tales*. Maria Lexton commissioned 'A Short History of the English Novel' for the *Time Out Book of London Short Stories*, and subsequently also published it in *Time Out*. Bill Buford ran a much abridged version of 'Scale' in *Granta*, although the piece was originally commissioned by Martin Jaques for a limited pictorial edition. All the other stories were written with this collection in mind.

Thanks are due to Sarah Milwidski who assisted with the preparation of the manuscript at a crucial juncture, to Liz Calder, Mary Tomlinson and all at Bloomsbury; and of course to Ed Victor and Morgan Entrekin for keeping the faith.

W.W.S., Suffolk 1994

FOR MY BROTHERS, NICK AND JONATHAN

Contents

'He had no interests but interest.'

– Dr Zack Busner's epitaph

Between the Conceits

T HERE ARE ONLY eight people in London and fortunately I am one of them.

Of course, when I make that statement I don't mean to be taken literally – heaven forbid! And what would be worse still, I shouldn't want you to think that I'm a snob of any kind. To discriminate between people on the basis of birth is inimical to me, always has been. I simply couldn't engage in that sort of conceit.

I can declare with some authority that there simply isn't a snobbish bone in my entire body. If there was I would feel quite confident that the good egalitarian tissue encasing it would tense up, like the lining of a chomping mouth, and spit the slimy thing out without more ado. There you have it in a nutshell: I should sooner be filleted than have it thought by you that I wish to elevate myself in some spurious, unmerited fashion.

But all of this being noted, the fact does remain that there are only eight people in London. Eight people who count, that is. Eight people who matter. I still find it strange to say this. It is so very strange to imagine, for example, that someone like Dooley – funny that his name should occur quite so readily – counts for anything at all. Even to some long-lost great-niece, or old army mate, what could the likes of Dooley possibly represent, save for an embarrassment? Even his family – I know that he had one, at one time – must have felt that being closely related to Dooley was like being trapped next to someone on a long plane flight, and having them force a glancing acquaintance into intimacy.

Furthermore Dooley smells. Of that much I am certain. Not that I know exactly where he lives, but I have narrowed it down to a particular grid of Victorian artisans' cottages in Lower Clapton. I can picture him in one of these ticky-tacky rabbit warrens readily enough. But I don't so much see him as scent him, reclining on a broken-down day bed, with layer after layer of urine-damp underwear compressed between his jaundiced arse and the worn nap of an old army blanket. I can guess as well that, all around him, resting on tables and chairs, the tops of heaters, the mantelpiece and the floor, there will be pots of prescription drugs: sedatives, hypnotics, tran-quillisers. For Dooley is a neurotic of the old school. He wouldn't be able to survive without such gross nostrums.

Of course, the reason why I don't know exactly where Dooley lives is because I don't want to. I don't want to know the precise location of any of them. Some might say that this is because I want to hold fast to my cherished illusion. But what does this illusion amount to really? That at such-and-such a time I might choose to see myself as a little more than an equal? A third amongst eight, rather than simply as one of eight? Well, why not?

I've never ever attempted to elevate myself above Lady Bob or the Recorder, but, by the same token, I'll never concede an iota of distinction to Lechmere, Colin Purves or the Bollam sisters. They could all rot in hell before I would give any one of them the satisfaction of believing that I think them quality.

And, of course, it's the same for them. I know – it's crazy. Crazy that the Bollam sisters – these virtually psychotic twins from St Nevis who sit all day, every day, in a Streatham bedsit knitting dolls of 'the Redeemer', and who share a bizarre kind of joint mind (speaking in unison, prescience and so forth) – should despite everything feel capable of being slighted socially! As if anyone would ever invite those two to any social function whatsoever. A turkey-pluckers' whist drive is as elevated and rarefied, in respect of the Bollam sisters, as one of Lady Bob's soirées would be for Dooley.

Yet, that being noted, it is an index of just how repugnant everything Dooley does is that even these two weirdo, humanoid knitting machines are still concerned to distance themselves from him.

So it goes on. We all tiptoe around one another, dancing our little dance, the two-step of arrogance and conceit. One of us will orchestrate a calculated snub, and then the rest of us will respond. There will be a rapprochement, an olive branch offered by one or perhaps two of us. A new clique will be constructed on the basis of mutually assured destruction.

We believe in it at the time. Believe that this collusion

of interests is for ever, as thick as family blood that has coagulated over centuries. Yet invariably it will all be picked away at within days, weeks at the outside, creating a ragged, exposed patch, a new area of potential healing.

Just occasionally these manoeuvres will get something like serious. There's a particular L-shaped axis of cliquishness that is dangerous. It begins with the Bollam sisters, snags in Lechmere – the insipid, compliant dunderhead – and then . . . and then (and you really would have thought that this would immediately act as a limpet mine planted on the very hull of their social ambition) . . . the three of them start extending their feelers towards Dooley. Dooley! What a joke, what a sick bloody joke!

To think of it, the Bollam sisters' people, many thousands of them – at least 150,000 individuals would be required – approaching Dooley's people at cocktail parties, union meetings, in bars and restaurants. Then, figuratively speaking, offering up to Dooley's lot the baboon's arse of acknowledged inferiority, in some crude way that even Dooley's people can understand. 147,000 invitations here, 270,000 confidences there, a myriad fatuous compliments in the middle. It doesn't matter. Perhaps twenty or thirty thousand of Lechmere's people will be deployed as well, to write grovel letters or open doors.

It should be funny, because they haven't a hope in hell of achieving anything. The minute they start deploying their people like this they drag them down to Dooley's level, rather than yanking his sots, moochers and social-security claimants up to theirs. But what I don't find funny at all is the way that this appears to place Colin Purves and me in some sort of clubbable relation to one another. Not that I dislike Colin Purves: in his own way he has a certain – albeit narrow – sympathy. It's just that his more *rentier* character-traits make him utterly and incontrovertibly unsuitable company for someone of Lady Bob's breeding.

What little progress I have made with Lady Bob over the years would be shot to pieces if she were to suspect that Colin Purves and I were anything more than acquaintances. Not that she would do anything crass – like have her people actively cut my people. It's just that I can imagine – visualise even – the tiny individual crystals of hoar frost that would begin to coalesce around her sense of *froideur* towards me. She is that subtle and refined a person.

But if I feel genuine venom to any particular individual over the way this scenario plays itself out, it's towards Lechmere. Lechmere, who should know better. Lechmere, who should be capable of being more steadfast. Lechmere, who has pretensions towards a higher kind of refinement. What with his collection of old silverware and his hunting prints. Lechmere, leaning against his invitation-encrusted mantelpiece, hands plunged deep into his grey-flannel bags, so he can jingle with his small change of maiden aunts and titled second cousins. Lechmere, who has the faint − but for all that distinct − whiff of new money about him.

This was dumped on him by a stepfather, of all people. A stepfather who made his money in construction, of all things. Con-struc-tion! Well, my dear, the word itself has a put-together feel about it. So you see, I cannot cede anything to Lechmere in the way of handicapping, even though on the face of it he's closer to Lady Bob and the Recorder (I believe many, many of their respective people are on Christian-name terms) than I am. For the truth of the matter is that he has secrets of his own to protect.

If only Lechmere's stepdaddy could have seen the uses his money has been put to. Lechmere gave up his job at the Treasury *tout de suite*. Now he fritters his time away between the bookanistes on the Farringdon Road and those chi-chi little antique joints in Camden Passage.

Can you squeeze in a little closer towards me? That's it, lean forward, because this really is intended for your ears alone. I would only dream of vouchsafing this to someone like yourself, someone with whom I have struck up an immediate rapport, someone who's a good listener. Further, you can take it as read that for me to divulge an intimate suspicion of this order is tantamount to my assuming that a corresponding intimacy exists between the two of us . . .

Anyway, the nub of it is this: I suspect Lechmere of being a practising homosexual. You don't seem shocked. Well, of course I suppose you know nothing of all this.

But let me tell you that among the eight of us it's common knowledge that more of Lechmere's people are homosexual than anyone else's. 15,394, to be precise.

What's more, I know that he has a fair few voyeurs on his books. No, dammit. That's the core of my suspicion – Lechmere's voyeurs. When I mull it over I don't think Lechmere's homosexuals are either here or there. After all, we all have our homosexuals (I have over half a million practising and getting on for a quarter of a million latent), and bloody useful they are at times. I wouldn't want to be without mine. They give more parties than the straights, and they're excellent for close, subtle work: the spreading of malicious gossip, the Chinese whispering of slurs, and the making of just the right kind of insinuations. Spend a great deal more of their time on office politics to boot.

So you see, I've nothing against a toad in the hole – even if he's one of Lechmere's. No, no, the thing is the voyeurs. Why has Lechmere acquired so many voyeurs, so many people who like to watch? The only answer I can come up with is that at some deep and magical level of thought he feels that if he can watch us more than we watch him we won't be able to find out what he's doing with his pork sword.

Personally, I'm rather stunned that he still has the energy for it. What's more, I'm sure that it corrupts his vision as far as dictating the more subtle movements of his people are concerned. If he's bumping and boring around like that, leaning over some bloody rent boy, how can he conceivably be alive to the nuances of 2,947 unreturned phone calls? Or 45,709 bad birthday presents? Let alone 17,578,582 gestures of dismissal.

The work demands attention. Being one of the only eight people in London is like some massive game of go. No, go isn't the right analogy at all, because people – whether controlled or not – are no mere counters. Each one, after all, has his or her own potentiality. It would be worse than pointless to deploy 4,732 throat-cutting gestures, where what was required were a mere 219 diplomatic overtures by the Right People.

No, perhaps a better way of understanding it is chess. But then, chess isn't played by eight players using thirteen million pieces between them. Who could possibly quantify the permutations that such a game represents; the googolplex available moves. I've heard it said that the brains of grand masters are uncoupled from time as ordinary people understand it. That the many many thousands of calculations they make, gambits they follow through, could only take place in parallel to one another, like many little rivulets of thought running down some hillside of cogitation.

Pah! I make more such calculations in an hour than Kasparov does in a year. I stretch, then relax – and 35,665 white-collar workers leave their houses a teensy bit early for work. This means that 6,014 of them will feel dyspeptic during the journey because they've missed their second piece of toast, or bowl of Fruit 'n' Fibre. From which it follows that 2,982 of them will be testy throughout the morning; and therefore 312 of them will say the wrong thing, leading to dismissal; hence one of these 312 will lose the balance of his reason and commit an apparently random and motiveless murder on the way home.

Now, to compute this, together with all the side issues, is unbelievably difficult. For this is not merely aimed at producing the effect of one homicide, oh no. There are many different outcomes that follow on from such a scenario. It isn't so much a decision tree as a decision forest, with branches parting, and parting and parting into twigs that divide and divide and divide again, some of them only then coming to fruition.

It takes more than mere brainpower, though, to undertake such infinitely subtle and ramified calculations. It takes a kind of flair. An ability to think laterally – and then zoom around a corner; an innate tendency to perceive the tactical move that one of the other seven hasn't grasped.

A good example of this is the massive double, triple, quadruple – all the way up to nonuple – bluffs that we all engage in, particularly on bank holidays. Naturally one would always like at least some of one's people to be able to get out of town on a bank holiday, see a little green grass, frolic with a few sheep, even splash off the shingle at Brighton or Shoreham. But at the same time one knows that a bank holiday with more than an hour spent in heavy traffic is worse than no bank holiday at all, especially if we're talking of people who have children. If this is to be the case it's far better that one direct the greater part of one's people to stay at home, if only so that a minority can gain greater utility.

You can see how it all shapes up. Like poker players the eight of us assess how many the others are likely to direct out of town, and how many by car, how many by bus or train. Sometimes one of the eight of us will go so far as to keep all of his or her people at home. The entire bunch! It can have only happened once or twice. I did it about five years ago, and the glee, let me tell you, the intense thrill of *schadenfreude* when I saw everyone else's: the Bollam sisters, Dooley, Colin Purves, Lechmere . . . damn it all, even a hell of a lot of Lady Bob and the Recorder's people . . . the whole lemming-load of them trapped sweating and bored in mile after mile of tailback after tailback.

But of course mostly it isn't so straightforward. I sit there, caressing my volumes and papers and discs, trying to sense the messages in the ether, the subtle modulations of intent that might indicate how many are on the move – and where to. I think about Lady Bob. Will she send her people out of town – and if so, how many? Or will she, like the Bollam sisters who are incorrigibly nervous and stay-at-home, respond to the numerous notices of roadworks on major routes that have been coming in all week, and leave the tarmac shimmering and empty, so most of my lot can make a dash.

Alternatively Lady Bob may react like the Recorder, whose fine lawyerly mind often attracts him to the triple bluff. He almost always sends a fair bunch of his people off, on the basis that we will think that he will think that we will think that he will think that it's not worth going. While it's true that this strategy has stood him in good stead, often allowing him to get as many as 694,672 people out of the city for the day (at any rate that's what he clocked last August bank holiday), I think it's as much to do with the fact that a high percentage of the Recorder's people debouch through the east of London as any great tactical achievement on his part.

Not that I mean to be disrespectful to the Recorder – nothing is further from my mind. And why would I? After all, it is the Recorder's people who have consistently increased the amount of 'Good mornings' they've bidden to my people over the past ten years. In the early eighties only about 900,000 of his people ever said 'Good morning' to my people, but now it more or less averages at that level, representing a compound increase year-on-year of over 0.96 per cent. Far greater – it has to be said – than the increase in salutations from Lady Bob's people.

It sounds complex, doesn't it? Quite a lot to take on board. Well, that's the way I work. But the saddest thing I have to tell you is that I fear it makes hardly any difference to the outcome. Dooley isn't capable of anything like this degree of foresight and calculation and yet I have to say that all too often as many of his people make it out of the city on bank holidays as mine; as many of his people get late reservations at Quaglino's as mine; as many of his people get a seat on the tube as mine. It just isn't fair. Simply by adopting the tactic that is no tactic, a kind of brutish *force majeure*, Dooley imposes himself on our society.

He farts – and 4,209 children are beaten and buggered. He coughs – and 68,238 sufferers from emphysema get promoted to cancer. He groans, turning on his day bed – and forty-seven of his people lose control of their vehicles and drive into the vehicles of forty-seven of my people. Dooley is a kind of elemental force. His weapons are pain, suffering, loneliness, and deprivation. He sneezes – and seven junkies overdose in squats off the Caledonian Road. Not for Dooley the subtleties of the snub, the cold shoulder, the dropped gaze and the backbite. He has no need of them, because he has no ambition save to remain as he is: Lord of the Underclass.

What is it with Lady Bob? Why is it so hard for me to get into work with her? Sometimes, lying awake on stormy nights, with the street lamps outside shining through the raindrops on the window, and making a stippled pattern across the floor of my bedroom, I begin to get the fear. The fear that somehow Lady Bob has mixed me up in her mind with Dooley. That she hasn't been paying attention to the infinite deference with which I have courted her favour.

It's my turn to toss and turn, to knead the duvet with my hands, as if it were some giant wad of sweating dough. Was it the 34,571 Valentine's Day cards that I sent to several of her many divisions of secretaries and data-processing clerks? Or perhaps the 14,408 ever so slightly forward air-kisses that I bestowed upon 7,204 of her hair stylists, sales assistants and gallery girls? Maybe she felt a deep and lingering rancour when – for reasons that I am unable to divulge – I was obliged to break off 415 of the extra-marital affairs that my people were having with hers?

Who can say. But the fact remains that Lady Bob consistently invites me to fewer dinner parties than even Dooley. That smarts – that hurts. Only 210,542 invitations to meals of any sort last year – and of those a good 40,000 were children's parties. Children's parties! I ask you. Worse still, at anything up to 22 per cent of these parties my kids failed to come away with a party bag. Tears before their bedtime – and mine.

What can I do? Any overt move would be misinterpreted, of that much I am sure. I can feel in the very limits of my seething collectivity of consciousness the peculiar inlets and isolated promontories of our interaction. The eight of us – the eight that matter, that is – are like the tectonic plates that cover the earth. If one of us rubs up against any other we produce mighty forces that reverberate, affecting the other six. Given this, perhaps I would do better to concentrate my efforts on the Recorder, once more.

In the past I assiduously courted him. I would even have my people in the City deliberately form shooting syndicates to which the Recorder's people could be invited. I made sure that the Recorder's people were always asked to be the godparents of my people's children. I formed suburban philatelic societies just so as to be able to invite some of the Recorder's loners along. If one of my people was doing the Samaritans and one of the Recorder's phoned in . . . well, you can be certain that they were given an excess of sympathy, a beaming out of true caring.

It was all to no avail. It wasn't so much that it didn't work (I know the Recorder thinks well of me, viz the 'Good mornings'), it's just that he didn't reciprocate in any meaningful fashion – unless you count 34,876 items of junk mail, far more than my people have ever received from any of the other six's lot.

I don't want to have to stoop to the tactics of Lechmere and the Bollam sisters. I don't want to have to associate with that perverse crew any more than I have to. Of course, I am protected to some degree by my covert association with Colin Purves. He's a worthy sort of chap – you know the kind – not that imaginative, a plodder really. He's the only one of the eight of us who commutes. He lives down at Tunbridge Wells with his wife. (He probably refers to her as 'my lady wife' whilst propping up the saloon bar in the local pub.) He takes the eight-twenty-two to Charing Cross every morning and then crosses via the footbridge to his office on the South Bank. I believe he's responsible (if that's the right word – 'responsibility' seems slightly too grand) for the stationery purchasing of one department, of one division, of one subsidiary of a multi-national oil company.

Lucky for Purves – having a desk job. It means that like me he has an opportunity to keep close to him the London phone directories, and the computer discs that hold pirated copies of all the electoral registers for London's constituencies. Of course, neither of us has to have the physical evidence of all the people we control to hand, oh no. It's just that Purves – like myself – finds it somewhat easier to get to grips with the job if he has some kind of a record of these multiplying blips of sentience.

I like to hold the directory that contains the listing of the biggest chunk of the people I am manipulating at any given time. It gives me the feeling that I am in some sense holding them, caressing them, tweaking the strings that shift their little arms and little legs, their little mouths and little heads.

I don't get out a lot any more. Tonight is an exception. It's nice just to sit here in the snug of the pub and watch the people laughing and drinking. It amuses me to try and guess which of them belongs to whom. That horsey-looking woman, yes her, the strawberry blonde with the Hermes headscarf drinking a ginger-beer shandy. Well, you would have thought she'd have to be Lady Bob's or the Recorder's, hmm? Well, you're wrong, she belongs to the Bollam sisters. I know, I know, but you see, look at the sides of her neck, there's a certain unresolved tension there in the tendons. It's ever so subtle, but it's enough for me to be able to tell.

And the man who collects the glasses. All stooped

17

over, with his drowned-rat beard, and that absurd mulberry-coloured quilted smoking jacket, the lapels of which are encrusted with silly badges. Lechmere's. In fact, he's one of Lechmere's voyeurs. A particularly gruesome one, I should imagine. What's that? You're surprised it doesn't make me paranoid having him here in my local . . . No, no, don't be ridiculous, it matters not a jot. We comingle freely – all of us. There are some of the other's people very close to me indeed. Couldn't get any closer if they tried.

No, no, I used to work, but I gave up my job at the bookshop to look after my mother. She's almost ninety now and quite bedridden. It's a fairly quiet life that Mother and I have. There's not a lot of money, but there are a lot of bedpans to empty. An exciting interlude for the two of us is a visit from the health visitor, or an extra sausage from the meals on wheels. I suppose you could say that Mother and I are close – perhaps too close. I can sometimes guess what she's thinking just by looking at her. The other way round? No, I don't think so. How can I put it, Mother is just a trifle *déclassé*, a tiny cut below myself. And anyway – she's one of Dooley's and that really scuppers it as far as I'm concerned.

It's strange the way that we all appear to have different motivations. Dooley acting apparently out of capriciousness; the Bollam sisters out of some perverted religiosity; Lechmere trying to see everything; Purves with his desire for orderliness – directing many many thousands of his rather dull little men to wash their cars every Saturday morning, and mow their lawns every Sunday afternoon, without fail . . . As for the Recorder and Lady Bob, well I wouldn't presume, but I think I can safely say that they have everyone's best interests at heart.

And then there's me. Acting, I would say, with absolute probity. Attempting to make sure that there is a kind of organic unity in London, that people have their right position and estate. It's entirely appropriate that it should be me who fulfils this role; occupying, as I do, a sort of middle-to-upper-middle niche. I can look in both directions, up and down the social scale, and check that to the best of my abilities everybody is in his correct place.

If 212 ethnic minority local councillors throughout the capital are getting a tad stroppy, then I make it my business to ensure that they're knocked down a peg or two. What exactly? We-ell, I might have their children arrested for drugs, something like that. And if there are 709 little Sloaney women who fancy they are about to get their name in some glossy magazine, then I'm on hand to make sure the proof readers make the correct error.

It can be still more subtle than this. In one blissful twenty-four-hour period, a month or so ago, I engineered it so that 45,902 of my people found themselves dropping the wrong name. Good, eh? I am good, good at the task in hand.

It's not snobbery! I thought I told you that at the

outset. I deplore snobbery and it constitutes no part of my motivation. I simply believe that there is a natural order of people just as there is of things. A kind of periodic table on to which every element within every person can be fitted.

Anyway, it's not a responsibility that most people would be prepared to shoulder. It can be gruelling work and of course there is no reward to speak of.

Yes, sometimes I do get depressed, very low. When I'm really down it amuses me to toy with this notion: that one of the little people might discover the truth. Discover not only that their freedom is a delusion; but that, furthermore, instead of being the hapless tool of some great deity, shoved up on a towering Titian-type cloud, they are instead jerked this way and that by a pervert in Bloomsbury, or a dullard in the Shell Centre, or an old incontinent in Clapton. Ye-es, it would be droll.

I'm sorry? Yes, yes, that's right, that's what I was leading up to. When it gets too claustrophobic at home, when Mother's rasping snore gets to me, and the old-woman smell of flannel, medicaments and cabbage is making me retch, I come here and engage someone like yourself in conversation. Someone bright, enquiring and interested. And then I do tell them – tell them everything.

What's that? Yes, of course, you are perceptive; naturally I can do this with impunity, because you'll never remember anything I've told you. It will depart from your tiny mind when we part. For as I told you at the outset: there are really only eight people in London. And whereas I am fortunately one of them – you are emphatically not.

The Indian Mutiny

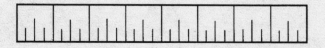

I KILLED A MAN when I was at school. I'm not just saying that, I really did. And you know the fact of it has eaten away at me for years. Even now, sitting in my office at the station, in the dead centre of a dead ordinary day, I get chilly and sweaty thinking about it.

It was a shit thing to do, a truly bad thing. When I was growing up – after it had happened – I didn't dwell on it that much. It wasn't as if I had beaten the back of his head in with a spade and watched his brains run out like grey giblets, or poisoned him so that he died kicking and thrashing, or stabbed him, shot him, or hung him ejaculating and shitting from a spindly tree.

Don't get me wrong – these aren't my imaginings. I don't visualise things like this. Like I say, when I was in my teens, my early twenties, I didn't think of it as actually murdering someone. I read my behaviour differently, innocently.

He was my history teacher, I was his pupil. He had a mental breakdown one day, actually in the class, while he was taking a lesson. He was hospitalised, but we heard that he killed himself a couple of weeks later. Killed himself by suffocation.

Years later I heard that what he had done was to shut himself in a tiny broom cupboard. He caulked up the cracks in the door. That's how he died, sitting in the close, antiseptic darkness. That's what triggered it, I suppose. Before that I might have suspected that I had more to do with his death than the other boys in 4b, but I didn't know. When I heard how he died I knew that I had killed him.

Soon after that the dreams came. The dreams where I'm looking at the blade of the spade, or fastening the elasticated belt around his thick, red neck. It's astonishing how many different ways I've murdered Mr Vello in my dreams. Murdered him and murdered him and murdered him again. I'd say that while I've slept I've probably killed Mr Vello at least two thousand times. And you wanna know the really queer thing about it? Every time I do him, I do him in a fresh way – an original way.

Some of the ways that I've dreamt I killed Mr Vello are positively baroque. Like shredding his buttocks to a pulpy mass, my weapon a common cheese grater. Or like pulling his head off. Just pulling it right off and sort of de-coring his body. Really icky stuff. I'm glad I can't express this too well in words because it's worse than any special effect you've ever seen. I don't know where the dreams come from because I don't see the world that way. I've never watched an operation, or been in an abattoir. I don't go to horror movies. I've never even seen a dead person. So I just don't know where I get all these vivid anatomical details.

Of course it's the guilt. I know that. I'm not stupid – far from it. I've got the real gift of the gab. I can talk and talk. That's what I do for a living: talk and talk. That's what the kids at school said about me, 'You can talk like a chat show host, Wayne,' that's what they said. And it was prophetic, because now I am a chat show host. I went straight from being a lairy kid to being a lairy adult. That's how I really killed Mr Vello, of course, I killed him with my big mouth. I killed him by winding him up. Winding him up so tight that he shattered. He just shattered.

Yeah, I did him all right. But I can tell you I didn't do it all by myself. I couldn't have managed it without the Indian Army. Mr Vello came to us as a supply teacher. He wasn't like the other teachers at the school. He didn't wear PVC car coats, or ratty corduroy jackets. He didn't speak with a cockney accent, or try and speak with one. He didn't read the *Guardian*, or the novels of D.H. Lawrence. Mr Vello dressed like a retired Indian Army officer. I think that's how he saw himself.

He was a solidly plump Yorkshireman in his mid-fifties. He always wore a blue blazer with brass buttons – the Yorkshire County Cricket Club badge was on the breast pocket. Mr Vello combed his hair back tight over his scalp. He had been using Brylcreem for so many years that the thin slick of his hair had become Brylcreem-coloured. Mr Vello's face was moley rather than vulpine, but when he got angry, which he did with increasing frequency, his apparently friendly, diffident wrinkles seemed to get smarmed back with his greasy hair.

With the benefit of culpable hindsight I can place myself behind Mr Vello's metal-framed spectacles and picture class 4b as it must have appeared to him when he first swung back the big wooden door and walked in on us.

Simmo was doing his drawing-pin trick. This was a bogus bit of fakirism whereby he placed three drawing pins on top of a desk and put his fat white hand over them. He then asked another boy to stamp on the back of his hand. On this occasion Simmo got it wrong – just as Mr Vello walked into the room he screamed and held up his hand. The three drawing pins were deeply embedded.

'What's all this?' said Mr Vello, setting a pile of textbooks down on the teacher's desk.

'Please, sir,' gurgled Simmo (blood was beginning to flow), 'please, sir, I've hurt my hand.'

'Nonsense, boy,' said Mr Vello, 'now sit down and shut up . . . all of you: sit down, shut up and pay attention.'

But we didn't. We never did. We just went on: flicking rubber bands; chasing one another around the desks; bashing and shouting. The majority, that is. But really there were three distinct minorities in class 4b: the Jews, the Gentiles and the Asians. 4b was a bipartisan culture, however, and power derived solely from the antagonism between the Jews and the Gentiles. We formed two gangs and called ourselves respectively The Yids and The Yocks.

The Asian boys were different. They were all first-generation immigrants, mostly East African Asians, expelled from Uganda and Kenya, but some Punjabis and Pakistanis as well. It could have been this factor alone, or perhaps it was because Asian families have a more pronounced tradition of respect for pedagogues, but none of the Asian boys was indisciplined or cheeky. On the other hand they didn't exactly stick together. They certainly didn't all sit together in the classroom. It was as if they had conspired to be unobtrusively unobtrusive. I reckon Mr Vello picked up on this immediately. Because it was the Asian boys who stopped buggering about first. They all sat down at their desks and got their books out.

Mr Vello saw the rest of us, immediately, for what we were: time-servers; time-wankers; ignorantly urbane boys – full of nasty decadences. The doomed scurf on the last polluted wave of our culture. He said as much, or rather shouted it.

'You boys are ignorant,' he shouted, 'ignorant of discipline.' He walked up and down the classroom batting the backs of heads with practised swipes of his wooden ruler. We yowled and yammered like the Yahoos we were. 'But it isn't your fault, you live in an undisciplined society and you are subjected to a banal cultural babble. You would do well to observe these Indian boys. They at least have been subjected in the more recent past to the rigours and responsibilities of imperial rule. Isn't that right, boy?' Mr Vello stopped by Jayesh Rabindirath, a thick oaf who was heavily moustachioed at fourteen.

'Err . . . yes, sir. I suppose so.'

Mr Vello tried to teach us. He tried for weeks. But he just couldn't hack it. Adolescent boys sense weakness in a teacher and go for it like piranhas sporting in offal. I think that in a quieter school, some nice prep where the kids were better behaved, Mr Vello would have been OK. But at Creighton Comprehensive he didn't have a chance.

I think he was overwhelmed by the militancy of our philistinism, the utter failure of our didactic urge. Naturally we played up to this – me in particular. It took only four maladministered lessons for the situation to deteriorate to such an extent that the poor man couldn't even talk for sixty seconds without being importuned by a battery of grubby paws, stuck out straining from the shoulder, at angles of forty-five degrees. 'Please, sir! Please, sir! Ple-ease, sir!' we all chorused, but as soon as he paid us any mind we would come up with some absurd request ('Please, sir, may I breathe?'), our subservience a grotesque parody of his assumed authority. Or if, in the course of attempting to instruct us, he managed to shout out a question, we would vie with one another to produce the most facile, the most patently weak, the most irrelevant answer.

I think I managed the worst example of this fairly early

on. Mr Vello was attempting to discourse on the Crimean War; back to the class, he mapped out the battlefield at Balaclava with a series of mauve chalk strokes. We had all fallen silent, the better to stand on our desks and wigglingly shimmy our contempt for him. Without bothering to turn he flung over his shoulder, 'Why were the Russian batteries positioned here?'

I came back triumphantly (God, have I ever been funnier?), 'Because that's where the little diagram said they should be positioned.'

We all fell about. I got eighteen consecutive detentions. God, how we (and me in particular) loved it when he got worked up. It was so comic, there was something cartoony about the colour contrast between his blue, blue blazer and his red, bursting, humiliated face. Rebellion was in the air.

It was during the lesson after that that Mr Vello first announced the establishment of the Indian Army. 'Now then, boy-yz!' He thwacked his desk with his ever-handy ruler to give his words emphasis.

'Now then, boy-yz!' we all chorused back, thwacking our desks with our rulers. Things really had got that bad. Worse still we all managed a pretty fair imitation of Mr Vello's idiosyncratic accent and enunciation. This was marked by a weird alternation in pitch between the swooping vowels of Yorkshire and the clipped consonants of received pronunciation. We were all pretty good at doing Mr Vello, but I was the best.

'Now then, boy-yz!' he came at us again. 'I have no

patience any more with your in-disci-pline. None at all. I have noticed that your Indian colleagues maintain a healthier respect for authority than the rest of you, so I am going to adopt my own Martial Races policy.'

He got all the Indian boys to stand up and then he lined them up in the aisle in order of height. Jayesh Rabindirath at the front, behind him Dhiran Vaz, behind him Krishna Patel and so on, all the way down to the minuscule Surrinyalingam (no one ever knew his first name), a tiny blackened block of a boy, who wasn't an Indian at all but a Tamil; however, Mr Vello chose to ignore this fine distinction.

'I commission all you Indian boyz into my Indian Army.' He paced the next aisle, ruler on one shoulder like an officer's swagger stick. 'It is no longer my task, but yours, to maintain ab-so-lute order amongst this miser-able, unlettered rabble – '

As he spoke my attention sideswiped out the window. A bus had pulled up and shook in mechanical ague by the concrete bus shelter. I could see fat old women coming out of the library across the road from the school and donning plastic rain hats. Life seemed to be proffer-ing a teasing and perhaps crucial juxtaposition. I raised my arm. Mr Vello whirled on me. 'Yes, Fein?'

'Please, sir – '

'Yes, boy?'

'Please, sir, I want to join the Indian Army.'

'Don't be bloody stupid, boy. Enlistment in the Indian Army is open only to boys of Indian descent. You, Fein,

32

are of Semitic descent, you are a Levantine, not an Aryan, therefore you shall not be called to the Colours.'

'Or the coloureds . . .' Simmo sniggered in the corner.

'But, sir, Mr Vello, sir,' I kept on at him, 'my dad says we're Ashkenazi Jews, not Sephardim. He says we aren't really Semites at all.'

And this was true. My father had a touch of the Mr Vellos about him as well, a fondness for the *Daily Telegraph* (ironed) and village cricket. A relentless auto-didact, he had been much taken by Arthur Koestler's theory that the Ashkenazi were in fact the descendants of the Scythian Khazars, Turkic tribesmen who had con-verted to Judaism in the seventh century. Dad discoursed on this in the garden of an evening, smoking a briar pipe (his plumed flag of utter assimilation).

'Oh, and what are you if you're not a Semite?'

'I'm an Aryan, sir. My ancestors were Turkic tribesmen. My dad told me so, he's really interested in Jewish history.'

Mr Vello was nonplussed, he left off drilling the Indian Army and took to his desk where he cradled his head in his hands. And here's one of the sickest bits of this sick, sad tale, for Mr Vello really was a conscientious and unbigoted man – he was giving this matter of my lineage real thought, heavy consideration. The class was strangely silent. At length he stirred.

'All right, Fein, I'll make an exception as far as you are concerned, and in deference to your father's scholarship. You may join the Indian Army.'

So it was that I became an Indian Army soldier. What a soldier I was: relentlessly enforcing the order I had so recently been determined to disrupt. With my fellow soldiers I patrolled the aisles of the classroom swiping hair-covered collars with my ruler, confiscating fags and sweets, strutting my skinny, flannel-legged stuff. I exulted in the power. My sharp tongue grew sharper still. And was discipline imposed? Did Mr Vello's writ run class 4b? Did it hell. For in as much as I was an Indian Army soldier I was also its principal mutineer. I was the Fletcher Christian to Mr Vello's Captain Bligh ('Why did the mutineers throw away the bread fruit plants?' 'Please, sir, please, sir,' 'Yes, Fein?' 'Because they were stale, sir!' Ha, ha, bloody ha).

Yes, it makes me sick now. Sick to think of it. Trim girlies come in and hand me things: write-ups and intelligence files on the guests I'm about to goose and humiliate, promote and patronise, fawn over and psychically fellate. That's my job. But if only I could get Mr Vello back, get him on the show. I'd recant, I'd apologise, I'd vindicate myself, and in doing so I'd make him whole again, make him live again, abolish the ghastly Vello golem that parades through my unconscious.

He got worse and worse. In one lesson he insisted on giving us a graphic description of the way he prepared his vegetable patch in the spring. In another he showed how, while on hazardous service during the latter war, he was taught to signal using a windproof lighter and a pipe. The Indian Army grew restless. It wasn't their idea, they just wanted to carry on being unobtrusively unobtrusive. After one particularly surreal lesson Dhiran Vaz and Suhail Rhamon got me in the corridor.

'You're a jerk, Fein,' said Vaz; he gripped and twisted my collar, 'the poor man's having a breakdown, he's really going nutty and you're just goading him, making it happen. D'you like watching people suffer?'

'Yeah,' Rhamon concurred, 'we've had enough of this, we're going to talk to the Headmaster – '

'Now hang on a minute, guys – guys.' I was emollient, placatory. 'I agree with you. I don't like it either, but I still think we should settle it ourselves. End the rule of the Indian Army in our own way.'

I won them round. I stopped them going to the Head. I implied that if they did the full weight of both the Yids and the Yocks would come down on them. They had no alternative.

The bubble burst the next Thursday. Mr Vello was ranting about the abandonment of the Gold Standard when I gave the signal. The soldiers of the Indian Army took up their prearranged positions: at the door, the windows, the light switches. While they flashed the lights on and off I strode to the front of the class and deprived Mr Vello of his ceremonial ruler. He blinked at me in amazement, his eyes huge and bulbous behind the concave lenses of his glasses.

'What are you doing, Fein?' I couldn't help giggling.

35

'This is it, sir,' I said. 'What we've been waiting for. It's the Indian mutiny.'

Mr Vello looked at my horrible, freckly little face. His eyes swung around the room to take in the rebellious sepoys. He sat down heavily and began to sob.

He sobbed and sobbed. His heavy shoulders heaved and shook. His wails filled the room. When Simmo opened the door to the corridor they filled the corridor as well. Eventually the Headmaster came with Mr Doherty, the gym teacher, and they led Mr Vello away, for ever.

So now you know how it was that I killed Mr Vello. Murdered him. You don't think that's enough? You think I'm being hard on myself? Children can be nasty after all – without meaning to be. But I meant to be, I really meant to be.

Last night I had one of my worst Mr Vello dreams yet. I was in Calcutta, it was 1857 – the Indian Mutiny was in full swing. Screaming fourteen-year-old sepoys broke into my villa and dragged me away. Their faces were distorted with blood lust and triumph. Dhiran Vaz hauled me along by the collar of my tunic. He and Rhamon took me and threw me in a cell, a tiny close cell, no more than twenty-feet square. And then they threw in the others, the other victims of the Mutiny: all my guests. All the guests I've ever had on *Fein Time Tonight*, one after another they came pressing into the cell, and each time one entered there was new roar of approval from the crowd of sepoy classmates massed on the dusty parade ground outside. I was pressed into the wall, tighter and tighter. My eyes filled with sweat but my throat was parched. I got a pain as sharp as a stuck bone when I tried to swallow. My thirst was oppressive, I longed for something, anything to drink.

And then Mr Vello arrived. He was in his Yorkshire County Cricket Club blazer, as ever. The chat-show guests passed him over their heads and then wedged him down beside me. He was still crying. 'Why did you do it, Fein?' he whimpered. 'Why did you do it?' And he was still whimpering when I buried my teeth into the leathery dewlap of his throat; still whimpering when I began to suck the life out of him.

A Short History
of the English Novel

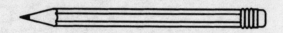

'ALL CRAP,' said Gerard through a mouthful of hamburger, 'utter shite – and the worst thing is that we're aware of it, we know what's going on. Really, I think, it's the cultural complement to the decline of the economy, in the seventies, coming lolloping along behind.'

We were sitting in Joe Allen and Gerard was holding forth on the sad state of the English novel. This was the only price I had to pay for our monthly lunch together: listening to Gerard sound off.

I came back at him. 'I'm not sure I agree with you on this one, Gerard. Isn't that a perennial gripe, something that comes up time and again? Surely we won't be able to judge the literature of this decade for another thirty or forty years?'

'You're bound to say that, being a woman.'

'I'm sorry?'

'Well, insomuch as the novel was very much a feminine form in the first place, and now that our literary culture has begun to fragment, the partisan concerns of minorities are again taking precedence. There isn't really an "English novel" now, there are just women's novels, black novels, gay novels.'

I tuned him out. He was too annoying to listen to. Round about us the lunchtime crowd was thinning. A few advertising and city types sipped their wine and Perrier, nodding over each other's shoulders at the autographed photos that studded the restaurant's walls, as if they were saluting dear old friends.

Gerard and I had been doing these monthly lunches at Joe Allen for about a year. Ours was an odd friendship. For a while he'd been married to a friend of mine but it had been a duff exercise in emotional surgery, both hearts rejecting the other. They hadn't had any children. Some of our mutual acquaintances suspected that they were gay, and that the marriage was one of convenience, a coming together to avoid coming out.

Gerard was also a plump, good-looking man; who despite his stress-filled urban existence still retained the burnish of a country childhood in the pink glow of his cheeks and the chestnut hanks of his thick fringe.

Gerard did something in publishing. That was what accounted for his willingness to pronounce on the current state of English fiction. It wasn't anything editorial or high profile. Rather, when he talked to me of his work – which he did only infrequently – it was of books as so many units, trafficked hither and thither as if they were boxes of washing powder. And when he spoke of authors, he managed somehow to reduce them to the status of assembly line workers, trampish little automata who were merely bolting the next lump of text on to an endlessly unrolling narrative product.

'. . . spry old women's sex novels, Welsh novels, the Glasgow Hard Man School, the ex-colonial guilt novel – both perpetrator and victim version . . .' He was still droning on.

'What are you driving at, Gerard?'

'Oh come on, you're not going to play devil's advocate on this one, are you? You don't believe in the centrality of the literary tradition in this country any more than I do, now do you?'

'S'pose not.'

'You probably buy two or three of the big prize-winning novels every year and then possibly, just possibly, get round to reading one of them a year or so later. As for anything else, you might skim some thrillers that have been made into TV dramas – or vice versa – or scan something issue-based, or nibble at a plot that hinges on an unusual sexual position, the blurb for which happens to have caught your eye – '

'But, Gerard' – despite myself I was rising to it – 'just because we don't read that much, aren't absorbed in it, it doesn't mean that important literary production isn't going on – '

'Not that old chestnut!' he snorted. 'I suppose you're going to tell me next that there may be thousands of unbelievably good manuscripts rotting away in attic rooms, only missing out on publication because of the diffidence of their authors or the formulaic, sales-driven narrow-mindedness of publishers, eh?'

'No, Gerard, I wasn't going to argue that – '

'It's like the old joke about LA, that there aren't any waiters in the whole town, just movie stars "resting". I suppose all these bus boys and girls' – he flicked a hand towards the epicene character who had been ministering to our meal – 'are great novelists hanging out to get more material.'

'No, that's not what I meant.'

'Excuse me?' It was the waiter, a lanky blond who had been dangling in the mid-distance. 'Did you want anything else?'

'No, no.' Gerard started shaking his head – but then broke off. 'Actually, now that you're here, would you mind if I asked you a question?'

'Oh Gerard,' I groaned, 'leave the poor boy alone.'

'No, not at all, anything to be of service.' He was bending down towards us, service inscribed all over his soft-skinned face.

'Tell me then, are you happy working here or do you harbour any other ambition?' Gerard put the question as straightforwardly as he could but his plump mouth was twisted with irony.

The waiter thought for a while. I observed his flat fingers, nails bitten to the quick, and his thin nose coped with blue veins at the nostrils' flare. His hair was tied back in a pony-tail and fastened with a thick rubber band.

'Do you mind?' he said at length, pulling half-out one of the free chairs.

'No, no,' I replied, 'of course not.' He sat down and

instantly we all became intimates, our three brows forming a tight triangle over the cruets. The waiter put up his hands vertically, holding them like parentheses into which he would insert qualifying words.

'Well,' a self-deprecatory cough, 'it's not that I mind working here – because I don't, but I write a little and I suppose I would like to be published some day.'

I wanted to hoot, to crow, to snort derision, but contented myself with a 'Ha!'.

'Now come on, wait a minute.' Gerard was adding his bracketing hands to the manual quorum. 'OK, this guy is a writer but who's to say what he's doing is good, or original?'

'Gerard! You're being rude – '

'No, really, it doesn't matter, I don't mind. He's got a point.' His secret out, the waiter was more self-possessed. 'I write – that's true. I think the ideas are good. I think the prose is good. But I can't tell if it hangs together.'

'Well, tell us a bit about it. If you can, quote some from memory.' I lit a cigarette and tilted back in my chair.

'It's complex. We know that Eric Gill was something more than an ordinary sexual experimenter. According to his own journal he even had sex with his dog. I'm writing a narrative from the point of view of Gill's dog. The book is called *Fanny Gill or I was Eric Gill's Canine Lover.*' Gerard and I were giggling before he'd finished; and the waiter smiled with us.

'That's very funny,' I said, 'I especially like the play on – '

'Fanny Hill, yeah. Well, I've tried to style it like an eighteenth-century picaresque narrative. You know, with the dog growing up in the country, being introduced to the Gill household by a canine pander. Her loss of virginity and so on.'

'Can you give us a little gobbet then?' asked Gerard. He was still smiling but no longer ironically. The waiter sat back and struck a pose. With his scraped-back hair and long face, he reminded me of some Regency actor-manager.

'Then one night, as I turned and tossed in my basket, the yeasty smell of biscuit and the matted ordure in my coat blanketing my prone form, I became aware of a draught of turpentine, mixed with the lavender of the night air.

'My master the artist and stone carver, stood over me.

' "Come Fanny," he called, slapping his square-cut hands against his smock, "there's a good little doggie." I trotted after him, out into the darkness. He strode ahead, whilst I meandered in his wake, twisting in the smelly skeins betwixt owl pellet and fox stool. "Come on now!" He was sharp and imperious. A tunnel of light opened up in the darkness. "Come in!" he snapped again, and I obeyed – poor beast – unaware that I had just taken my last stroll as an innocent bitch.'

★   ★   ★

Later, when we had paid the bill and were walking up Bow Street towards Long Acre, for no reason that I could think of I took Gerard's arm. I'd never touched him before. His body was surprisingly firm, but tinged with dampness like a thick carpet in an old house. I said, trying to purge the triumph from my tone, 'That was really rather good – now wasn't it?'

'Humph! S'pose so, but it was a "gay" novel, not in the mainstream of any literary tradition.'

'How can you say that?' I was incredulous. 'There was nothing obviously gay about it.'

'Really, Geraldine. The idea of using the dog as a sexual object was an allegory for the love that dare not speak its name, only wuffle. Anyway, he himself – the waiter, that is – was an obvious poof.'

We walked on in silence for a while. It was one of those flat, cold London days. The steely air wavered over the bonnets of cars, as if they were some kind of automotive mirage, ready to dissolve into the tarmac desert.

We normally parted at the mouth of the short road that leads to Covent Garden Piazza. I would stand, watching Gerard's retreating overcoat as he moved past the fire-eaters, the jugglers, the stand-up comedians; and on across the parade ground of flagstones with its manoeuvring battalions of Benelux au pair girls. But on this occasion I wouldn't let him go.

'Do you have to get back to the office? Is there actually anything pressing for you to do?'

He seemed startled and turning to present the oblong sincerity of his face to me – he almost wrenched my arm. 'Erm . . . well, no. S'pose not.'

'How about a coffee then?'

'Oh all right.'

I was sure he had meant this admission to sound cool, unconcerned, but it had come out as pathetic. Despite all his confident, wordy pronouncements, I was beginning to suspect that Gerard's work might be as meaningless as my own.

As we strolled, still coupled, down Long Acre, the commercial day was getting into its post-prandial lack of swing. The opulent stores with their displays of flash goods belied what was really going on.

'The recession's certainly starting to bite,' Gerard remarked, handing a ten-pence piece to a dosser who sat scrunched up behind a baffler of milk crates, as if he were a photographer at one of life's less sporting events.

'Tell me about it, mate.' The words leaked from the gaps in the dosser's teeth, trickled through the stubble of his chin and flowed across the pavement carrying their barge-load of hopelessness.

The two of us paused again in front of the Hippodrome.

'Well,' said Gerard, 'where shall we have our coffee then? Do you want to go to my club?'

'God, no! Come on, let's go somewhere a little youthful.'

'You lead – I'll follow.'

We passed the Crystal Rooms, where tense loss adjusters rocked on the saddles of stranded motor cycles, which they powered on through pixilated curve after pixilated curve.

At the mouth of Gerrard Street, we passed under the triumphal arch with its coiled and burnished dragons. Around us the Chinese skipped and altercated, as scrutable as ever. Set beside their scooterish bodies, adolescent and wind-cheating, Gerard appeared more than ever to be some Scobie or Brown, lost for ever in the grimy Greeneland of inner London.

Outside the Bar Italia a circle of pari-cropped heads was deliberating over glasses of *caffe latte* held at hammy angles.

'Oh,' said Gerard, 'the Bar Italia. I haven't been here in ages, what fun.' He pushed in front of me into the tiled burrow of the café. Behind the grunting Gaggia a dumpy woman with a hennaed brow puffed and pulled. '*Due espressi*!' Gerard trilled in cod-Italian tones. '*Doppio*!'

'I didn't know you spoke Italian,' I said as we scraped back two stools from underneath the giant video screen swathing the back of the café.

'Oh well, you know . . .' He trailed off and gazed up as the flat tummy filling the hissing screen rotated in a figure-eight of oozing congress. A special-effect lipoma swelled in its navel and then inflated into the face of a warbling androgyne.

A swarthy young woman with a prominent mole on her upper lip came over and banged two espressos down on the ledge we were sitting against.

'I say,' Gerard exclaimed; coffee now spotted his shirt front like a dalmatian's belly. 'Can't you take a little more care?' The waitress looked at him hard, jaw and brow shaking with anger, as if some prisoners of consciousness were attempting to jack-hammer their escape from her skull. She hiccupped, then ran the length of the café and out into the street, sobbing loudly.

'What did I say?' Gerard appealed to the café at large. The group of flat-capped Italian men by the cake display had left off haggling over their pools coupons to stare. The hennaed woman squeezed out from behind the Gaggia and clumped down to where we sat. She started to paw at Gerard's chest with a filthy wadge of J-cloths.

'I so sorry, sir, so sorry . . .'

'Whoa! Hold on – you're making it worse!'

'Iss not her fault, you know, she's a good girl, ve-ery good girl. She have a big sadness this days – '

'Man trouble, I'll be bound.' Gerard smirked. It looked like he was enjoying his grubby embrocation.

'No, iss not that . . . iss, 'ow you say, a re-jection?'

I sat up straighter. 'A rejection? What sort of rejection?'

The woman left off rubbing Gerard and turned to me. 'She give this thing, this book to some peoples, they no like – '

'Ha, ha! You don't say. My dear Gerard' – I punched him on the upper arm – 'it looks like we have another scrivenous servitor on our hands.'

'This is absurd.' He wasn't amused.

'My friend here is a publisher, he might be able to help your girl, why don't you ask her to join us?'

'Oh really, Geraldine, can't you let this lie? We don't know anything about this girl's book. Madam – '

But she was already gone, stomping back down the mirrored alley and out the door into the street, where I saw her place an arm round the heaving shoulders of our former waitress.

Gerard and I sat in silence. I scrutinised him again. In this surrounding he appeared fogeyish. He seemed aware of it too, his eyes flicking nervously form the carnal cubs swimming on the ethereal video screen to their kittenish domesticated cousins, the jail bait who picked their nails and split their ends all along the coffee bar's counter.

The waitress came back down towards us. She was a striking young woman. Dark but not Neapolitan, with a low brow, roughly cropped hair and deep-set, rather steely eyes that skated away from mine when I tried to meet them.

'Yes? The boss said you wanted to talk to me – look, I'm sorry about the spillage, OK?' She didn't sound sorry. Her tears had evaporated, leaving behind a tidal mark of saline bitterness.

'No, no, it's not that. Here, sit down with us for a minute.' I proffered my pack of cigarettes; she refused with a coltish head jerk. 'Apparently you're a writer of sorts?'

'Not "of sorts". I'm a writer, full stop.'

'Well then,' Gerard chipped in, 'what's the problem with selling your book? Is it a novel?'

'Ye-es. Someone accepted it provisionally, but they want to make all sorts of stupid cuts. I won't stand for it, so now they want to break the contract.'

'Is it your first novel?' asked Gerard.

'The first I've tried to sell – or should I say "sell-out" – not the first I've written.'

'And what's the novel about – can you tell us?'

'Look' – she was emphatic, eyes at last meeting mine – 'I've been working here for over a year, doing long hours of mindless skivvying so that I have the mental energy left over for my writing. I don't need some pair of smoothies to come along and show an interest in me.'

'OK, OK.' For some reason Gerard had turned emollient, placatory. 'If you don't want to talk about it, don't, but we are genuinely interested.' This seemed to work, she took a deep breath, accepted one of my cigarettes and lit it with a *fatale*'s flourish.

'All right, I'll tell you. It's set in the future. An old hospital administrator is looking back over her life. In her youth she worked for one of a series of hospitals that were set around the ring road of an English provincial town. These had grown up over the years from being small cottage hospitals serving local areas to becoming the huge separate departments – psychiatry, oncology, obstetrics – of one great regional facility.

'One day a meeting is held of all the Region's administrators, at which it is realised that the town is almost completely encircled by a giant doughnut of health facilities. At my heroine's instigation policies are fomented for using this reified *cordon sanitaire* as a means of filtering out undesirables who want to enter the town and controlling those who already live in it. Periods of enforced hospitalisation are introduced; troublemakers are subjected to "mandatory injury". Gradually the administrators carry out a slow but silent coup against central as well as local government.

'In her description of all these events and the part she played in them, my heroine surveys the whole panorama of such a herstory. From the shifting meaning of hygiene as an ideology – not just a taboo – to the changing gender roles in this bizarre oligopoly – '

'That's brilliant!' I couldn't help breaking in. 'That's one of the most succinct and clearly realised satirical ideas I've heard in a long time – '

'This is not a satire!' she screamed at me. 'That's what these stupid publishers think. I have written this book in the grand tradition of the nineteenth-century English novel. I aim to unite dramatically the formation of individual character to the process of social change. Just because I've cast the plot in the form of an allegory and set it in the future, it has to be regarded as a satire!'

'Sticky bitch,' said Gerard, some time later as we stood on the corner of Old Compton Street. Across the road in the window of the catering supplier's, dummy waiters stood, their arms rigidly crooked, their plastic features permanently distorted into an attitude of receptivity, preparedness to receive orders for second helpings of inertia.

'Come off it, Gerard. The plot sounded good – more than good, great even. And what could be more central to the English literary tradition? She said so herself.'

'Oh yeah, I have nothing but sympathy for her sometime publishers, I know just what authors like that are to deal with. Full of themselves, of their bloody idealism, of their pernickety obsession with detail, in a word: precious. No, two words: precious and pretentious.

'Anyway, I must get – ' but he bit off his get-out clause; someone sitting in the window of Wheeler's – diagonally across the street from us – had caught his eye. 'Oh shit! There's Andersen the MD. Trust him to be having a bloody late lunch. I'll have to say hello to him, or else he'll think that I feel guilty about not being at the office.'

'Oh I see, negative paranoia.'

'Nothing of the sort. Anyway, I'll give you a ring, old girl – '

'Not so fast, Gerard, I'll come and wait for you. I want to say goodbye properly.'

'Please yourself,' he shrugged in the copula of our linked arms.

I stood just inside the entrance while Gerard went and fawned over his boss. I was losing my respect for him by the second. Andersen was a middle-aged stuffed suit with a purple balloon of a head. His companion was similar.

Gerard adopted the half-crouch posture of an inferior who hasn't been asked to join a table. I couldn't hear what he was saying. Andersen's companion gestured for the bill, using that universal hand signal of squiggling with an imaginary pen on the sheet of the air.

The waiter, a saturnine type who had been lingering by a half-open serving hatch in the oaken mid-ground of the restaurant, came hustling over to the table, almost running. Before he reached the table he was already shouting, 'What are you trying to do! Take the piss!'

'I just want the bill,' said Andersen's companion. 'What on earth's the matter with you?'

'You're taking the piss!' the waiter went on. He was thin and nervy, more like a semiologist than a servant. 'You know that I'm really a writer, not a waiter at all. That's why you did that writing gesture in the air. You heard me talking, talking frankly and honestly to some of the other customers, so you decided to make fun of me, to deride me, to put me down!' He turned to address the whole room. The fuddled faces of a few lingering lunchers swung lazily round, their slack mouths O-ing.

'I know who you are!' The waiter's rapier finger pointed at Andersen's companion. 'Mister-bloody-Hargreaves. Mister big fat fucking publisher! I know you as well, Andersen! You're just two amongst a whole school of ignorami, of basking dugongs who think they know what makes a jolly fucking good read. Ha!'

Gerard was backing away from the epicentre of this breakdown in restraint, backing towards me, trying to make himself small and insignificant. 'Let's get the hell out of here,' he said over his shoulder. The waiter had found some uneaten seafood on a plate and was starting to chuck it around: 'flotch!' a bivalve slapped against the flock wallpaper, 'gletch!' a squiggle of calimari wrapped around a lamp bracket.

'I'll give you notes from underwater! I'll give you a bloody lobster quadrille' – he was doing something unspeakable with the remains of a sea bream – 'this is the *fin* of your fucking *siècle*!' He was still ranting as we backed out into the street.

'Jesus Christ.' Gerard had turned pale, he seemed winded. He leant up against the dirty frontage of a porn vendor. 'That was awful, awful.' He shook his head.

'I don't know, I thought there was real vigour there. Reminded me of Henry Miller or the young Donleavy.' Gerard didn't seem to hear me.

'Well, I can't go back to the office now, not after that.'

'Why not?'

'I should have done something, I should have intervened. That man was insane.'

'Gerard, he was just another frustrated writer, it seems the town is full of them.'

'I don't want to go back, I feel jinxed. Tell you what, let's go to my club and have a snifter – would you mind?' I glanced at my watch, it was almost four-thirty.

'No, that's OK, I don't have to clock-on for another hour.'

★ ★ ★

As we walked down Shaftesbury Avenue and turned into Haymarket the afternoon air began to thicken about us, condensing into an almost palpable miasma that blanked out the upper storeys of the buildings. The rush-hour traffic was building up around us, Homo Sierra, Homo Astra, Homo Daihatsu, and all the other doomsday sub-species, locking the city into their devolutionary steel chain. Tenebrous people thronged the pavements, pacing out their stay in this pedestrian purgatory.

By the time we reached the imposing neo-classical edifice of Gerard's club in Pall Mall, I was ready for more than a snifter.

In the club's great glass-roofed atrium, ancient bishops scuttled to and fro like land crabs. Along the wall free-standing noticeboards covered in green baize were hung with thick curling ribbons of teletext news. Here and there a bishop stood, arthritic claw firmly clamped to the test score.

I had to lead Gerard up the broad, red-carpeted stairs and drop him into a leather armchair, he was still so sunk in shock. I went off to find a steward. A voice came from behind a tall door that stood ajar at the end of the gallery. Before I could hear anything I caught sight of a strip of nylon jacket, black trouser leg and sandy hair. It was the steward and he was saying, 'Of course, *Poor Fellow My Country* is the longest novel in the English language, and a damn good novel it is too, right?' The meaningless interrogative swoop in pitch – an Australian. 'I'm not trying to do what Xavier Herbert did. What I'm trying to do is invigorate this whole tired tradition, yank it up by the ears. On the surface this is just another vast *Bildungsroman* about a Perth boy who comes to find fame and fortune in London, but underneath that – '

I didn't wait for more. I footed quietly back along the carpet to where Gerard sat and began to pull him to his feet.

'Whoa! What're you doing?'

'Come on, Gerard, we don't want to stay here – '

'Why?'

'I'll explain later – now come on.'

As we paced up St James's Street I told him about the steward.

'You're having me on, it just isn't possible.'

'Believe me, Gerard, you were about to meet another attendant author. This one was a bit of a dead end, so I thought you could give him a miss.'

'So the gag isn't a gag?' He shook his big head and his thick fringe swished like a heavy drape against his brow.

'No, it isn't a gag, Gerard. Now let's stroll for a while, until it's time for me to go to work.'

We re-crossed Piccadilly and plunged into fine-art land. We wandered about for a bit, staring through window after window at gallery girl after gallery girl, each one more of a hot-house flower than the last.

Eventually we turned the corner of Hay Hill and there we were, on Dover Street, almost opposite the job centre that specialises in catering staff. What a coincidence. Gerard was oblivious as we moved towards the knot of dispirited men and women who stood in front. These were the dregs of the profession, the casual waiters who pick up a shift here and a shift there on a daily basis. This particular bunch were the failures' failures. The ones who hadn't got an evening shift and were now kicking their heels, having a communal complain before bussing off to the 'burbs.

Stupid Gerard, he knocked against one shoulder, caromed off another.

'Oi! Watch your step, mate – can't you look out where you're going?'

'I'm awfully sorry.'

' "Aim offly sorry".' They cruelly parodied his posh accent. I freed my arm from his and walked on, letting him fall away from me like the first stage of a rocket. He dropped into an ocean of Babel.

Terrified Gerard, looking from face to face. Old, young, black, white. Their uniform lapels poking out from their overcoat collars; their aprons dangling from beneath the hems of their macs. They sized him up, assessed him. Would he make good copy?

One of them, young and lean, grabbed him by the arm, detaining him. 'Think we're of no account, eh? Just a bunch of waiters – is that what you think?' Gerard tried to speak but couldn't. His lips were tightly compressed, a red line cancelling out his expression. 'Perhaps you think we should be proud of our work. Well we are matey, we fucking are. We've been watching your kind, noting it all down, putting it in our order pads while you snort in your trough. It may be fragmentary, it may not be prettified, it may not be in the Grand Tradition, but let me tell you,' and with this the young man hit Gerard, quite lightly but in the face, 'it's ours, and we're about ready to publish!'

Then they all waded in.

I was late for work. Marcel, the *maître d'*, tut-tutted as I swung open the door of the staff entrance. 'That's the third time late this week, Geraldine. Hurry up now, and change – we need to lay up.' He minced off down the corridor. I did as he said without rancour. Le Caprice may no longer be the best restaurant in London to eat at, but it's a great place to work. If you're a waiter, that is.

Incubus
or
The Impossibility of
Self-Determination as to Desire

JUNE LAUGHTON, a prize-winning gardener, and Peter Geddes, her husband, a philosopher no less, were having an altercation in the kitchen of their ugly house.

The house was indubitably ugly but it had an interesting feature which meant that English Heritage paid for its maintenance and upkeep. The altercation was on the verge of getting ugly – although not quite so ugly as the house. It concerned Peter Geddes's habit of employing the very tip of his little finger as a spatula with which to scoop out the fine, white rheum from the corners of his pink eyes. This he transferred to his moist mouth, again and again. Each fingerful was so Lilliputian a repast that he required constant refreshment.

It was one of those aspects of her husband that June Laughton could stomach on a good day but only on a good day.

'It's disgusting – ' she expostulated.

'I can't help it,' he retorted, 'it's a compulsion.'

'Don't be stupid. How can something like that be a compulsion?'

'Oh, all right – I don't mean compulsion. I mean that

it's an involuntary action, I don't have any control over it.'

'Sometimes I think that you don't have any control over anything,' and she banged the egg-encrusted frying pan into the sink to give her judgement proper emphasis.

The action was a failure. Her husband didn't pay any attention and the frying pan broke a glass. A glass dirtied with stale whisky that was lingering in the bottom of the aluminium trough. Naturally it was June who had to pick the fragments out, extract them from the slurry of food and cutlery that loitered around the plughole.

'Of course, strictly speaking you could be right about that . . . Mmm.' Peter's head was bent as he fiddled on the table top.

'Ouch!' June registered intense irritation and intense pain simultaneously: her husband's edifying tone lancing up under her fingernail alongside a sliver of glass from the broken vessel. 'Why can't you do your own washing up? Look what you've done to me.' She turned from the sink to face him, holding up her wounded paw, fingers outstretched.

Peter Geddes regarded his wife and thought: How like the Madonna she is, or Marcel's description of the Duchesse de Guermantes, the first time he sees her in the church at Combray. He had a point, June Laughton was formidably beautiful. Behind her face bone tented flesh into pure arabesque. Her neck was long and undulant. So long that she could never hold her head straight. It was always at an angle, capturing whatever wash of prettifying light was on offer. Now, in this particular pose, with her hand spread, red rivulet running down her index finger, she was even beatified by the commonplace.

'But, darling, that's what Giselle is for, in part at any rate. She'll do all the washing up.'

'Don't be absurd, Peter. You can't expect a research assistant to labour at your turgid book all day and do domestic service as well – '

'That's what she's for. That's what she's offered to do. Look, I know you find it very difficult to believe but I'm actually well thought of, respected, in what I do – '

'What's that you're doing now?'

'What?'

'You're writing on the table. You're writing on the bloody table! I suppose you're going to tell me that's an involuntary action as well.'

'What, this, this? H-hn, h-hn-hn, ha-hn.' He went into his affected, fat-man's chortle. 'Oh no, no no. No, this is a truth table. A truth table as it were on a truth table. H-hn h-hn, insofar as when we sit at this table we attempt to tell the truth. And this, this' – he gestured at the square grid of letters and symbols that he had inscribed on the formica surface – 'is a truth table expressing the necessary and sufficient conditions of an action being intentional, being willed. Do you want me to explain it further, old girl?'

'No, I don't. I want you out of here. And that girl, research assistant, au pair, factotum or scullery maid.

Whatever she is – you'll have to pick her up from Grantham yourself in the Renault. Unless you've forgotten, the twins get back today.'

'No, I hadn't forgotten. How long will they be here for?'

'A week or two, and then they're off to Burgundy for the grape picking.'

'Together?'

'Of course.'

They cracked up in the synchronised spasm that only comes after souls have been engrafted, bonded by white rheum, cemented by dusty semen, glued by placenta. The funniest thing in their lives was the fact of their children, the non-identical twins, the girl tall and opulently beautiful like her mother, the boy short, fat, cardigan-cuddly like his dear old buffer-dad.

The twins' inseparability had resisted all their parents' attempts to drive them apart, to wedge them into individuality. When they came home together, from their university, or their predictable travels – Inter-railing, inefficiently digging irrigation ditches for peasants, offending Muslims – their parents laughed again at the funhouse image of their young selves incestuously bonded.

'Had you thought of putting them in the Rood Room?' Peter flung this over his shoulder as he worked his way round the awkward curved corridor that led from the kitchen to the rest of the house.

'Oh no, your Giselle must have the Rood Room.

After all she has to have some compensation for becoming an indentured serf.'

Later that day Peter Geddes waited in his crap car for Giselle to exit from Grantham Station. There were never many passengers on this mid-afternoon stopper from King's Cross so he knew he wouldn't miss her. Despite this he adopted a sort of sit-up-and-beg posture in the hard, functional seat of the car, as if he were a private detective waiting to follow a suspect. He did this because he had the heightened self-consciousness of an intelligent person who has drunk slightly too much alcohol in the middle of the day.

'Sorry,' said Giselle, coming up on Peter unawares and hallooing in the characteristic manner of an English bourgeois.

'Whossat!' he started.

'Sorry,' she reiterated, 'I was late and got stuck in the rear carriage. It's taken me ages to lug this lot up the platform. I couldn't find a porter or anyone.'

It didn't occur to Peter to cancel out her superfluous apology with one more justified. But he did get out and load her luggage through the back hatch. There was a lot of it. Two scuffed, functional suitcases, two straw baskets that wafted pot-pourri, a rolled Peruvian blanket and so on.

They drove through Grantham. A plump man and a plump girl. Both philosophers and therefore necessarily free in spirit, yet still mundanely hobbled by avoirdupois, like battery porkers being fattened up to do metaphysics.

Peter spoke first. 'It's a dull little town, we hardly bother to come in here. You can get just about everything you need in Bumford.'

'Is your house right in the village?'

'No, it's on the outskirts, on the Vale of Belvoir side.'

'Oh, that must be lovely.'

'No, not exactly. You'll see what I mean.'

She did. The town of Grantham gave way to the unmade, unfinished countryside of South Notts. The scrappy alternation of light industry and industrial farming gave the area a sort of kitchen-where-no-one-has-washed-up feeling. The Vale of Belvoir, which was the only eminence for miles around, was little more than a yellow, rape-filled runnel, spreading out towards a hazy horizon, giving the distinct impression that all of England was a desultory plateau, falling away to the north.

'Well, Giselle, this is your home for the foreseeable future, or at least until we can get this bloody book finished.' Peter abruptly braked the Renault, scrunching the gravel. They sat for a moment, still in the monochrome of a dull summer afternoon, listening to an electric mower and each other's breathing.

Even Giselle couldn't summon up much more of a comment about the house than, 'Ooh, what an interesting house. It must have been quite unique when it was built.' As good an example of the enigma of the counterfactual as any.

Peter took her inside. June was off getting the twins from Stansted. He led her through the cramped rooms on the ground floor and up the back stairs. They entered the Rood Room.

'Good heavens!' cried Giselle. 'I don't think I've ever seen anything like this before. How? I mean what −?'

'Yes, yes, well, the Rood Room often does take people this way. I'll give you the edited lecture, then if you want to know more you can read the pamphlet English Heritage have done on it.'

'Is this −?'

'Where you'll be sleeping, yes, that is, if you think you can cope with it?'

'Cope with it, why, it's beautiful.'

'Perhaps that's putting it a bit strongly but it is an unusual room, a characterful room. It was built by a local craftsman called Peter Horner, in the mid-seventeenth century. As you can see, the room is dominated by an outsize version of a traditional rood screen. Originally this feature would have separated the nave of the church from the chancel and been surmounted by a crucifix. Its status as a symbolic dividing off of the congregation from the priest is obvious, but here in the Rood Room the symbolism of the screen has been subverted.

'Horner was a member of a local Manichaean sect called the Grunters. He probably built the room as a secret worshipping place for the sect. The screen itself, instead of being topped by a crucifix, is capped by a number of phalluses. Some of these descend from the ceiling, like plaster stalactites, some ascend from the screen like wooden stalagmites. The overall effect is rather toothy, wouldn't you say?'

'It's astonishing. And all the carving, painting and plasterwork. It's all so fresh and vivid.'

'Yes, well, of course the Rood Room has been extensively restored. As a matter of fact by a team of unemployed architectural graduates working under the direction of our own dear Dr Morrison. Nevertheless it was remarkably preserved to begin with. It is without doubt the foremost example of seventeenth-century vernacular architecture still extant in England.'

'Actually, Dr Geddes, it does seem odd . . . I mean not that I don't want to . . . but sleeping in a place of worship – '

'Oh I shouldn't give it another thought. We've been living here for years, since the twins were ten, and they always slept here. And anyway, you have to consider what the Grunters' probable form of worship was. Like other Manichaeans they believed that, as the Devil was co-eternal with God, forms of behaviour that orthodox Christians regarded as sinful were in fact to be enjoined. Hence all these rude, rather than "rood", paintings and carvings.'

Giselle fell to examining the panels of the rood screen and Peter, remembering his more material duties as host and employer, went off to fetch her cases from the car.

Standing in front of the house Peter looked up at its façade and shook his head in weary enjoyment. It never fails, he thought, it never fails to surprise them. Had he troubled to analyse his glee at exposing the Rood Room to Giselle, he might have found it to be a more complicated and troublesome emotion. After all, shocking guests with the Rood Room was akin to a sophisticated form of flashing.

Because the exterior of the Geddes–Laughton house was so uncompromisingly Victorian – two shoeboxes of dark-red London brick, topped off with a steeply gabled tiled roof – any visitor was bound to expect its interior to correspond. But it was only a cladding, a long mackintosh that could be twitched aside to reveal a priapic core. For really the house was a collection of seventeenth-century cottages and hovels that had been cemented together over the centuries by a mucilage of plaster, wattle, daub and stonework. The only room of any substance was the Rood Room; all the others were awkward moulded cells, connected by bulging, serpentine corridors.

But Peter didn't trouble to analyse his emotions – it wasn't his style. It's difficult to imagine what the interior scape of a philosopher's mind might be like. Modern works of analytic philosophy are so arid. How could anyone hold so many fiddly Fabergé arguments in his or her mind for so long? Without the drifting motes of decaying brain cells – used-up thoughts and prototypical thoughts never to be employed – beginning to fill the atmosphere and cloud the clarity of introspection with intellectual plaster dust.

To get around the problem, Peter's mind was akilter

to real time. Like a gyroscope spinning slowly, set inside another gyroscope spinning faster, Peter's mind went on churning through chains, puzzles and tables of ratiocination, while the world zipped by him: a time-lapse film with a soundtrack of piping, irrelevant Pinky and Perky voices. And while not exactly fecund, the similes required to describe his mental processes were sterile rather than decaying. They were like three-dimensional word puzzles: propositions, premises, theses and antitheses, all were manipulated in free fall, coaxed into place with a definite 'click'. It was if Peter's will were a robotic claw that lanced into a radioactive interior in order to perform subtle manipulations.

But then the greatest paradox of all is that nothing is farther off from self-knowledge than introspection, and nothing more remote from wisdom than pure intellect.

On re-entering the house, Peter found Giselle in the kitchen. She was arranging some freesias in a jamjar full of water as he popped puffing through the narrow door.

'You must let me help you with those – they're awfully heavy.'

'Oh no – no. Don't worry. You sit down. Bung on the kettle if you like.' He was already mounting the awkward steps.

Back upstairs he placed her cases and baskets by the big pine bedstead set beneath the largest window. He sat on the edge of the bed and lost himself for a while in the Rood Room's gullet confines.

It really was an astonishing place, hardly like a room in a house at all, more of a grotto. There was one large diamond-mullioned window over the bed and another, much smaller, on the opposite wall, the other side of the rood screen. The light from these came in in thick shafts, given body by swirls of golden dust motes. But it was the ceiling that gave the room its organic feel. It was thrown over the top like a counterpane and tied down by each corner to a respective corner. The middle of the billowing roof was held aloft, over the dead centre of the rood screen, supported there by its petrified folds. Between these folds, studding the rippling walls, were hundreds of plaster mouldings.

Running up from the room's corners to its apex, were seams of lozenges entwined by ivy. But this simple decoration was nothing compared to the profusion of body parts – gargoyle heads, thrusting breasts, dangling penises; as well as a comprehensive bestiary, griffins and sphinxes, bulls rampant, lions couchant – that sprouted across the rest of the curved surfaces. The eye could not take in the whole of this decoration – there were over four hundred individual reliefs – instead it reduced them to a warty effect.

Each side of the rood screen itself was adorned with some thirteen individual painted panels. Dr Morrison may have assured English Heritage that his assistants had used authentic reformulations of the original pigments to retouch the screen, yet the result was advertisingly garish. The white and flat bodies of the Grunters lay entwined in naive tableaux of sexual abandon. They sported in distorted copses of painful viridity and dug from the excremental earth the falsely dead cadavers of their brethren, dragging them back into the one and only world.

Peter Geddes couldn't bear to look at the rood screen for too long. When he and June had bought the house some fifteen years ago, the Rood Room had been impressive, but in grimy decay. The screen was blackened and the images faint. The stippling of explicit carvings covering the walls had been chipped and disfigured into insignificance.

Dr Morrison and his crew had only finished their restoration work that spring. Now, in the glory of midsummer, with the garden outside groaning in prefructive labour, the Rood Room had acquired a pregnant burnish. The walls bellied pink, the screen glared. Even Peter was susceptible to the rioting colour and the strange sensation of heretical worship resonating down the ages. He wondered, idly, if the room might have an adverse psychological effect on his new research student.

This reverie was cut into by the sound of the family Volvo pulling up outside, and shortly after, the shouts of his teenage twins resounded through the house. He came back down the cramped stairway and found the four of them already at tea.

Peter wasn't fazed as the four sets of eyes swivelled towards him. He knew that in his family's eyes he cut a somewhat embarrassing figure. Not exactly a looker: his duck-egg body defied his clothes to assume recognisable forms. On him, trousers ceased to be bifurcated, shirts stopped being assemblies of linen planes and tubes; and shoes became hopelessly adrift – merely functional stops to his roly-poly body – wedged underneath, as if to stop him from toppling over.

None of this mattered to Peter, for he was one of those men who had managed in adolescence wilfully to disregard his physical form – for good. So, he entered the kitchen unabashed and crying, 'Here you are, you rude mechanicals!' He cupped the head of his daughter and drew her cheek to his lips, then did the same with his son. Giselle, whose father's touch was nothing but wince-provoking, was struck by the fact that neither twin struggled to avoid him. Quite the reverse: they seemed to lean into his kiss.

'Well, and how were the Masai?' Peter went on, sitting down at the head of the table and reaching for a cup of tea. 'Did they let you drink milk and blood? Did you learn their eighty-seven different words to express the shape of their cattle's horns?'

'We haven't been with the Masai, Dad,' said Hal, the son. 'We haven't even been in Africa – '

'Oh, I see, not in Africa. Next you're going to tell me that you didn't even leave England.'

'We did leave England,' said Pixie, the daughter, 'but we went north rather than south. We've been at a rural development project, working with the Lapps in northern Sweden – '

75

'Drinking reindeer pee. And we've learnt fifteen different words to express the shape of a reindeer's antlers.' Her brother finished the account for her.

Giselle was charmed by this demonstration of familial good humour. Cuddling, nicknames, banter, all were alien to the privet-lined precincts of her proper parents.

They ate lardy cake and drank a lot of tea. The sounds of the B road that ran through the village reached them but faintly, drowned out by the rising evening chorus of the birds.

'Well!' June exclaimed. 'I can't sit here for the rest of the day. For one thing I shan't have room for dinner. I don't know if you had forgotten, Peter, but Henry and Caitlin are coming this evening – '

'Of course I hadn't. I've got some suitably caustic Burgundy. It's just dying to climb right out of its bottles and scour that self-satisfied man's mind.'

'Of course, darling. I'm going to get back to work now, or I shan't be able to finish re-turfing that lawn before dusk.' June rubbed her hands on her trouser legs, as if she could already feel the peat on her palms. 'You twins can do the cooking. Christ knows, you're better at it than I am.'

'Oh but, Ma, we're jet lagged,' they chorused.

'Nonsense. Lapland is, as we all know, due north of here.'

There was a brief groaning duet, but no further protest. The twins went off to inhabit their rooms. Giselle stood up and began to tidy away the tea things.

'Don't worry about that,' June called out from the front door, 'leave it for the twins.'

'Oh, ah, OK. Well,' she giggled nervously, 'what to do? Should we . . .? I mean I have some notes relating to Chapter Four. It's the rather technical stuff – you know, where you demolish the compatiblist arguments. If you'd like to – '

'Ah no. Don't worry about that now,' Peter sighed, looking up from the cake corpse he was feeding on. 'Free will and determinism will still be incompatible come the morning. You just relax. Breathe in the country air. I have some correspondence to deal with that'll take me the rest of today.'

Giselle followed June out into the garden. The older woman was already plying a long-handled spade, picking up the turfs from a neat pile and laying them out in rows on the brushed bare soil. Giselle, rather than disturb her, walked in the opposite direction.

June Laughton had transformed the half-acre or so of conventional ground into a miniature world of land-scaping. Prospects had been foreshortened, or artificially lengthened, by clever earthworks, reflective pools and the planting of the obscurer varieties of pampas grass. On hummocks and in little dells she had embedded sub-tropical flowers and shrubs, varieties that survived in the local climate.

Giselle wandered enchanted. Like a lot of intellectuals she felt herself to be hopelessly impractical. This was an affectation that she had wilfully fostered, rather than a true trait. It allowed her to view the physical (and therefore inferior) achievements of others with false modesty, as heroic acts, as if they were plucky spastics who had entered a marathon.

So deceived was she by the clever layout of the garden, that Giselle was startled, on rounding a clump of flora, to come upon June.

'Oh sorry!' she barked, compounding her own surprise with June's. June dropped her spade.

'That's OK,' she said. 'Enjoying the evening?'

'Oh it's lovely, really lovely. And it's amazing what you've done with this garden – I don't think I've ever seen anything quite like it.'

'No, it's not exactly your traditional English garden, is it? For years Peter and I were stuck in England, he with his work and I with the twins. I was determined to bring something of the foreign and the exotic into our lives, so I created this garden.' June bent and picked up her turfing spade. She stood and turned to give Giselle her profile. Standing there in her peat-dusted corduroys, with her gingham shirt unbuttoned to the warm roots of her breasts, her thick blonde hair falling away in a drape from its hooking grips, June was like a William Morris Ceres, gesturing to the fruits of her labours.

For ten minutes she strolled the garden with Giselle, pointing out the individual plants and describing their properties. Her manner was so gracious, so unselfconscious, that the younger woman felt entirely at ease.

Giselle had been terribly worried about coming to stay

78

with Dr Geddes. She was too young to be able to divorce the potency of the mind from that of the body, and when, in his capacity as her postgraduate supervisor, Peter enthused over ideas, slinging out arguments like conceptual clays, Giselle had been seduced, and longed for his wet mouth to clamp on hers.

She thought them a good match – they could be cuddly together. This was a dream she had harboured, but she was far too ethical, too upstanding, ever to imagine that anything would come of it. And anyway, she could tell that he didn't even regard her as belonging to the same species as himself. In his disinterested gaze she saw only zoological interest.

While June and the twins made dinner Giselle was parcelled off to have a bath. She sported in the tub. She laved herself and laved herself and laved herself. Working up lather after lather after lather, until when at last she stood, steaming on the mat, her skin smelt of nothing but lavender; her personal, indefinable odour was eradicated, sluiced away.

Back in the Rood Room, Giselle unpacked. She interleaved her chemises, blouses, slips and underwear in the broad drawers of a large dresser. She placed her books on the footstool by the double bed, together with a candle, shaped and scented like an orange. With little touches such as these, the Rood Room soon began to seem to Giselle like her room. She had that ability to feel almost instantly at home simply by the application to a new place of a small coating of personal artefacts.

Giselle had a tea ceremony that completed her un-packing. It was part of her divine indwelling, her personal mythology. She primed the tiny spirit burner, lit it, set a diminutive kettle on its stand, and unpacked some translucent bowls from their tissue paper. Then she slipped a silk dressing gown over her round shoulders. All of this had a ritual quality, a sacred rhythm.

Here in Peter Geddes's house, in the Rood Room, the whole tea ceremony took on a potent aura. The sun was sinking down and the thick beams of light that entered the room from the smaller western window were combed by the top of the rood screen. Carious shadows snaked across the quilt, and over Giselle's crossed thighs, where she sat in its dead centre, her bowl of tea cradled in her lap.

Giselle felt drugged by bath and tea, ready to abandon herself to the Rood Room, to become just another painted panel.

Am I free? she thought, with an access of introspection as slight as a woodchip. That's what I'm here for: to consider that question in its widest and narrowest senses. But am I? Wouldn't it be an achingly reductive proposition for one who was truly un-free even to bother to consider the grounds of that un-freedom? Giselle hunched further upright on the lumpy softness of the mattress.

Her features were pretty enough. She had a fine-bridged nose, long and flaring into *retroussé*. Her eyes were large and dark violet. The smallness of her brow was well disguised by her long pelt of hair, which, falling inwards to her collarbone, served also to flatter the fullness of her figure.

The irony was that, seated there on her round haunches, although Giselle may not have possessed the sort of freedom that implies full moral responsibility, she nonetheless had plenty of that very prosaic power: the power of fey sexual self-awareness.

Pixie came scuttling under the low lintel and into the Rood Room. She was free. Entirely free of the painful shyness Giselle remembered blustering her way through at that age.

'Ooh, what a clever little thing.' Pixie was fiddling with the copper kettle on its spirit lamp, tipping it this way and that so splashes of still steaming water fell on to the windowsill.

'Careful –' said Giselle.

'Don't worry,' snapped back Pixie. 'I won't break it.' She took a turn around the Rood Room, looking closely at the panels and the plaster reliefs. 'Don't mind me,' she threw out after a while, 'I always like to come up and check on the Rood Room after I've been away for a while – you don't mind, do you?'

'No, no, of course – '

'So you're a philosopher like Daddy, are you?'

'Hardly,' Giselle demurred, 'your father is extremely eminent. He's very likely to get the Pelagian Professorship next year, especially if this book is a success.'

'And that's what you're here for?'

'To help him with the book, yes. Dr Geddes is my postgraduate supervisor. He very kindly offered me a couple of months' work, both helping him out and helping your mother around the house – '

'So you're not here to screw him then?'

'Phsss No!' Giselle sprayed the quilt with Lapsang Souchong.

'Well, that's just as well' – Pixie was halfway out of the door – 'because Mum says that he's got so fat he's hardly capable of it anymore.' While Giselle was still too stunned to frame a rejoinder Pixie poked her blonde head back under the lintel. 'The guests are here, by the way. You'd better dress and come down.'

As she hurriedly dressed, Giselle put Pixie's behaviour down to precocity rather than conscious rudeness. The other possibility – that the girl had somehow sensed Giselle's desire – was too awful to contemplate.

In the drawing room she found Peter Geddes and another man drinking whisky.

'Giselle Dawson,' said Peter, gesturing at her, 'this is Henry Beckwood.' He indicated the man, who was twitchily thin, sporting bifocals and wire-wool hair. 'Henry, Giselle is my new research assistant. Giselle, Henry is big in plastics.'

'And not much else besides,' said the man called Henry, offering Giselle his hand. Seeing that she looked perplexed he added, 'What Peter means is that I'm a polymer scientist.'

'D'you want a drop of coloured water then, Giselle?'

Peter was holding the bottle around its shoulders and thrusting it at her, as if it were a club with which he was going to beat her into sedation.

'Err . . . no thank you.'

'If you want something else, some wine, say, you'll find it in the kitchen, on the truth table.'

As she left the room Giselle could hear Peter explaining to Henry why he called it the truth table. She found Peter's manner disconcerting. The bottle of whisky had been half-empty, but she couldn't believe that the two of them had already drunk that much, it was only eight o'clock.

'Pissed already, are they?' said June as Giselle came into the kitchen. 'I know it's only eight but once you get Peter and Henry together there's no stopping them, is there, Caitlin?' Giselle saw that there was another woman in the kitchen. She was middle-aged but with the figure of a gamine. She had pretty little features and an uncomfortably sharp, trowel-like chin. Giselle proffered her hand.

'Hi, I'm Giselle Dawson.'

'And I'm Caitlin Beckwood – and that's the only straight statement you're likely to get out of me all evening. June, d'you have a corkscrew, I'm sure Giselle is dying for a glass of wine, I know I am.'

Dinner was accorded a great success.

A success as far as the two couples were concerned, perhaps, but Giselle felt distinctly sidelined. The older people took one end of the table and the twins consorted at the other. Giselle was stuck in the middle, faced with either having to force herself into the grown-ups' conversation, which was raucous and full of shared allusions, references to a communal history, or else relapse into her teens and the kind of join-the-dots self-assertion and clumsily plotted intimacy that was still all too fresh from her days as an undergraduate.

She got up after courses to help June and the twins with the clearing, but each time she was shooed back down into her seat. Not even this form of ordinary intercourse was allowed her.

It wasn't anything intentional on anyone's part – she knew that. It was just that the two older women had a lot to talk about – and so it seemed did the men. As for the twins, their communication consisted almost entirely of near-telepathic nods and lid dips, betokening leisured centres of self but thinly partitioned-off from one another.

Giselle was struck by the way that neither of the men offered to assist in any way. Caitlin Beckwood had got up to do a late whip of the syllabub because she was 'good at that sort of thing', but the only contribution Peter made throughout the evening was to open bottle after bottle of the caustic Burgundy, and the only contribution Henry made was to drink them. By the time the cheese board was passed round, the plot of the table that lay between them had been over-developed with empty bottles. They stood about like glass missile silos that had already shot their wad.

The wine had got to Peter and Henry's faces. It was particularly remarkable in Peter's case, because he was wearing an intense, burgundy-coloured smoking jacket with quilted lapels. His white shirt was a wedge of light between the two blobs of vinous darkness.

It looked ridiculous, this posh bit of plush cast over his teddy-bear torso, and Peter seemed to regard it accordingly as a joke prop, occasionally flicking invisible particles of dust from the cuffs, as if punctuating his interminable philosophical wrangles with Henry by alluding to the insubstantiality of matter itself.

Throughout dinner, and even when they moved next door to have coffee and After Eights, they had talked Free Will. This was capitalised – in Giselle's mind – because so intense were their clashes that they might have been arguing the tactics relating to some Amnesty International campaign to liberate a freedom fighter of that name.

'Look, Henry.' Peter plunked the table with outspread pudgy fingers. 'It doesn't matter at what point you introduce indeterminacy into the material world, that isn't the issue. The impossibility of free will rests on a misconception of what it is to be truly free; and indeed, the irony of the great superstructure of argument that has been built on top of this category error is that it – in and of itself – represents the very acting-out of unfreedom –'

'Bollocks,' Henry countered expertly. 'Total crap. You go round and around, Peter, up and down the rhetorical escalator like a child, but really your arguments are a naive outgrowth of adolescent cynicism. Your refusal to face up to the freedom of the will is a wish to avoid full moral responsibility – '

'For Christ's sake, Henry, give it a bloody rest.'

And so they went on. To begin with Giselle had listened to the argument with close attention. Her eyes flicked over the net of Burgundy bottles, from player to player, as they volleyed rubberised sophistries back and forth, struggling to win the *bon point*. Eventually she grew weary.

The paradox that it was Beckwood, the polymer scientist working with the testable proofs of science, who clung on to the moral essence of free will, wasn't lost on her. And although she was disappointed by Peter's unwillingness to include her in the debate – apart from an occasional 'Giselle will back this up, she's a philosopher too, y'know' – she couldn't help being thrilled once more, as she had been in his seminars, by the audacity of his pronouncements, the sure rigidity of his mental projections.

Peter kept on creating truth tables to illustrate his more technical points. At the dinner table these were constructed from rolled-up pellets of bread, lain out on the mahogany surface like edible Go counters. From time to time, Caitlin and June broke off from their intimate conversation to say things like, 'Really, Peter, playing with your food like an infant, is this what you do at High Table . . .'

Giselle was amazed by how dismissive the women

were of their menfolk. They either ignored them, or joshed them unmercifully. Their remarks betrayed such condescension, such refusal to admit any equality with Peter and Henry, that she was surprised that the men didn't retaliate in any way. But perhaps they were simply too drunk.

'That's what Jowett used to say.' They were in the drawing room and Henry and Peter were drinking Rémy Martin out of mismatched tumblers. 'Are you a two-bottle man, or a three-bottle man!' They guffawed at this.

'Joyce doesn't realise what she's putting up with,' Caitlin was saying to June. 'If she did, she wouldn't allow them to bully her in this fashion.' It had transpired that Caitlin was a landscape gardener as well – and a successful one. Giselle could work this out from the famous names that were inadvertently kicked between them as they discussed ideas, billings, possible commissions, the impossibility of getting good workers.

Giselle had had more wine that she should. She was almost drunk. When she turned her head, from the bookcase to the men's mulberry faces, from these faces to those of the animated women, her eyes followed on lazily, lurching against the insides of their sockets as if intoxicated in their own right.

The voices burred and lowed. Giselle tried to imagine her hosts as cattle. They fitted the role well, set down on the field of carpet by the pools of wavering light, grazing on conversation.

'You look ready to drop, Giselle.' It was June, her voice maternal, gently concerned.

'I'm, I'm sorry . . .?'

'You'd better go up to bed, my dear, you'll need a good night if you're going to cope with Peter and his hangover in the morning.'

'Oh, yeah, um, s'pose so.' Giselle struggled to her feet, the distance from the bottom of the low armchair to being upright was an Everest ascent.

She said her good-nights. Peter and Henry barely interrupted their conversation, they just waved their glasses at her and made valedictory noises. The women were more polite.

'I do hope you'll be all right in the Rood Room,' said June. 'It can be a bit draughty.'

'Oh I'm sure I will; please don't worry.'

As she tunnelled her way up through the house Giselle felt nothing but relief – relief to have escaped the adults. Even though she was going to bed, she might have been on her way to join the twins, who she could hear chattering and playing records in some mid-distanced room. But what Giselle really wanted was sleep. Sleep and dreams.

In the Rood Room she felt her way gingerly around the shoulder-high screen and across the warped floor-boards to the bed. She snapped on the bedside lamp and in that instant the whole space was defined with startling clarity, the Grunters jumbled together in jangling co-pulation on the screen, its penile coping writhing in the shadows, the plaster reliefs giving a serried leer.

Giselle sat down heavily on the bed and absorbed the charge gathered in the room, the accumulated gasps of time. They bounced off the walls and came into her, nuzzling down into the warm pit off her lower belly. Giselle was shocked by the feeling – the immediacy of her lust. The Rood Room seemed to hold her like a lover, cupping her body within its own warm confines.

Giselle had never had any real difficulties with sex. She had moved from riding ponies and horses to riding men and boys easefully, just going up on her sensual stirrups to absorb the shift from a merely physical trot to a psychic canter. But while she could will herself to climax, power herself up on to some kind of free-floating plateau, she knew that the constrictions of her upbringing still remained. Some way inside her, like a twist in a party balloon, they strangled abandon, choked off the flow of desire.

If only someone like Peter Geddes – not Geddes himself, of course – but someone like him, someone who plaited the psychic with the physical into a rigid rope, could pull himself into her. Here, in the Rood Room, her orange candle lit and pulsing soft light over the curved ceiling, Giselle could dare to imagine such a possibility – it coming and lancing into her, a naked libertine will, imploding from the noumenal realm into the phenomenal body of her world.

Outside the night insects scratched their legs, as Giselle caressed her own. She ran her palms up from her knees, snagging and then furling back the material of her skirt, conscious of it as a curtain being raised on a living puppet show; her hands – the players – descended from the boards of her belly to the pit of lust.

Her fingernails snagged at the rubber-band waist of her tights. She peeled them off, together with her pants. The warm coil was dropped by the side of the bed. It was the same with her blouse and her bra. She removed them with the hands of another person. It was the hands that made love to her, the hands that grasped her buttocks and pitched Giselle's body back against the headboard. They whooshed around her breasts, pulling the nipples out to precise points of sensation. They moulded her body with worshipful art, as if it were a wet gobbet of clay being shaped into a votary statue of a fertility goddess.

From the other time of the twins' room, Giselle could faintly hear and dimly recognise the chanting of a current hit: 'Doo-wa yi, yi, yi, dooo-waaa. Yeah–yeah, mm-m-, yeah-yeah.' The painted Grunters flexed their Hanna-Barbera bodies in time to the music, while the foreign fingers – wet now with a gastronome's delight – picked at tit-bits of Giselle.

When she came it was with a hot flush. So much so, that as she lay on the disordered bed Giselle could almost imagine that she saw steam rising from the juncture of her thighs.

Downstairs Peter Geddes was pissed. The Beckwoods had long gone, and with them the necessity for the propriety performance that masks unhappiness for the well-bred English family.

June and Peter had reverted to their intimate selves, their rude selves, their hateful and hating selves. The fresh start they had made that morning, the honest attempt to use happy memories as scaffolding for a brave new marital building, had subsided into the churned-up mud of the present.

June was in the kitchen stacking the dishwasher when Peter's pencilled doodles on the table caught her eye. She went over and peered down at them. This is what she saw:

$p(M)$	$\forall m(F)j$	$\rightarrow p(F)j$
T	T	F
F	T	F
T	F	F

She wiped it out with a sweep of her damp J-cloth, and called into the next room, 'You're not free any more, Peter!'

'Whassat?' His burning brow poked round the door-jamb.

'You're not free any more.'

'Whyssat?' he slurred.

'Because I've obliterated your stupid truth table. You're always saying that the truth about the world is a revealed thing. Well now it's unrevealed. In fact, it's gone altogether.' She was at the sink. Scraping filaments of veal from the dinner plates with horrid knife squeals.

'Oh no, June, you shouldn't have done that, really you shouldn't . . .' Peter was genuinely distressed. He staggered across to the table. In the overhead lighting of the kitchen his drunkenness was even more apparent. 'June, June . . . That was the matrix, the functional cradle that contains us both. Now it's gone . . . Well, I don't know, I just don't know . . .' and in concerto with his voice trailing away, his pudgy finger trailed across the damp surface. He raised it up to his brimming eyes and contemplated the greyish stain on its pad – all that was left of his freedom.

June slammed the door of the dishwasher. She was, Peter reflected with the hackneyed heaviness of the drunk, even more beautiful when she was angry. 'Right! That's it. I'm not going to listen to this maudlin drivel all night, I'm going to bed. I would suggest you do the same instead of sitting downstairs until 5 a.m., the way you did when Henry and Caitlin last came over. Honestly, chucking back brandy and listening over and over to the Siegfried Idyll.

'Half of your waking life you seem to think that you're wearing a horned helmet and sitting with the gods in Valhalla, not sporting a greasy mop of thinning hair and drunkenly slumped in your family-fucking-home in Notting-bloody-hamshire.' With that she departed, stamping up the stairs.

For a couple of minutes after she had left the kitchen

Peter did nothing. He just swayed back and forth, listening to the gurgling of alcohol in his brain, heavy oil slopping in a rusty sump. Then he summoned himself and dabbing at the light switch with his numb hand managed to kill the lights. He went next door to the sitting room and with great deliberation turned on the record player, selected an album from the old-fashioned free-standing rack that stood by it, and put it on.

As Wagner's billowing orchestration filled the room, Peter subsided into an armchair. He spilt a few measures of brandy on to his trousers, but three more managed to hit the tumbler. These he chucked down. The music swelled to fill the space, lowering like a heliotrope grizzly bear. Peter poured himself another brandy, then another and then a fourth.

Some time later he was truly drunk, orbiting his own consciousness in a tiny capsule of awareness that was shooting backwards at speed. He watched, awed, as the dawn of his own sentience sped away from him towards the great slashed crescent of the horizon. Then the toxic confusional darkness came upon him, swallowing him entirely.

The synaptic gimbals had been unslung and Peter's splendidly meticulous gyroscope of ratiocination fell to the jungly floor of his id. He rose and did not know that he did so. He went to the record player and snapped it off – not knowing that he did so. He quit the room. Standing in the misshapen vestibule, the oddly angled point of entry to this disordered household, the philosopher stared into an old mirror – not knowing that he did so.

From out of the mirror there loomed the face of a Grunter. It was dead white, shaped by the utter foreignness of the distant past. The Civil War recusant looked at Peter for a while and then slid away into the mirror's bevelled edge. Peter's head shook itself – hard. His body felt the painful anticipation of the morning and took its mind upstairs.

In the Rood Room Giselle lay in a deep swoon. After climaxing she had relapsed thus, and gone to sleep with the twins' pop records still sounding in her ears. But the twins were now asleep as well, and her fine body was still banked up on top of the disordered covers, forming cumulus piles of sweet flesh. A beam of starlight fell across her upper thighs, then extended itself towards the rood screen, where it illuminated the central panel, which depicted five Grunters in a loose bundle of copulation, a fasces of fornication.

Giselle was gorgeous, the fullness of her refulgent in the silvery light. Her auburn pubic hair glowing as if lit from within. Her breath disturbed her breast, only just sufficiently to reinforce the impression that she was an artist's model trapped since the Regency in suspended inanimation.

There was a creaking from the corridor, a groaning of larynx and wood. The door squealed on its hinges and Peter Geddes's brandy golem entered the Rood Room.

94

Giselle awoke at once and sat up. The diamond light from the window was scattered across his brow – outsize spangles. The incubus rubbed at them carelessly. She didn't need to ask who it was, she could see that immediately. She shifted herself back under the covers, adroitly, as if inserting a sliver of ham into a half-eaten sandwich.

'D-Doctor Geddes, is that you?'

'Please,' said the incubus, his voice clear now, un-slurred, 'call me Peter.' And then he went on, 'I'm terribly sorry, I must have taken the wrong turning at the top of the stairs. Quite easy to do, y'know – even after many lifetimes' residence.'

'Th-that's OK – are you all right?'

'Fine, thanks – and you?' He had turned away from her now and was confronting the rood screen. 'Not finding it too hard to sleep in this strange old place?' His voice came to her now as it had done in tutorials, focused, crisply edged by intellect. His outstretched hand traced the line of a Grunter back, in the same way she remembered it tracing the sinuous connectives of his scrawled logical formulae.

As if it were the most natural thing in the world to do, the incubus then moved away from the rood screen and towards where Giselle lay.

'Do you mind if I sit down for a moment?' he said, looking down at her.

'No, not at all.' The words pooted from her kissable lips, inappropriate little farts of desire. The incubus sat, inhabiting the warm vacant V between the ranges of Giselle's calves and thighs. He canted round, his unfocused eyes squeezing their watery gaze into the dilation of her pupils.

'If it wasn't such a trite remark,' the incubus quipped, 'I would tell you how vitally lovely you are at this precise moment – right now.' He bent to kiss her, her urge to resist was as insubstantial as the air that escaped from between their marrying bodies.

His hands unwrapped the covers, her hands unfurled his woolly bunting, until they lay, two tubby people, damp with desire, in the heat of an English summer night.

He kissed her clavicle – the pit of it neatly fitted the trembling ball of his tongue. He tasted the salt of her skin as he ice-cream-licked the whole of her upper body, lapping her up. His face went down on her trembling belly and his hands cupped first her round face, then her round shoulders and lastly her rounded breasts. Cupped and kneaded, cupped and kneaded.

To her, the incubus and his touch were more than a release. She couldn't have said why – for she had no reason left now – but he was beautiful. His pendulous belly, his bow legs, the scurf on his high forehead, the stubble on his jowls, all of it moved her. She grasped the flesh on his back, feeling moles like seeds beneath her palms; she worked at them to cultivate still more of his lust.

The mouth of the incubus was presently in her pubic

hair, the tip of his tongue describing ancient arabesques and obscure theurgical symbols on her mons, the deep runnels of her groin, the babyflesh of her inner thighs. The incubus drew in a gout of the urine and mucous smell of her, and savoured it noisily, as if it were the nose of some particularly rambuncious Burgundy.

Then his horizontal lips were firmly bracketing her vertical ones, his hands were under her, holding her by the apex of her buttocks, and he ate into her, worried at the very core of her, as if she were some giant water-melon that he must devour to assuage an unquenchable thirst.

Later still the incubus addressed her with the incon-trovertible fact of his penis. Entered into her with the logical extension of himself. She was curled up like a copula, a connective, her kneecaps almost in her eye sockets, as he placed himself on top of her. And Giselle went into him, went out of herself, travelled over the curved roof. The incubus was lancing into her from out of that other realm – he was pure, ineffable will, freeing her up with each stroke, dissolving her corporeal self.

His tongue was in her mouth, marauding around the back of her throat. His penis was in her vagina, knocking forcefully at the mouth of her cervix. The shadows of the phalluses on top of the rood screen fell across both their bodies, tiger-striping them in the luminous darkness. The Grunters stared down at the wreckless, wrecking bodies with gnostic inappetency.

She came; and the incubus yanked her up in her

orgasm, hooking her higher by the pubic bone, until she span in giddy baroque loops and twirls – pain for pleasure and pleasure for pain. Her cries, her groans, her molar-grinds, all were grace notes, useless embroideries on the fact of her abandonment. 'S–s–s–sorry!' It was almost a scream; this remembering, even at the point of no return, the refinements of her upbringing.

They lay in each other's arms for a while, but only a short one. Then the incubus, kissing her to stay silent, departed. Some while afterwards Giselle heard the sound of a shower pattering in a distant bathroom.

The following morning Giselle went downstairs knowing that this could be the hardest entrance of her life. She had no idea how Peter Geddes was going to play it. His lovemaking the night before had been so demonic, so intense. It had beached her on the nightmare coast of the dreamland. Would he acknowledge what had passed between them in some way? Would he already have confessed to his wife? Would she find herself back at Grantham station within the hour, her vacation job over and her academic career seriously compromised?

Peter and June were altercating in the kitchen of their ugly house as Giselle appeared at the bottom of the stairway.

'Honestly, Peter.' The gardener was even more beautiful this morning, her long blonde hair loose in a sheaf around her shoulders. 'You should be ashamed of yourself, getting pissed like that on a weekday. What's Giselle' – she gestured towards the guilty research assistant – 'going to think of this household?'

Peter dropped the upper edge of his *Guardian* and looked straight into those guilty eyes. Looked forthrightly and yet distantly. Looked at her, Giselle realised with a shock, as if she were a member of some other species. He said – and there was no trace of duplicity or guile in his voice, 'Sleep well, Giselle? Hope Richard and I didn't disturb you during the night?'

'R–Richard?'

'He means Wagner,' said June, placing a large willow-patterned plate of eggs and bacon on the table. 'He always plays Wagner when he gets pissed – thinks it's romantic or something. Silly old fool.' She rumpled Peter's already rumpled hair with what passed for affection, then went on, 'Here's your breakfast, Giselle, better eat it while it's hot.'

'Oh, er . . . sorry, thanks.' Giselle sat down.

Peter rattled his paper to the next page. He was feeling pretty ghastly this morning. I really oughtn't, he mused internally, get quite that drunk. I'm not as young as I used to be, not as resilient. Still, lucky the old autopilot's so efficient, can't remember a thing after putting on the Idyll . . . He glanced up from the paper and felt the eyes of his research assistant on him, full of warm love. Silly girl, thought Peter wryly.

Difficult to imagine why but she must fancy me or something. His eyes went to the straining spinnakers of

her contented bosoms. Still, she is a handsome beast . . .
pity that I'm not free – in a way.

Appendix

Peter Geddes's Truth Table

p(M)	∀m(F)j	→p(F)j
T	T	F
F	T	F
T	F	F

or:

Peter is a man. All men want to fuck June. Therefore
Peter wants to fuck June.
T = the truth of a component or concluding proposition.
F = the falsity of a component or concluding proposition.

Scale

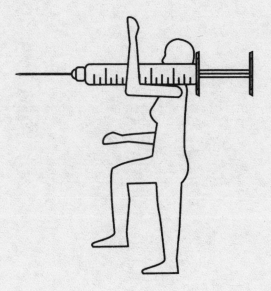

Prologue

(to be spoken in conversational tones)

THE PHILOSOPHER FREDDIE Ayer was once asked which single thing he found most evocative of Paris. The venerable logical positivist thought for a while, and then answered, 'A road sign with "Paris" written on it.'

Kettle

S OME PEOPLE LOSE their sense of proportion; I've lost my sense of scale. Arriving home from London late last night, I found myself unable to judge the distance from the last exit sign for Junction 4 to the slip road itself. Granted it was foggy and the bright headlights of oncoming vehicles burned expanding aureoles into my view, but there are three white-bordered, oblong signs, arranged sequentially to aid people like me.

The first has three oblique bars (set in blue); the second, two; and the third, one. By the time you draw level with the third sign you should have already begun to appreciate the meaning of the curved wedge, adumbrated with further oblique white lines, that forms an interzone, an un-place, between the slip road, as it pares away, and the inside carriageway of the motorway, which powers on towards the Chiltern scarp.

The three signs are the run-in strip to the beginning of the film; they are the flying fingers of the pit-crew boss as he counts down Mansell; they are the decline in rank (from sergeant, to corporal, to lance corporal) that indicates your demotion from the motorway. Furthermore, the ability to co-ordinate their sequence with the falling needles on the warmly glowing instrument panel of the car is a sound indication that you can intuitively apprehend three different scales at once (time, speed, distance), and that you are able to merge them effortlessly into the virtual reality that is motorway driving.

But for some obscure reason the Ministry has slipped up here. At the Beaconsfield exit there is far too long a gap between the last sign and the start of the slip road. I fell into this gap and lost my sense of scale. It occurred to me, when at last I gained the roundabout, and the homey, green sign (Beaconsfield 4) heaved into view, that this gap, this lacuna, was, in terms of my projected thesis, 'No Services: Reflex Ritualism and Modern Motorway Signs (with special reference to the M40)' – an aspect of what the French call *délire*. In other words that part of the text that is a deviation or derangement, not contained within the text, and yet defines the text better than the text itself.

I almost crashed. By the time I reached home (a modest bungalow set hard against the model village that is Beaconsfield's principal visitor attraction), I had just about stopped shaking. I went straight to the kitchen. The baking tray I had left in the oven that morning had become a miniature Death Valley of hard-baked morphine granules. The dark brown rime lay in a ruckled surface, broken here and there into regular patterns of scales, like the skin of some moribund lizard. I used a steel spatula to scrape the material up and placed it carefully in a small plastic bowl decorated with leaping bunnies. (After the divorce my wife organised the division of the chattels. She took all the adult-size plates and cutlery, leaving me with the diminutive ware that our children had outgrown.)

I have no formal training in chemistry, but somehow, by a process of hit and miss, I have developed a method whereby I can precipitate a soluble tartrate from raw morphine granules. The problem with the stuff is that it still contains an appreciable amount of chalk. This is because I obtain my supplies in the form of bottles of kaolin and morphine purchased in sundry chemists. If I leave the bottles to sit for long enough, most of the morphine rises to the top. But you can never eradicate all the kaolin, and when the morphine suspension is siphoned off, some of the kaolin invariably comes as well.

Months of injecting this stuff have given my body an odd aspect, as with every shot more chalk is deposited along the walls of my veins, much in the manner of earth being piled up to form either an embankment or a cutting around a roadway. Thus the history of my addiction has been mapped out by me, in the same way that the road system of South-East England was originally constructed.

To begin with, conscious of the effects, I methodically worked my way through the veins in my arms and legs, turning them first the tannish colour of drovers' paths, then the darker brown of cart tracks, until eventually they became macadamised, blackened, by my abuse. Finally I turned my attention to the arteries. Now, when

I stand on the broken bathroom scales and contemplate my route-planning image in the full-length mirror, I see a network of calcified conduits radiating from my groin. Some of them are scored into my flesh like underpasses, others are raised up on hardened revetments of flesh: bloody flyovers.

I have been driven to using huge five-millilitre barrels, fitted with the long, blue-collared needles necessary for hitting arteries. I am very conscious that, should I miss, the consequences for my circulatory system could be disastrous. I might lose a limb and cause tailbacks right the way round the M25. Sometimes I wonder if I may be losing my incident room.

There's this matter of the thesis, to begin with. Not only is the subject matter obscure (some might say risible), but I have no grant or commission. It would be all right if I were some dilettante, privately endowed, who could afford to toy with such things, but I am not. Rather, I both have myself to support and have to keep up the maintenance. If the maintenance isn't kept up, my ex-wife – who is frequently levelled by spirits – will become as obdurate as any consulting civil engineer. She has it within her power to arrange bollards around me, or even to insist on the introduction of tolls to pay for the maintenance. There could be questions in the bungalow – something I cannot abide.

But last night none of this troubled me. I was lost in the arms of Morphia. As I pushed home the plunger she spoke to me thus: 'Left hand down. Harder . . . harder

. . . harder!' And around I swept, pinned by g force into the tight circularity of history. In my reverie I saw the M40 as it will be some 20,000 years from now, when the second neolithic age has dawned over Europe.

Still no services. All six carriageways and the hard shoulder are grassed over. The long enfilades of dipping halogen lights, which used to wade in concrete, are gone, leaving behind shallow depressions visible from the air. Every single one of the distance markers 'Birmingham 86' has been crudely tipped to the horizontal, forming a series of steel biers. On top of them are the decomposing corpses of motorway chieftains, laid out for excarnation prior to interment. Their bones are to be placed in chambers, mausoleums that have been hollowed out from the gigantic concrete caissons of moribund motorway bridges.

I was conscious of being one of these chieftains, these princelings of the thoroughfare. And as I stared up into the dark, dark blue of a sky that was near to the end of history, I was visited by a horrible sense of claustrophobia – the claustrophobia that can come only when no space is great enough to contain you, not the involution that is time itself.

I have no idea how long I must have lain there, observing the daily life of the simple motorway folk, but it was long enough for me to gain an appreciation of the subtlety with which they had adapted this monumental ruin. While the flat expanse of the carriageways was used for rudimentary agriculture, the steeply raked embankments were left for aurochs, moufflon and other newly primitive grazers.

The motorway tribe was divided up into clans or extended families, each of which had made its encampment at a particular junction and taken a different item of the prehistoric road furniture for its totem. My clan – Junction 2, that is – had somehow managed to preserve a set of cat's eyes from the oblivion of time. These were being worn by the chieftain, bound into his complicated head-dress, when he came to see how I was getting on with decomposing.

'You must understand,' he said, observing the Star Trek convention, whereby even the most outlandish peoples still speak standard English, 'that we view the M40 as a giant astronomical clock. We use the slip roads, maintenance areas, bridges and flyovers azimuthally, to predict the solstices and hence the seasons. Ours is a religion both of great antiquity and of a complexity that belies our simple agrarian culture. Although we are no longer able to read or write ourselves, our priesthood has orally transmitted down the generations the sacred revelations contained in this ancient text.' With this he produced from a fold in his cloak a copy of 'No Services: Reflex Ritualism and Modern Motorway Signs (with special reference to the M40)', my as yet unwritten thesis.

Needless to say, this uncharacteristically upbeat ending to my narcotic vision left me feeling more melioristic than usual when I awoke this morning. Staggering to the kitchen I snapped on the radio. A disc jockey ululated an intro while I put on the kettle. The sun was rising over the model village. From where I sat I could see its rays reflected by a thousand tiny diamond-patterned windows. I sipped my tea; it tasted flat, as listless as myself. Looking into the cup I could see that the brown fluid was supporting an archipelago of scale. Dirty grey-brown stuff, tattered and variegated. I went back to the kitchen and peered into the kettle. Not only was the interior almost completely choked by scale, but the de-scaler itself was furred over, transformed into a chrysalis by mineral deposits. I resolved that today I would visit the ironmonger's and purchase a new de-scaler.

It's on my route – the ironmonger's – for I've burnt down every chemist in Beaconsfield in the last few months, and now I must head further afield for my kaolin and morphine supplies. I must voyage to Tring, to Amersham and even up the M40, to High Wycombe.

Relative

'CAN I PAY for these?'
        'Whassat?'
'Can I pay for these – these de-scalers?' Time is standing still in the ironmonger's. Outside, a red-and-white-striped awning protects an array of brightly-coloured washing-up bowls from the drizzle. Inside, the darkness is scented with nails and resinous timber. I had no idea that the transaction would prove so gruelling. The proprietor of the ironmonger's is looking at me the same way that the pharmacist does when I go to buy my kaolin and morphine.

'Why d'you want three?' Is it my imagination, or does his voice really have an edge of suspicion? What does he suspect me of? Some foul and unnatural practice carried out with kettle de-scalers? It hardly seems likely.

'I've got an incredible amount of scale in my kettle; that's why.' I muster an insouciance I simply don't feel. Since I have been accused, I know that I am guilty. I know that I lure young children away from the precincts of the model village and subject them to appalling, brutal, intercrural sex. I abrade their armpits, their kneepits, the junctures of their thighs, with my spun mini-rolls of wire. That's why I need three.

Guilt dogs me as I struggle to ascend the high street, stepping on the heels of my shoes, almost tripping me up. Guilt about my children – that's the explanation for the scene in the ironmonger's. Ever since my loss of sense of scale, I have found it difficult to relate to my children. They no longer feel comfortable coming to visit me here in Beaconsfield. They say they would rather stay with their mother. The model village, which used to entrance them, now bores them.

Perhaps it was an indulgence on my part – moving to a bungalow next to the model village. It's true that when I sat, puffing on my pipe, watching my son and daughter move about amongst the four-foot-high, half-timbered semis, I would feel transported, taken back to my own childhood. It was the confusion in scale that allowed this. For if the model village was to scale, my children would be at least sixty feet tall. Easily big enough, and competent enough, to re-parent me.

It was the boy who blew the whistle on me, grassed me up to his mother. At seven, he is old enough to know the difference between the smell of tobacco and the smell that comes from my pipe. Naturally he told his mother and she realised immediately that I was back on the M.

In a way I don't blame him – it's a filthy habit. And the business of siphoning off the morphine from the bottles and then baking it in the oven until it forms a smokable paste. Well I mean, it's pathetic, this DIY addiction. No wonder that there are no pleasure domes for me, in my *bricolage* reverie. Instead I see twice five yards of fertile ground, with sheds and raspberry canes girded round. In a word: an allotment.

When my father died he subdivided his allotment and left a fifth of it to each of his children. The Association wouldn't allow it. They said that allotments were only leased rather than owned. It's a great pity, because what with the subsidies available and the new intensive agricultural methods, I could probably have made a reasonable living out of my fifth. I can just see myself . . . making hay with a kitchen fork, spreading silage with a teaspoon, bringing in the harvest with a wheelbarrow, ploughing with a trowel tied to a two-by-four. Bonsai cattle wind o'er the lea of the compost heap as I recline in the pet cemetery . . .

It was not to be.

Returning home from High Wycombe I add the contents of my two new bottles of kaolin and morphine to the plant. Other people have ginger-beer plants; I have a morphine plant. I made my morphine plant out of a plastic sterilising unit. It would be a nice irony, this transmogrification of taboo, were it not for the fact that every time I clap eyes on the thing I remember with startling accuracy what it looked like full of teats and bottles, when the children were babies and I was a happier man. I think I mentioned the division of chattels following the divorce. This explains why I ended up, here in Beaconsfield, with the decorative Tupperware, the baby-bouncer, sundry activity centres and the afore-mentioned sterilising unit. Whereas my ex-wife resides in St John's Wood, reclining on an emperor-size bateau-lit. When I cast off and head out on to the sea of sleep my vessel is a plastic changing mat, patterned with Fred Flintstones and Barney Rubbles.

It's lucky for me that the five 'police procedurals' I wrote during my marriage are still selling well. Without the royalties I don't think I would be able to keep my family in the manner to which they have unfortunately become accustomed. I cannot imagine that the book I am currently working on, *Murder on the Median Strip*, will do a fraction as well. (I say that confidently, but what fraction do I mean? Certainly not a half or a quarter, but why not a fiftieth or a hundredth? This is certainly conceivable. I must try and be more accurate with my figures of speech. I must use them as steel rulers to delimit thought. Woolliness will be my un-doing.)

In Murder on the Median Strip (henceforth *M on the MS*), a young woman is raped, murdered and buried on the median strip of the M40 in between Junction 2 (Beaconsfield) and Junction 3 (High Wycombe). As shall become apparent, it is a howdunnit, rather than a whodunnit. The murder occurs late on a Friday evening when the motorway is still crowded with ex-urbanites heading for home. The police are patrolling, looking for speeders. Indeed, they have set up a radar trap between the two principal bridges on this section of road. And yet no one notices anything.

When the shallow, bitumen-encrusted grave is discovered, the police, indulging in their penchant for overkill, decide to reconstruct the entire incident. They put out a call on *Crimewatch UK* for all those who were on the motorway in that place, at that time, to reassemble at Junction 2. The public response is overwhelming, and by virtue of careful interviewing – the recollection of number plates, makes of car, children making faces and so forth – they establish that they have managed to net all the cars and drivers that could have been there. The logistics of this are immensely complicated. But such is the ghastliness of the crime that the public demands that the resources be expended. Eventually, by dint of computer-aided visualisations, the police are able to re-enact the whole incident. The cars set off at intervals; the police hover overhead in helicopters; officers in patrol cars and on foot question any passers-by. But, horror of horrors, while the reconstruction is actually taking place, the killer strikes again – this time between Junction 6 (Watlington) and Junction 7 (Thame). Once more his victim is a young woman, whom he sexually assaults, strangles, and then crudely inters beneath the static steel fender of the crash barrier.

That's as far as I've got with *M on the MS*. Sometimes, contemplating the *MS*, I begin to feel that I've painted myself into a corner with this convoluted plot. I realise that I may have tried to stretch the credulity of my potential readers too far.

In a way the difficulties of the plot mirror my own difficulties as a writer. In creating such an unworkable and fantastic scenario I have managed, at least, to fulfil my father's expectations of my craft.

'There's no sense of scale in your books,' he said to me shortly before he died. At that time I had written only two procedurals, both featuring Inspector Archimedes, my idiosyncratic Greek Cypriot detective. 'You can have a limited success,' he went on, 'chipping away like this at the edges of society, chiselling off microscopic fragments of observation. But really important writing provides some sense of the relation between individual psychology and social change, of the scale of things in general. You can see that if you look at the great nineteenth-century novels.' He puffed on his pipe as he spoke, and, observing his wrinkled, scaly hide and the way his red lips and yellow teeth masticated the black stem, I was reminded of a basking lizard, sticking its tongue out at the world.

A letter came this morning from the Municipality, demanding payment of their property tax. When I first moved here, a man came from the borough valuer's to assess the rateable value of the bungalow. I did some quick work with the trellises and managed to make it look as if Number 59, Crendon Road, was in fact one of the houses in the model village.

To begin with, the official disputed the idea that I could possibly be living in this pocket-sized dwelling, but I managed to convince him that I was a doctoral student writing a thesis on 'The Apprehension of Scale in *Gulliver's Travels*, with special reference to Lilliput', and that the operators of the model village had leased the house to me so that I could gain first-hand experience of Gulliver's state of mind. I even entered the house and adopted some attitudes – head on the kitchen table, left leg rammed through the french windows – in order to persuade him.

The result of this clever charade was that for two years my rates were assessed on the basis of 7ft 8in sq. of living space. I had to pay £11.59 per annum. Now, of course, I am subject to the full whack. Terribly unfair. And anyway, if the tax is determined by the individual rather than by the property, what if that individual has a hazy or distorted sense of self? Shouldn't people with acute dissociation, or multiple personalities, be forced to pay more? I have resolved not to pay the tax until I have received a visit from the borough clinical psychologist.

The Ascent

'Affected as well as asinine' *TLS*

SOME OF MY INNOVATIONS regarding the new genre of 'Motorway Verse' have been poorly received, both by the critics and by the reading public. My claim, that what my motorway verse is trying to do represents a return to the very roots of *poetas*, an inspired attempt to link modish hermeneutics to the original function of oral literature, has been dismissed *sans phrase*.

I myself cannot even understand the thrust of this criticism. It seems to me self-evident that the subconscious apprehension of signs by motorway drivers is exactly analogous to that act whereby the poets of primitive cultures give life, actually breathe reality into the land.

Taking the M40 as an example of this:

> Jnctn 1. Uxbridge. Jnctn 1A. (M25) M4.
> Jnctn 2. Slough A365. No Services.
> On M40 . . .

would be a very believable sample of such a 'signing up' of the country. Naturally, in order to understand the somewhat unusual scansion, it is necessary that readers imaginatively place themselves in a figurative car that is actually driving up the aforementioned motorway. Metrical feet are, therefore, to be determined as much by feeling through the pedals the shift from macadamised to concrete surfaces, and by hearing the susurration produced by alterations in the height and material construction of the crash barrier, as by the rhythm of the words themselves.

Furthermore, a motorway verse that attempts to describe the ascent of the Chiltern scarp from the Oxfordshire side will, of course, be profoundly different to one that chronicles the descent from Junction 5 (Stokenchurch) to Junction 6 (Watlington). For example:

> Crawling, crawling, crawling. Crawler Lane
> Slow-slow O'Lorry-o. Lewknor. 50 mph max.
> 11T! Narrow lanes, narrowing, narr-o-wing,
> na-rro-wing.

as opposed to:

> F'tum. F'tum. F'tum.
> Kerchunk, kerchunk (Wat-ling-ton) . . .

Well, I'm certain no one reading this had any difficulty in divining which was which!

On the Continent they are not afflicted by the resistance to the modern that so entirely characterises

English cultural life. In France, '*Vers Péage*' is a well-respected genre, already making its way on to university syllabuses. Indeed I understand that a critical work is soon to be published that concerns itself solely with the semantic incongruities presented by the term 'soft vierge'.

It has occurred to me that it could be my introduction of motorway symbology itself, as if it were an extension of the conventional alphabet, that has hardened the hearts of these penny-ante time-servers, possessors of tenure (but no grip), and the like. But it seems to me that the white arrow pointing down, obliquely, to the right; the ubiquitous '11T' lane-closing ideogram; the emotive, omega-like, overhead '[X]'; and many many others all have an equal right to be considered capable of meaningful combination with orthodox characters.

On bad days, days when the tedium and obscurity of my life here at Beaconsfield seem almost justified, I am embarrassed to say that I console myself with the thought that there may be some grand conspiracy, taking in critics, publishers, editors and the executives in charge of giant type-founders such as Monotype, to stop my verse from gaining any success. For, were it to do so, they would have to alter radically the range of typefaces that they provide.

Is it any wonder that I look for consolation – partly in draughts of sickly morphine syrup (drunk straight off the top of bottles of kaolin and morphine), and partly in hard, dedicated work on my motorway saga, entitled

From Birmingham to London and Back Again Delivering Office Equipment, with Nary a Service Centre to Break the Monotony?

There's that, and there's also the carving of netsuke, at which I am becoming something of an expert. I have chosen to concentrate on rendering in ivory the monumental works of modern sculptors. Thus, I have now completed a set of early Caros and Henry Moores, all of which could be comfortably housed in a pup tent.

The ebb and flow of my opiate addiction is something that I have come to prize as a source of literary inspiration. When I am beginning a new habit, my hypnagogic visions are intricate processions of images that I can both summon and manipulate at will. But when I am withdrawing, I am frequently plunged into startling nightmares. Nightmares that seem to last for eons and yet of which I am conscious – at one and the same time – as taking place within a single REM.

Last night's dream was a classic case of this clucking phenomenon. In it, I found myself leaving the bungalow and entering the precincts of the model village. I wandered around the forty-foot-long village green, admiring the precision and attention to detail that the model makers have lavished on their creation. I peeked first into the model butcher's shop. Lilliputian rashers of bacon were laid out on plastic trays, together with sausages, perfect in every respect, but the size of mouse droppings. Then I sauntered over to the post office. On the eight-inch-high counter sat an envelope the size of a postage stamp. Wonder of wonders, I could even read the address on the envelope. It was a poll-tax demand, destined for me.

Straightening up abruptly I caught sight of two model buildings that I was unfamiliar with. The first of these was a small, but perfectly formed, art gallery. Looking through the tall windows I could see, inside, on the polished wooden floor, a selection of my netsuke. The Caros rather than the Moores. Preposterous, I thought to myself, with one of those leaps of dream logic; a real village of this size would never have an art gallery. Let alone one exhibiting the works of an internationally renowned sculptor.

The second building was my own bungalow. I couldn't be certain of this – it is after all not that remarkable an edifice – until I had looked in through the kitchen window. There, under the dirty cream melamine work surface surrounding the aluminium sink, I could see hundreds of little kaolin and morphine bottles, serried in dusty ranks. That settled it.

As soon as I had clapped eyes on them, I found myself miraculously reduced in size and able to enter the model bungalow. I wandered from room to room, more than a little discomfited at my phantasmagoric absorption into Beaconsfield's premier visitor attraction. Stepping on to the sun porch I found another model – as it were, a model model. Also of the bungalow. Once again I was diminished and able to enter.

I must have gone through at least four more of these

vertiginous descents in scale before I was able to stop, and think, and prevent myself from examining another model bungalow. As it was I knew that I must be standing in a sun porch for which a double-glazing estimate would have to be calculated in angstroms. From the position I found myself in, to be 002 scale would have been, to me, gargantuan. How to get back? That was the problem.

It is fortunate indeed that in my youth I spent many hours tackling the more difficult climbs around Wastdale Head. These rocky scrambles, although close to the tourist tramps up the peaks of Scafell Pike and Helvellyn, are nevertheless amongst the most demanding rock climbs in Europe.

It took me three months to ascend, back up the six separate stages of scale, and reach home once more. Some of the pitches, especially those involving climbing down off the various tables the model bungalows were placed on, I would wager were easily the most extreme ever attempted by a solo climber. On many occasions, I found myself dangling from the rope I had plaited out of strands of carpet underlay, with no apparent way of regaining the slick varnished face of the table leg, and the checkerboard of lino – relative to my actual size – some six hundred feet below.

Oh, the stories I could tell! The sights I saw! It would need an epic to contain them. As it is I have restrained myself – although, on awakening, I did write a letter to the Alpine Club on the ethics of climbers, finding themselves in such situations, using paper clips as fixed crampons.

The final march across the 'true' model village to my bungalow was, of course, the most frightening. When contained within the Russian-doll series of ever diminishing bungalows, I had been aware that the ordinary laws of nature were, to some extent, in abeyance. However, out in the village I knew that I was exposed to all the familiar terrors of small-scale adventuring: wasps the size of zeppelins, fluff-falls the weight of an avalanche, mortar-bomb explosions of plant spore, and so on and so forth.

My most acute anxiety, as I traversed the model village, was that I would be sighted by a human. I was aware that I could not be much larger than a sub-atomic particle, and as such I would be subject to Heisenberg's Uncertainty Principle. Were I to be in any way observed, not only might I find the direction of my journey irremediably altered, I could even cease to exist altogether!

It happened as I picked my way over the first of the steps leading up from the village to my bungalow. The very grain of the concrete formed a lunar landscape which I knew would take me days to journey across. I wiped the sweat that dripped from my sunburnt brow. Something vast, inconceivably huge, was moving up ahead of me. It was a man! To scale! He turned, and his turning was like some geological event, the erosion of a mountain range or the undulation of the Mohorovicic Discontinuity itself!

It was one of the maintenance men who works in the model village. I knew it because, emblazoned across the back of his blue boiler suit, picked out in white as on a motorway sign, was the single word 'MAINTENANCE'. His giant eye loomed towards me, growing bigger and bigger, until the red-and-blue veins that snaked across the bilious ball were as the Orinoco or the Amazon, to my petrified gaze. He blinked – and I winked out of existence.

I don't need to tell you that when I awoke sweating profusely, the covers twisted around my quaking body like a strait-jacket, I had no difficulty at all in interpreting the dream.

To the Bathroom

'LIKE, WE'RE CONSIDERING the historic present –?'
    'Yeah.'
    'And David says, "I want to go to the bathroom."'
    'Yeah.'
    'So, like we all accompany him there and stuff. Cos in his condition it wouldn't like be a . . . be a – '
    'Good idea for him to be alone?'
    'Yeah, thassit. So we're standing there, right. All four of us, in the bathroom, and David's doing what he has to do. And we're still talking about it.'
    'It?'
    'The historic present. Because Diane – you know Diane?'
    'Sort of.'
    'Well, she says the historic present is, like . . . er . . . like, more emotionally labile than other tenses. Yeah, thass what she says. Anyways, she's saying this and David is, like, steaming, man . . . I mean to say he's really plummeting. It's like he's being de-cored or something. This isn't just Montezuma's revenge, it's everyone's revenge. It's the revenge of every deracinated group of indigenes ever to have had the misfortune to en-

counter the European. It's a sort of collective curse of David's colon. It's like his colon is being crucified or something.'

'He's anally labile.'

'Whadjewsay?'

'He's anally labile.'

Labile, labile. Labby lips. Libby-labby lips. This is the kind of drivel I've been reduced to. Imaginary dialogues between myself and a non-existent interlocutor. But is it any surprise? I mean to say, if you have a colon as spastic as mine it's bound to insinuate itself into every aspect of your thinking. My trouble is I'm damned if I do and I'm damned if I don't. If I don't drink vast quantities of kaolin and morphine I'm afflicted with the most terrifying bouts of diarrhoea. And if I do – drink a couple of bottles a day, that is – I'm subject to the most appalling undulations, seismic colonic ructions. It doesn't really stop the shits either. I still get them, I just don't get caught short. Caught short on the hard shoulder, that's the killer.

Say you're driving up to High Wycombe, for example. Just out on a commonplace enough errand. Like going to buy a couple of bottles of K&M. And you're swooping down towards Junction 3, the six lanes of blacktop twisting away from you like some colossal wastepipe, through which the automotive crap of the metropolis is being voided into the rural septic tank, when all of a sudden you're overcome. You pull over on to the hard shoulder, get out of the car, and squat down. Hardly dignified. And not only that, destructive of the motorway itself. Destructive of the purity of one's recollection.

That's why I prefer to stay home in my kaolin-lined bungalow. I prefer to summon up my memories of the motorway in the days before I was so afflicted. In the days when my vast *roman-fleuve* was barely a trickle, and my sense of scale was intact. Then, distance was defined by regular increments, rather than by the haphazard lurch from movement to movement.

This morning I was sitting, not really writing, just dabbling. I was hunkered down inside myself, my ears unconsciously registering the whisper, whistle and whicker of the traffic on the M40, when I got that sinking feeling. I hied me to the bathroom, just in time to see a lanky youth disappearing out of the window, with my bathroom scales tucked under his arm.

I grabbed a handful of his hip-length jacket and pulled him back into the room. He was a mangy specimen. His head was badly shaven, with spirals of ringworm on the pitted surface. The youth had had these embellished with crude tattoos, as if to dignify his repulsive skin condition. His attire was a loose amalgam of counter-cultural styles, the ragged chic of a redundant generation. His pupils were so dilated that the black was getting on to his face. I instantly realised that I had nothing to fear from him. He didn't cry out, or even attempt to struggle.

I had seen others like him. There's quite a posse of them, these 'model heads'. That's what they call themselves. They congregate around the model village, venerating it as a symbol of their anomie. It's as if, by becoming absorbed in the detail of this tiny world, they hope to diminish the scale of society's problems. In the winter they go abroad, settling near Legoland in Belgium.

'Right, you,' I said, in householder tones. 'You might have thought that you'd get away with nicking something as trivial as those bathroom scales, but it just so happens that they have a sentimental value for me.'

'Whadjergonna do then?' He was bemused – not belligerent.

'I'm going to put you on trial, that's what I'm going to do.'

'You're not gonna call the filth, are you?'

'No, no. No need. In Beaconsfield we have extended the whole principle of Neighbourhood Watch to include the idea of neighbourhood justice. I will sit in judgment on you myself. If you wish, my court will appoint a lawyer who will organise your defence.'

'Err – ' He had slumped down on top of the wicker laundry basket, which made him look even more like one of Ali Baba's anorectic confrères. 'Yeah, OK, whatever you say.'

'Good. I will represent you myself. Allow me, if you will, to assume my position on the bench.' We shuffled around each other in the confinement of tiles. I put the seat down, sat down, and said, 'The court may be seated.'

For a while after that nothing happened. The two of us sat in silence, listening to the rising and falling flute of the Vent-Axia. I thought about the day the court-appointed officer had come to deliver my decree nisi. He must have been reading the documents in the car as he drove up the motorway, because when I encountered him on the doorstep he was trying hard – but failing – to suppress a smirk of amusement.

I knew why. My wife had sued for divorce on the grounds of adultery. The co-respondent was known to her, and the place where the adultery had taken place was none other than on these selfsame scales. The ones the model head had just attempted to steal. At that time they were still located in the bathroom of our London house. After the decree absolute, my ex-wife sent them to me in Beaconsfield, together with a caustic note.

It was a hot summer afternoon in the bathroom. I was with a lithe young foreign woman, who was full of capricious lust. 'Come on,' she said, 'let's do it on the scales. It'll be fun, we'll look like some weird astro-logical symbol, or a diagram from the *Kama Sutra*.' She twisted out of her dress and pulled off her underwear. I stood on the scales. Even translated from metric to imperial measure, my bodyweight still looked un-impressive. She hooked her hands around my neck and jumped. The flanges of flesh on the inside of her thighs neatly fitted the notches above my bony hips. I grasped the fruit of her buttocks in my sweating palms. She braced herself, feet against the wall, toenails snagging on the Artex. Her panting smoked the mirror on the medicine cabinet. I moved inside her. The coiled spring inside the scales squeaked and groaned. Eventually it broke altogether.

That's how my wife twigged. When she next went to weigh herself she found the scales jammed, the pointer registering 322 lb. Exactly the combined weight of me and the family au pair . . .

Oh, *mene, mene, tekel, upharsin*! What a fool I was! Now fiery hands retributively mangle my innards! The demons play upon my sackbut and I am cast into the fiery furnace of evacuation. I am hooked there, a toilet duck, condemned for ever to lick under the rim of life!

The model head snapped me out of my fugue. 'You're a Libra,' he said, 'aren't you?'

'Whassat?'

'Your sign. It's Libra, innit?' He was regarding me with the preternatural stare of a madman or a seer.

'Well, yes, as a matter of fact it is.'

'I'm good at that. Guessing people's astrological signs. Libra's are, like, er . . . creative an' that.'

'I s'pose so.'

'But they also find it hard to come to decisions – '

'Are you challenging the authority of this court?' I tried to sound magisterial, but realised that the figure I cut was ridiculous.

'Nah, nah. I wouldn't do that, mate. It's just . . . like . . . I mean to say, whass the point, an' that?'

I couldn't help but agree with him, so I let him go. I even insisted that he take the bathroom scales with him. After all, what good are they to me now?

Lizard

Epilogue. Many years later . . .

I F YOU WANT to walk round the Lizard Peninsula,
you have to be reasonably well equipped. Which is
not to say that this part of Cornwall is either particularly
remote (the M5 now goes all the way to Land's End) or
that rugged. It's just that the exposure to so much wind
and sky, and so many pasties, after a winter spent huddled
on the urban periphery (somewhere like Beaconsfield,
for example), can have an unsettling effect. I always
advise people to take an antacid preparation, and also
some kaolin and morphine. There's no need any more to
carry an entire bottle, for Sterling Health have thought-
fully created a tablet form of this basic but indispensable
remedy.

One other word of warning before you set out. Don't
be deceived by the map into thinking that distances of,
say, eight to ten miles represent a comfortable afternoon's stroll. The Lizard is so called because of the many
rocky inlets that are gouged out of its scaly sides, giving
the entire landmass the aspect of some giant creature,
bound for the Atlantic vivarium. The coastal path is

constantly either ascending or descending around these inlets. Therefore, to gain a mile you may have to go up and down as much as six hundred feet.

I myself haven't been to the Lizard for many years, in fact not since I was a young man. Even if I felt strong enough to make the journey now, I wouldn't go. For those younger than I, who cannot remember a time before the current Nationalist Trust Government took power, the prospect may still seem inviting. But personally, I find that the thought of encountering the Government's Brown Shirts, with their oak-leaf epaulettes, sticks in my craw. I would bitterly resent being compelled by these paramilitary nature wardens to admire the scenery, register the presence (or even absence) of ancient monuments, and propitiate the wayside waste shrines with crumpled offerings.

Of course, we aren't altogether immune from the depredations of the Trust here in Beaconsfield. Last month, after a bitterly fought local election, they gained power in almost all of the wards, including the one that contains the model village itself. There have been rumours, discreet mutterings, that they intend to introduce their ubiquitous signs to the village. These will designate parts of it areas of (albeit minute) 'outstanding natural beauty'.

But I am old now, and have not the stomach for political infighting. Since the publication of the last volume of my magnum opus, *A History of the English Motorway Service Centre*, I have gained a modest eminence. People tell me that I am referred to as 'the Macaulay of the M40', a sobriquet that, I must confess, gives me no little pleasure. I feel vindicated by the verdict of posterity. (I say posterity, for I am now so old that hardly anyone realises I am still alive.)

I spend most my the days out on the sun porch. Here I lie naked, for all the world like some moribund reptile, sopping up the rays. My skin has turned mahogany with age and melanoma. It's difficult for me to distinguish now between the daub of cancerous sarcoma and the toughened wattle of my flesh. Be that as it may, I am not frightened of death. I feel no pain, despite having long since reduced the indulgence of my pernicious habituation to kaolin and morphine to a mere teaspoonful every hour.

With age have come stoicism and repose. When I was younger I could not focus on anything, or even apprehend a single thought, without feeling driven to incorporate it into some architectonic, some Great Design. I was also plagued by lusts, both fleshly and demonic, which sent me into such dizzying spirals of self-negation that I was compelled to narcosis.

But now, even the contemplation of the most trivial things can provide enough sensual fodder to last me an entire morning. Today, for example, I became transfixed, staring into the kettle, by the three separate levels of scale therein. First the tangible scale, capping the inverted cradle of the water's meniscus. Secondly, the crystalline accretions of scale that wreathed the element.

And thirdly, of course, the very abstract notion of 'scale' itself, implied by my unreasoned observation. It's as if I were possessed of some kind of Escher-vision, allowing me constantly to perceive the dimensional conundrum that perception presents.

I am also comforted in my solitude by my pets. One beneficial side-effect of the change in climate has been the introduction of more exotic species to this isle. But whereas the *nouveaux riches* opt for the Pantagruelian spectacle of giraffes cropping their laburnums, and hippopotamuses wallowing in their sun-saturated swimming pools, I have chosen to domesticate the more elegant frill-necked lizard.

This curious reptile, with its preposterous vermilion ruff, stands erect on its hind legs like a miniature dinosaur. When evening comes, and the day's visitors have departed, I let it out so that it may roam the lanes and paths of the model village. The sight of this pocket Godzilla stalking the dwarfish environs, its head darting this way and that, as if on the look-out for a canapé-sized human, never fails to amuse me.

However, not every aspect of my life is quite so easeful and reposed. The occasional dispute, relating to a lifetime of scholarly endeavour, still flares up occasionally. It is true that my work has a certain status here in England, but of course all this means in practice is that although many have heard of it, few have actually read any of it.

In the ex-colonies the situation is different. A Professor Moi wrote to me last year, from the University of

Uganda, to dispute the findings of my seminal paper 'When is a Road Not a Road?'*, in which – if you can be bothered to recall – I established a theory that a motorway cannot be said to be a motorway unless it is longer than it is broad. I was inspired to this by my contemplation of the much maligned A41(M), which at that time ran for barely a mile. Moi took issue with the theory, and after I had perused the relevant Ugandan gazetteer it became clear to me why.

The ill-fated Lusaka Bypass was to have been the centrepiece of the Ugandan Government's Motorway Construction Programme. However, resources ran out after only one junction and some eighty feet of road had been built. Faced with the options of either changing the nomenclature or admitting failure, the Ugandans had no alternative but to take issue with the theory itself.

But such episodes are infrequent. Mostly I am left alone by the world. My children have grown up and disappointed me; my former friends and acquaintances have forgotten me. If I do receive any visitors nowadays, they are likely to be young professional couples, nascent ex-urbanites, come to enquire whether or not the bungalow is for sale.

It is a delicious irony that although when I first moved to Beaconsfield the bungalow was regarded as tacky in the extreme, over the years it has become a period piece. The aluminium-framed picture windows, the pebble-dash façade, the corrugated-perspex carport: all of these

* *British Journal of Ephemera*, Spring 1986

are now regarded as delightfully authentic and original features. Such is the queer humour of history.

And what of the M40 itself, the fount of my life's work? How stands it? Well, I must confess that since the universal introduction of electric cars with a maximum speed of 15 mph, the glamour of motorway driving seems entirely lost. Every so often I'll take the golf buggy out and tootle up towards Junction 5 (Stokenchurch), but my motives are really rather morbid.

Morbid, for it is here that I am to be buried. Here, where the motorway plunges through a gunsight cutting and the rolling plain of Oxfordshire spreads out into the blue distance. Just beyond the Chiltern scarp the M40 bisects the Ridgeway, that neolithic drovers' path which was the motorway of Stone Age Britain. It is here that the Nationalist Trust has given gracious permission for me to construct my mausoleum.

I have opted for something in the manner of an ancient chamber tomb. A long, regular heap of layered stones, with corbelled walls rising to a slab roof. At one end the burial mound will tastefully elide with the caisson of the bridge on which the M40 spans the Ridgeway.

It is a fitting memorial, and what's more, I am convinced that it will remain long after the motorway itself has become little more than a grassed-over ruin, a monument to a dead culture. The idea that perhaps, in some distant future, disputatious archaeologists will find themselves flummoxed by the discovery of my tomb, together with its midden of discarded motorway signs, brings a twitch to my jowls.

Will the similarities in construction between my tomb and the great chamber tombs of Ireland and the Orkneys lead them to posit a continuous motorway culture, lasting some 7,000 years? I hope so. It has always been my contention that phenomena such as Silbury Hill and the Avebury stone circle can best be understood as, respectively, an embankment and a roundabout.

And so it seems that it is only by taking this very, very, long-term view that the answer to that pernicious riddle 'Why are there no services on the M40?' will find an answer.

In conclusion, then. It may be said of me that I have lost my sense of scale, but never that I have lost my sense of proportion.

Repeat this exercise daily, or until you are
thoroughly proficient.

Chest

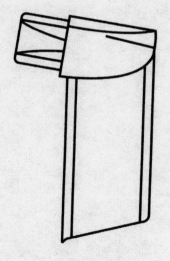

THE PAVEMENT OUTSIDE Marten's the newsagent was streaked with sputum. In the outrageously dull light of a mid-afternoon, in midwinter, in middle England, the loops and lumps of mucus and phlegm appeared strangely bright, lurid even, as if some Jackson Pollock of the pneumo-thorax had been practising Action Hawking.

There was an incident – of sorts – going on in the entrance to the shop. A man in the middle of his middle years, dressed not so much warmly as tightly in a thick, hip-length jacket, corduroy trousers, brogues, and anaconda of woollen scarf, was upbraiding the shop manager. His voice – which was in the middle of middle-class accents – would start off at quite a reasonable pitch, but as he spoke it would creep up the scale until it was a melodramatic whine. The shop manager, blue-suited, nylon-shirted, with thinning hair and earnest expression, kept trying – albeit with appropriate deference – to break in, but without success.

'I can't put up with this any more, Hutchinson,' said the man, whose name was Simon-Arthur Dykes. 'I've two sick children and an invalid wife, as well as other dependants. God knows how many times I've told your boy to bring the paper to the door and knock, but he still won't do it. The paper is vital for my work – it's useless to me if it's damp and soggy, but every single day it's the same, he just chucks it over the fence. What the hell does he think it's going to do, grow legs and scamper up to the house?'

'But Mr Dykes – '

'Don't "but" me, Hutchinson, I'm paying you for a service that I don't receive. I'm a sensitive man, you know, a man who needs some caring and consideration. My nerves, you see, they're so very . . . so very . . . stretched, I feel that they might snap. Snap! D'you appreciate that? The nerves of the artist – '

'I'm not un – '

'You're not what? Unaware? Unsympathetic? Unaffected? All of the above? Oh, I don't know – I don't know – it's all too much for me. Perhaps my wife is right and we need a redeemer of some kind, Hutchinson, a reawakening . . .' And with this, Simon-Arthur Dykes's voice, instead of climbing up towards hysteria, fell down, down into his chest where it translated itself into a full-bodied coughing. A liquid coughing, that implied the sloshing about of some fluid ounces of gunk in his lungs.

The shop manager was left free to talk, which he did, fulsomely. 'No, Mr Dykes,' he began, sounding placatory, 'I'm not unsympathetic, I do feel for you, really I do. I can imagine what it must be like only too well. Out there at the Brown House, isolated, with the wet,

exposed fields all around you, damp and encompassing.'
His fingers made combing motions, ploughing dismal
little furrows in the air. 'I can see what a torment it must
be to receive a wet newspaper every morning' – now the
manager's own voice had begun to quaver – 'knowing
that it may be the only contact that you will have with
the world all day, the only thing to touch your sense of
isolation. I don't know. Oh Christ! I don't know.'

And with that the manager's voice cracked, and he
began to weep openly. But the weeping didn't last for
long, for having given way to the flow in one form, the
manager's will to resist the ever present tickling in his
own chest was eliminated. Soon, both of the men were
hacking away, producing great caribou-cry honks, followed by the rasping eructation of tablespoon-loads of
sputum, which they dumped, along with the rest of the
infective matter, on the pavement fronting the newsagent's.

A group of adolescents was hanging about outside
Marten's, for this was where the buses stopped, picking
up passengers for Oxford, High Wycombe and Princes
Risborough. They wore padded nylon anoraks, decorated with oblongs of fluorescent material and the
occasional, apparently random, selection of letters and
figures: 'ZX POWER NINE', was written on one boy's
jacket; and 'ARIZONA STATE 4001' on his girl companion's. With their squashy vinyl bags at their rubber-
ridged feet and their general air of round-shouldered
indifference, the adolescents gave the impression of

being a unit of some new kind of army – in transit. Part of a pan-European formation of Jugend Sportif.

None of them paid any attention to the two men, who were now reaching the rattling end of their joint coughing fit. They were all focused on one of the older boys, who held a small red cylinder attached to a valved mouthpiece. Mostly he kept the mouthpiece clamped in his teeth and breathed through the double-action valve with a mechanical 'whoosh', but every so often he would pass it to one of the others, and they would take a hit.

Straightening up the manager said, 'What's that you've got there, Kevin-Andrew?'

'It's oxygen, Mr Hutchinson,' said the lad, removing the mouthpiece.

'Well, give us both a go, Kevin, for the love of God. Can't you see the state poor Mr Dykes and I are in?'

'I don't know if I can, Mr Hutchinson . . .' The lad paused, looking shamefaced. 'You see, it's the family cylinder. I just got it recharged at the health centre and it's got to last us till the weekend.'

'If that's the case, why are you giving it out to your pals like a tube of bloody Smarties!' This was from Simon-Arthur Dykes. He too had straightened up, but was still gasping and visibly blue in the face. He shouldn't really have expostulated with such vigour, for it got him wheezing again, and he began to double over once more, one hand clutching at the doorjamb, the other flopping around in the air.

'Come on, Kevin-Andrew,' said the manager, 'give him the mouthpiece, for heaven's sake. Tell you what, you can all have a belt off of my Ventalin inhaler, if Mr Dykes and I can just get ourselves straight.'

Grudgingly, and with much shoulder-shrugging and foot-shuffling, the youth handed over the small red cylinder. In return Hutchinson passed him the angled plastic tube of the Ventalin inhaler.

For a while there was a sort of calm on the wan stage of the pavement. The two men helped one another to take several much needed pulls from the oxygen cylinder, while the group of adolescents formed a circle around which they passed the inhaler. There was silence, except for the whirring whizz of the inhaler and the kerchooof! of the oxygen cylinder.

All the parties began to look slightly better than formerly. Their pale cheeks acquired an ulterior glow, their eyes brightened, their countenances took on the aspect of febrile health that only comes to those who have temporarily relieved a condition of chronic invalidism.

Simon-Arthur Dykes drew himself up in the doorway, passing the oxygen cylinder back to Kevin-Andrew. 'Thank you, Mr Hutchinson, really I thank you most sincerely. You are a man of some honour, sir, some Christian virtue in a world of ugliness and misery.' Dykes clutched the manager's upper arm. 'Please, please, Mr Dykes, don't upset yourself again – think of your poor chest.' The manager gave Dykes his copy of the *Guardian*, which he had dropped during the coughing fit.

Dykes looked at the paper as if he couldn't remember what it was. His rather protruberant grey eyes were darting about, unable to alight on anything. His thick brown hair was standing up in a crazy bouffant on top of his high, strained forehead.

He took the manager by the arm again, and drew him back into the shop a couple of paces. Then he leant towards him conspiratorially saying, 'It's Dave Hutchinson, that's your name, isn't it?'

'Ye-es,' the manager replied uneasily.

'And your patronymic?'

'Dave as well.'

'Well, Dave-Dave, I want you to call me Simon-Arthur. I feel this little episode has brought us together, and I stand in debt on your account.'

'Really, Mr Dykes – '

'Simon-Arthur.'

'Simon-Arthur, I don't think it's at all – '

'No, I do. Listen, I've just picked up a brand-new nebuliser in Risborough. I've got it in the car. Why don't you come around this evening, and give it a try – bring your wife if you like.'

This invitation, so obviously felt and meant, softened the manager's resistance, broke down his barriers of social deference and retail professionalism. 'I'd like that, Simon- Arthur,' he said, grasping the artist's right hand firmly in both of his, 'really I would. But I'm afraid my wife is bed-bound, so it would only be me.'

'I am sorry — but that's OK, just come yourself.'

'I've got a few mils of codeine linctus left over from the monthly ration — shall I bring it with me?'

'Why not . . . we can have a little party, as best we can.'

The two men finished, smiling broadly, in unison. Simon-Arthur took Dave-Dave Hutchinson's hand warmly in his and gave it several pumps. Then they parted; and whilst Dave-Dave Hutchinson turned back into the interior of the shop, Simon-Arthur Dykes crossed the road to where his car was parked in the middle of the town square.

As he gained the herringbone of white lines that designated the parking area, Simon-Arthur felt a whooshing sensation behind him. He turned to see the 320 bus bearing down on the stop outside Marten's. Observing the way the rows of yellow windows shone through the murky air, he jolted into greater haste. Darkness was coming; and with it the great bank of fog, that had hung two hundred feet above the ground all day, was beginning to descend, falling around the shoulders of the grey stone houses like some malodorous muffler.

Simon-Arthur kept his mouth clamped shut, but sniffed the fog judiciously with a connoisseur's nose. Lots of sulphur tonight, he thought, and perhaps even a hint of something more tangy . . . sodium, maybe? He turned on the ignition. His headlights barely penetrated the thick fog. As he pulled out and drove off down the road Simon-Arthur avoided looking at the fog too closely. He knew from experience that if he peered into it for too long, actually concentrated on its twistings, its eddies, its endless assumptions of insubstantial form, that it could all too easily draw him down a darkling corridor, into more durable, more horribly solid visions.

But halfway home he had to stop. A heavy mizzle was saturating the air. The A418 was a tunnel of spray. Heavy lorry after heavy lorry churned up the fog and water. Simon-Arthur was jammed between two of these grunting beasts as he gained the crest of the hill at Tiddington. The vacuum punched in the air by the one ahead was sucking his flimsy 2cv forward, whilst the boil of turbulence pushed up by the one behind propelled him on. The wheels of the car were barely in contact with the tarmac. He dabbed the brakes and managed to slide off the road into a lay-by.

Sort of safe, Simon-Arthur slumped over the Citroën's steering wheel. He felt more than usually depleted; and the thought of facing his family produced a hard, angular sensation in his gorge. Without quite knowing why he opened the door of the car and got out. If he had felt unsafe in the car – he was now totally exposed. Lorry after lorry went on slamming by, throwing up clouds of compounded gas and liquid.

Simon-Arthur lurched round to the other side of the car and stood transfixed by the hard filthiness of the verge. The bank of grass and weeds was so stained with pollutants that it appeared petrified. It was as if the entire lay-by had been buried in a peat bog for some thousands of years and only this moment disinterred.

Simon-Arthur stood, lost in time, ahistoric. He looked along the A418 towards his house. The road manifested itself as a serpent of yellow and orange, winding its way over the dark country. Each ploughing vehicle was another muscular motion, another bunching and un-coiling in its anguiform body. But if he turned away from the road he was enclosed in his lay-by burial ship. A Sutton Hoo of the psyche. The armour of mashed milk cartons and crushed cans, the beadwork of fag butts, the weaponry of buckled hub caps and discarded lengths of chromium trim. They were, Simon-Arthur reflected, entirely useless – and therefore entirely apt – funerary gifts, for his sustenance in this current afterlife.

He would have stayed longer, savouring this mordant feeling, but the fog was seeping into his chest, producing acute sensations of rasp and tickle that grew and grew until he began to cough. When he was underway again he had to drive with the Citroën's flap window open so that he could spit out of it. And by the time he turned off the main road, up the track to the Brown House, he was as blue as any Saxon – chieftain or otherwise.

The house stood about twenty yards back from the track, in an orchard of diseased apple trees; their branches were wreathed in some type of fungus that resembled Spanish moss. The impression the Brown House gave was of being absolutely four-square, like a child's drawing of a house. It had four twelve-paned windows on each side. As its name suggested, it was built from brown brick; atop the sloping brown-tiled roof was a brown brick chimney.

As Simon-Arthur got out of the car, he looked up at this and noted with approval that it was gushing thick smoke. The fog was so dense now that he could barely make out the point at which this smoke entered the atmosphere; it looked, rather, as if the Brown House were sucking in the murk that wreathed it.

He took a tightly sealed cardboard box from the back of the Citroën, and tucking this under one arm and his *Guardian* under the other he struggled over the buckled wire fence. There was a gate, but it was awkward to open and as Simon-Arthur was the only member of the family who now left the immediate purlieus of the Brown House, he hadn't bothered to fix it. The fence and the gate had been Simon-Arthur's stab at being a countryman. It was summer when he built it and Simon-Arthur, stripped to the waist, spent a sweaty afternoon hammering in the stakes and attaching the netting. He imagined himself like Levin, or Pierre, communing through labour with the spirit of Man. It was a vain delusion.

Even then the fog had been in evidence – albeit as a shadow of what it later became. That afternoon it gave the air a bilious tint. It made everything seem disturbingly post-nuclear, irradiated. When Simon-Arthur had finally finished and stood back to admire his work he saw an aching disjunction between what he had imagined he had achieved – and what was actually there.

The fence zigged and zagged and sagged its way along the track's tattered verge. It looked like a stretch of wire looming up across the shell-holed sludge of no man's land in an old photograph of the Somme.

For as long as the children had played in the garden the fence had acted more as a psychic barrier than a physical one. While it prevented them from getting on to the farm track, it also turned them in on themselves, in on the sepia interior of the Brown House. The fog came. Now it had been over two years since any of them had even ventured out of the house for more than a few minutes. Every time Simon-Arthur contemplated the fence he thought of pulling it down, but to do so was to counsel defeat on too many different levels.

Simon-Arthur opened the front door and stepped into the small vestibule. The first sound that met his ears was of some child plainting in the sitting room. He ignored it and kicking off his muddy boots went into the parlour and set the nebuliser box down on the table. He was unpacking it when his wife's cousin, Christabel-Sharon, came wafting in.

'Is that the nebuliser?' she said, without preamble. He grunted assent. 'Well, as soon as you've got it up and running we'd better put Henrykins on it for a while – the poor child is panting like a steam engine.'

'What about Stormikins?'

'Stormikins is fine, she can have second go. It's Henrykins who's really acting up.' Christabel-Sharon pulled one of the cane-backed chairs out from the table and slumped down on it with a sigh. A sigh that turned into a choke, a splutter and then a full-blown rasping cough. A bronchitic cough that was of such sub-sonic, juddering intensity that Simon-Arthur, as always, could hardly believe her narrow chest capable of producing – or containing – it.

He watched her out of the corner of his eye, whilst continuing to ready the nebuliser. Christabel-Sharon was very thin – almost anorectic. Her ginger-blonde hair was done up in a chignon, revealing what once must have been a graceful swoop of pale, freckled neck, but what was now a scrawny shank of a thing with grease-proof skin stretched over a marbling of vein. She had once been very pretty, in a sylphlike way. Her grey eyes were deep-set, like Simon-Arthur's own, although he could no longer remember whether they had always been so. They glittered under her brows, sending out a coruscating beam with each heave of her chest. Her breasts, fuller than the rest of her, moved under the stretchy fabric of her pullover; the nipples were erect and to Simon-Arthur they betokened nothing more than an autonomous and involuntary sexuality, parasitic on its hacking host.

He had the nebuliser assembled now and he plugged it in to the mains and switched it on. The rubber suction pads moved up and down in the glass chambers of

Salbutimol and steroid. He turned on the stopcock of the oxygen cylinder and pressed the mask to his mouth. The sense of relief was overpowering. He could feel the electric engine adjusting itself to the motion of his ribcage, so that with each of his trembling and ineffectual inhalations it pushed more drug-laden oxygen into him.

It was bliss – like breathing normally again. The sensation marched at the head of a procession of memories: windows flung open and deep gouts of ozone-flavoured air drawn in unimpeded; running up hills and gasping with joy – not pain; burying his head in the bosom of the earth and drawing its warm fungal odour in through flaring nostrils. These pneumo-recollections were so clear that Simon-Arthur could visualise each molecule of scent and gas burying itself in the pinkness of his membranes.

Christabel-Sharon's woollen bosoms came into the corner of his eye. 'Come on, Simon-Arthur, don't you think you're being a little selfish with that thing?'

'Selfish! What the hell do you mean?' As suddenly as the gift had been bestowed it was snatched away. Simon-Arthur's anger rose up in him unbidden. 'Listen, Christabel-Sharon, I'm the person in this house who has to go out, to engage with the brutal commerce of the world. I come back after a gruelling trip, blue in the face, on the verge of expiring, and just because I dare to take a few breaths – a few trifling puffs – on this nebuliser, this nebuliser which I abased myself to get . . . you call me selfish. Selfish! I won't stand for it!'

Christabel-Sharon had recoiled from him and was pressing herself up against the side of the tiled Dutch stove that stood in the corner of the parlour. Simon-Arthur noted through stinging tears of self-pity and frustration that she was doing something he found particularly disgusting: jettisoning sputum from her full lips into a pad of gauze that she had pressed against her mouth. She had quantities of these fabricated pads hidden about her person, and after use, deposited them – together with their glaucous contents – in a bucket lined with a plastic bag that she kept in her room. The dabbing practice further erased her beauty. For Simon-Arthur could never look at her without seeing little parcels of infective matter studding her body.

Simon-Arthur's wife, Jean-Drusilla, came hurrying into the kitchen. In her arms she carried Henry-Simon, their son, a child of about eight.

'Simon, thank God, thank God! The nebuliser. Praise be to the Father and to the Son. Praise be to the Mother of God especially, for granting us this deliverance.' She set the child down on a chair and attached the mask, which was still giving out little 'poots' of oxygen, to his pallid face. Then she fell to her knees on the cold stone flags. 'Simon-Arthur, Christabel-Sharon . . . You will join me.' It was a command, not a request.

Looking sheepishly at one another Simon-Arthur and Christabel-Sharon knelt on the flags. The three adults joined hands. 'Oh merciful Mother,' Jean-Drusilla chanted, 'giver of all bounty, repository of all grace, we thank you for this gift of a nebuliser. Be sure, oh Blessed One, that we will employ it solely in furtherance of your Divine Will. So that our children and ourselves might breathe freely, and so that my dear husband might create beautiful art, the greater to glorify your name.'

Simon-Arthur had knelt grudgingly, and cynically observed the way that this spiritual intensity shaped his wife's rather homely features. Her thick black hair was cut so as to frame her broad brow and firm chin, but the flesh hung slackly on her and there was a yellowish tinge to the whites of her eyes when she rolled them up to stare beatifically at the fire-resistant tiles. Even so, the effect of her measured chanting, which adapted itself to the background chuffing of Henry-Simon and the nebuliser, was mesmeric.

Perhaps there is a Redeemer, Simon thought. Perhaps He will come in a cloud of eucalyptus, freeing up all our passages, gusting through us with the great wind of the Spirit. And before he knew it tears were coursing down his cheeks. Jean-Drusilla, seeing this, leant forward and, taking his head, cradled it against her breast. Christabel-Sharon leant forward as well and stretched her thin arms around the both of them, and for quite a while they stayed like that, gently rocking.

When Dave-Dave Hutchinson, the manager of Marten's the newsagent, arrived at the Brown House about three hours later, the *ecstasis* had somewhat subsided. He knocked, and waited on the metal bootscraper, treading gingerly from one foot to the other. After a few minutes Simon-Arthur himself came to the door. 'My God, it's you,' he said. 'I didn't think you'd make it over tonight, the fog's ridiculously thick.'

'I've got the new radar in the car. It's a bit tricky but once you've got the hang of it you can drive well enough.'

'Come in, come in.' Simon-Arthur almost yanked Dave-Dave in off the doorstep. 'The children aren't quite in bed yet and I don't want them getting a lungful of this.' He grabbed at the air outside the door and brought a clutch of the fog inside, which stayed intact, foaming like a little cloud on the palm of his hand for some seconds.

'I brought this along with me.' Dave-Dave pulled a small brown bottle from the side pocket of his sheepskin jacket.

'Is that the codeine?'

'Yeah, I'm afraid I've only about sixty mils left, but I pick up tomorrow.'

'Sixty mils!' Simon's face lit up. 'That's splendid, that'll bring us some warm cheer, but' – and here his face fell – 'what about your poor wife?'

The newsagent's face adopted a serious expression. 'I'm afraid she gets Brompton's now.'

'Oh, I see. Well, that's too bad. Anyway, come in now, come in here to the drawing room, where it's warm.'

Simon-Arthur ushered Dave-Dave into a long room

that took up half of the Brown House's ground floor. Dave-Dave could see at once that this was where the family spent the bulk of their time. There were two separate groupings of over-stuffed armchairs and sofas, one at either end of the room. Mahogany bookcases went clear along one of the walls, interrupted only by two windows in the centre and a door which presumably led to the garden.

On the other wall there was a vast collection of icons set on a number of shelves that were unevenly spaced, giving the impression that the icons were somehow radiating from the smouldering fire in the grate. Everywhere in the room, set on little tables – occasional, coffee and otherwise – on the arms of the chairs, and even the floor itself, were votive objects: crucifixes, incense burners, hanks of rosary beads, statuettes of the Blessed Virgin. The long room vibrated with the hum of so many patterns flowing into one another: wallpaper into carpet; carpet into seat-cover; seat-cover into cushion; cushion into the gilded frame of an icon. It was like a peacock's tail under the glass dome of a taxidermist's collation.

The overwhelming clutteredness of the room so impressed itself upon Dave-Dave Hutchinson that it wasn't until Simon-Arthur said, 'Jean-Drusilla, I want to introduce Mr Hutchinson, he manages the newsagent's in Thame,' that he realised there was anyone in it besides the two of them. A rather gaunt woman with severely chopped black hair and a prominent, red-tipped nose rose from behind the moulting back of a horsehair armchair where she had been seated.

'I am so pleased to meet you, Mr Hutchinson,' she said, holding out her hand. Dave-Dave Hutchinson advanced towards her, picking his way between the outcroppings of religionalia. She was wearing a crushed velvet, floor-length dress. Both the lace at her throat and that of her handkerchief broadcast the caramel smell of Friar's Balsam.

He kissed her hand, and releasing it looked up into her eyes, which were deep brown. There, he caught a glimpse of her graphic religiosity: circling the two diminutive Hutchinson heads, reflected in her pupils, hovered imps, satyrs, minor demons and hummingbird angels. 'A-and I you, Mrs Dykes,' he stammered.

'Simon-Arthur told me about the help you gave him this afternoon – and the concern you showed him as well.'

'Really, Mrs Dykes, it was nothing, nothing at all.'

'No, not nothing, Mr Hutchinson, far from it. It was a truly Christian act, the behaviour of a man of true feeling. A Samaritan casting aside the partisan claims of place, people and estate, selflessly to aid another.'

She was still holding his hand and she used it to draw him round and pilot him into an armchair that faced her own. 'I fear my husband was asthmatic even before the fog, and he will let his emotions run away with him. Like all artists he is so terribly sensitive. When he gets upset . . .' She tailed off and shrugged expressively, both of her hands held palm-upwards. Dave-Dave Hutchinson stared at the many heavy gold rings, studded with amethysts and emeralds, that striped her fingers.

'What exactly is it that you paint, Mr Dykes?' Dave-Dave Hutchinson asked, turning in his chair to face Simon-Arthur, who was still hovering by the door. Even as the newsagent said it, he felt that the question was both too prosaic and too forward. He was painfully aware that his own social position was quite inferior to that of the Dykeses, and while it didn't matter when he and Simon Dykes had formed that spontaneous bond of friendship at Marten's – which was after all his own preserve – here at the Brown House he felt awkward and gauche, on guard lest he commit some appalling gaffe, or utter a solecism that would point up his humble origins.

'Oh, I don't paint much besides icons nowadays. These are some of mine around the fireplace.'

The newsagent rose from his chair and walked over to the wall. The icons were really very strange indeed. They featured all the correct elements of traditional icons, but the Trinity and the saints depicted were drawn not from life, nor imagination, but from the sort of photographs of public personages that are printed in the newspapers. These bland faces and reassuring eyes had been done in oils with total exactitude. The artist had even rendered the minute moiré patterning of coloured dots that constituted the printed image.

'I can see why you're so concerned to get your newspaper in good condition each day, Mr Dykes,' he said – and immediately regretted it, it sounded so trite, so bourgeois a comment.

'Ye-es,' Simon-Arthur replied, 'it's very difficult to get that level of detail if you're working from a soggy paper.'

'Is there much of a demand for icons at the moment?'

'A huge demand,' said Jean-Drusilla Dykes, 'a vast demand, but Simon-Arthur doesn't sell his. He paints them for the greater glory of our Saviour, for no other client.'

Just then the door of the room swung open and Christabel-Sharon came in, carrying her three-year-old daughter Storm in her thin arms. The little girl was feverish. She was murmuring in a distracted way and had two bright, scarlet spots high up on her cheeks. Christabel-Sharon herself was in tears. 'Henry has thrown Storm out of the oxygen tent again, Simon-Arthur; really, you must do something about it, look at the state she's in.'

Simon-Arthur didn't say anything, but left the room immediately. Dave-Dave Hutchinson could hear heavy feet thudding up the stairs and then voices raised in the room above, one deep, the other reedy.

'Christabel-Sharon,' said Jean-Drusilla Dykes when her husband had gone, 'this is Mr Hutchinson who manages the newsagent's in Thame. Mr Hutchinson, this is my cousin Christabel-Sharon Lannière.'

'I'm delighted to meet you, Ms Lannière,' said Dave Hutchinson, and waited for her to put the child down somewhere so that he might kiss her hand. She dumped the little girl quite unceremoniously on a *chaise-longue*, and advanced towards him smiling broadly, hand outstretched, the tears already drying on her cheeks, like snail trails in the morning sun.

And as he took the hand, and noticed how small and fine it was, Dave-Dave Hutchinson decided that she was unquestionably the most beautiful woman he had seen in a very long time. He was, after all, so conditioned to accepting emaciation as a body-type, that he could dwell on the hollow beneath a woman's clavicle, even if it threatened to bore through her thorax. Christabel-Sharon must have sensed this silent homage on his part, for, as she curtsied, she gave an extra little bob, as if acknowledging this new allegiance to her attractions.

They stood like that for a while, looking at one another, whilst Jean-Drusilla Dykes tended to the little girl, propping her up on some cushions, finding a coverlet for her, and eventually placing the nebuliser mask over her whispering mouth and turning the machine on.

'Oh, is that the nebuliser?' Dave-Dave Hutchinson asked. 'It looks absolutely fantastic.'

'Isn't it,' said Christabel-Sharon, with equal enthusiasm. 'We've been on the waiting list for one now for months, but somehow Simon-Arthur managed to get priority – '

'We don't talk about that, Christabel-Sharon,' Jean-Drusilla Dykes cut in. 'It isn't seemly.'

'I'm dreadfully sorry,' Dave-Dave Hutchinson said hurriedly. 'I didn't mean to seem intrusive.'

'No, no, Mr Hutchinson, it's not your fault, but the truth of the matter is that Simon-Arthur did use connections to get hold of the nebuliser; and even though I'm delighted to have it I can't help feeling that the way in which it was obtained will tell against us eventually. Oh Mr Hutchinson, what a shoddy, cheap world we live in when a fine man like my husband, a moral man, a just man, has to resort to such expedients merely in order to aid his suffering family – ' Her voice broke, quite abruptly, and she began to sob, screwing the handkerchief soaked with Friar's Balsam into her eye.

Then the large, velvet-robed woman started to cough. It was, Dave-Dave Hutchinson noted – being now as adept at judging the nature of a cough as any doctor – a particularly hoarse and rattling cough, with an oil-drum resonance about it, admixed with something like the sound of fine shingle being pulled this way and that by breakers on a beach.

'Now there – there, Mrs Dykes, please don't upset yourself, please . . .' He pulled the little brown bottle of codeine linctus from his pocket and showed it to her. 'I have some linctus here – that'll help us all to stop coughing for a while.'

'Ach-cach–cach-cach-Oh Mr ach-cach- Hutchinson, you are too kind, too kind. Christabel-Sharon, kindly fetch the linctus glasses.' Christabel-Sharon exited. The two of them were left regarding one another over the *chaise-longue*; on which the child lay, her laboured breath wheezing contrapuntally to the choof-choof of the nebuliser.

'Did you say,' asked Dave-Dave Hutchinson, by way of making polite conversation, 'that you had an oxygen tent?'

'It's nothing really,' she replied, 'hardly a tent at all, more of an oxygen fly-sheet.' They both laughed at this, and it was a laughter that Dave-Dave Hutchinson was profoundly grateful for. It ruptured the rather fraught atmosphere of the room, earthing the static sheets and flashes of his hostess's spiritual intensity. But his gratitude didn't sustain for long, because even this trifling response to her witticism, this strained guffaw, was enough to give him a coughing fit – this time a bad one.

He sat back down on the armchair, both hands clasped against his mouth. Dave-Dave's lungs heaved so, they threatened to turn themselves inside out. He laboured to retain some element of composure, or at any rate not to void himself on the Dykes' Persian carpet. The edges of his visual field turned first pink, then red, and eventually purple. He felt himself losing control, when a cool, white hand was placed on his arm and he heard a voice say, 'Here, Mr Hutchinson, pray take one of these, it looks as if you could do with one.' It was Christabel-Sharon. She had materialised back inside the room and was proffering him a neat pad of gauze. 'You'll doubtless need it for the – '

'Buh, buh –' he laboured through his hands to express his shame and embarrassment.

'Now, now, Mr Hutchinson, you musn't worry about a bit of sputum with us,' said Jean-Drusilla Dykes firmly. 'We know how it is, we understand that the normal proprieties have had to be somewhat relaxed during the current situation.' He gratefully seized the pad and as discreetly as he was able deposited several mouthfuls of infective matter into its fluffy interior. When he had finished Christabel-Sharon passed him a bucket lined with a plastic bag.

Simon-Arthur Dykes came back into the room. 'Did you sort the children out, Simon-Arthur?' asked his wife.

'Ye-es,' he sighed wearily. 'Henry and Magnus are back in the small room, so Storm can go up to the oxygen tent whenever she's ready; and then Dave-Dave can take a turn with the nebuliser. He obviously has need of it – and I'm not surprised, coming out on this vile night.'

'Is the humidifier on in the boys' room?'

'Yes, of course.'

'And the ioniser in ours?'

'Yes, yes, dear Jean-Drusilla, please don't trouble yourself.' He crossed the room to where his wife stood, and taking her arm, bade her sit beside him on a divan covered with brocade cushions. Their two heads leaned together and the four feverish spots on their cheeks reached an uneasy alignment.

'Look, Simon-Arthur,' said Christabel-Sharon, gesturing towards the round silver tray she had brought in from the kitchen, 'doesn't the linctus look pretty?'

It did look pretty. She had poured the thick green liquid out into tiny, cut-glass linctus glasses. In the yellow-and-blue light from the fire the whole array sparkled the spectrum. She offered the tray to Dave-Dave Hutchinson. 'Mr Hutchinson, will you have some?'

'Thank you, Ms Lannière.'

'Please, do use my matronymic – and may I use your patronymic?'

'Certainly . . . Christabel –'

'Christabel-Sharon,' she said with her ever-so-slightly affected voice, 'and you are Dave-Dave, aren't you?'

'That's right.' He blushed.

Taking one of the tiny glasses, Dave-Dave sipped judiciously, savouring the thickness and sweetness of the stuff, whilst assaying the weight of the crystal it came in. At home he and Mrs Hutchinson drank their linctus from Tupperware. Christabel-Sharon handed two glasses of linctus to the Dykeses and took one herself. Then they all sat together in silence for a while, contentedly tippling.

It was a good little party. One of the best evenings that any of the inhabitants of the Brown House could remember having in a long time. After Storm-Christabel had gone up to the oxygen tent and Dave-Dave had had a good long go on the anaboliser, Simon-Arthur set up a small card table and they played whist for a couple of hours. Christabel-Sharon paired off with Dave-Dave, and there was an agreeably flirtatious character to the way they bid together, often taking tricks through shared high spirits rather than any skill at the game.

There was no discussion of weighty matters or what really preoccupied them all. The mere presence of Dave-Dave at the Brown House was a sufficient reminder. The codeine linctus helped to free up the constrictions in their four pairs of lungs, which did necessitate frequent recourse by all parties to Christabel-Sharon's supply of gauze pads and the attendant bucket. But such was the *bonhomie* that the linctus engendered that none of them felt much embarrassment, or awkwardness.

Only when Jean-Drusilla went out to the kitchen to ask the maid to make them some ham sandwiches, and her husband followed her to get a bottle of port from the cellar, was there any exchange that alluded to the wider issue. 'It is strange, is it not, my dear,' said Simon-Arthur, leaning his head against the wall and fighting the dreadful torpor that threatened to encase him, 'to have a news-agent for company of an evening.'

'Yes, dear, I suppose it is,' she replied distractedly – she was helping the maid to de-crust some slices of bread, 'but he is a very nice man, a very Christian man. I don't imagine for a second that simply because we receive him in this fashion that he imagines we think him quality for an instant.'

'Quite so, quite so.'

'Christabel-Sharon seems to have taken quite a shine to him – is he married?'

'Oh yes, but I fear the poor man's wife is *in extremis*. He told me this afternoon that she was getting Brompton's – hence his oversufficiency of linctus.'

'I see. Well, while in the normal course of things such a flirtation might not be seemly, I think that in these times we live in, almost anything – within the bounds of propriety, of course – that serves to inculcate good feeling can be accepted.'

'You are entirely right, my dear,' replied Simon-Arthur, who had, like so many men of his age and class, long since abandoned the matter of making these practical moral judgements to his wife.

But late that night when Simon-Arthur was in his dressing room, readying himself for bed, the fog and all the awful misery that hung about it began to impose itself on him once more. He slumped down in a broken rattan chair that he kept in the little room – which was barely more than a vestibule. The codeine linctus was wearing off and he could feel the tightness in his chest, the laval accumulation of mucus, flowing down his bronchi and into each little sponge bag of an alveolus. Felt this fearfully, as his nervous system reintroduced him to the soft internality of his diseased body, its crushable vulnerability.

He remembered reading somewhere – God knows how many years ago – that if the human lungs were unfolded in their entirety, each little ruche and complicated pleat of veined tissue, then the resulting membrane would cover two football pitches. 'Or two damp, exposed fields,' Simon-Arthur murmured to himself, remembering Dave-Dave's eloquent description of the Brown House and its environs earlier that day. He pulled off his socks by the toe, wheezing with the effort.

In the bedroom next door he could hear his wife breathing stertorously. She was going through a cycle in her sleep that was familiar to him. First she would inhale, the twists and loops of mucus in her throat soughing like electricity cables in a high wind. Then she would exhale through her nose. This sounded peculiarly like a waste-disposal unit being started up.

The noises would get closer and closer together until they were continuous: 'Soouuugh-grnngchngsoouuugh-grnnchng.' Eventually she would seize up altogether and begin coughing, coughing raucously, coughing and even spluttering like some beery fellow in a bar, who's taken a mouthful of lager and then been poked in the ribs by a drinking buddy: 'Kerschpooo-kerschpooo-kerschpooo!' Over and over again. He couldn't believe that this colossal perturbation of her body didn't wake her – but it never seemed to. Whereas he was invariably yanked into consciousness by his own coughing in the night, or by that of the children, or Christabel-Sharon.

He could, he realised, hear all of them coughing and snoring and breathing in the different rooms of the Brown House. To his left there was the sharp rasp of Christabel-Sharon, to the right there were the childishly high and clattery coughs of his two sons, and in the small room immediately opposite the door to his dressing room he could even detect the more reposeful sighs of Storm-Christabel. He even thought – but couldn't be certain – that he could just about hear the maid, hacking away in the distant attic room. But on consideration he decided this was unlikely.

Yes, it wasn't the maid he could hear, but the furthest reaches of his lungs, playing their own peculiar, patho-logical fugue. Clearly each of the innumerable little pipes and passages had its own viscous reed, and as the air passed around them they produced many hundreds – thousands even – of individual sounds. Simon-Arthur concentrated hard on this and found himself able to differentiate quite subtle tones. He could screen the background noise out, so as to be able to pick up the individual notes being blown in the pipes of his internal organ. Or else he could relax, and taking in breaths as deep as he could manage, produce swelling chords.

This discovery of the hidden musicality of his own lungs transfixed Simon-Arthur. He sat breathing in and out, attempting to contort his thorax in various ways, so as to bring off various effects. He even fancied that a particular sort of scrunching up in the rattan chair, combined with a two-stage inhalation, and long, soft exhalation, could, if pulled off properly, make his lungs play the magisterial, opening chords of Mozart's Mass in C major.

So peculiar and absorbing was this new game that Simon-Arthur became enveloped in it, fancying that he was himself inside a giant lung. The coughing and breathing of the other inhabitants of the house were integrated into his bronchial orchestration. He could no longer tell which noises were inside him and which outside. Then senses merged in the painter's disordered mind. Looking around him at the many tiny icons – icons he himself had painted – that studded the walls of the dressing room, Simon-Arthur no longer saw them for what they were. Everything, the pattern of the carpet, the texture of the walls, was transmogrifying into a gothic scape of pulsing red tubes and stretched, semi-transparent membranes.

In the midst of this fantasy the despair clamped down on him. The black bear bumped under the bed of his mind. He saw that the walls were studded with carci-nomas, the corridors lined with angry scars and lesions. Up and down the stairs of the lung-house ran rivulets of infective matter. The thoracic property was choking with disease. The alveolar bricks that made up its structure were embedded in nacreous mortar. And then the final horror: the carcinomas took on the faces of people Simon-Arthur had known, people he had not done right by.

The contrast between his light-hearted silliness of a split-moment ago and the sickening despair of this image plunged Simon-Arthur into retching tears. He ground his fists into the sockets of eyes. Bam! Bam! Bam! Bam! The ugly realisations came winging in on him, each scything into his chest from a different trajectory. He buckled as the images of his loved ones choking on their own blood, drowning in it, impinged on him with dread force, awful certainty.

The fog was never going to lift, just thicken and thicken and thicken, until the air curdled. Stopping up the mouths of babies as surely as if they were smothered in the marshmallow folds of a pillow. Simon-Arthur knew this. Knew it as his tears called forth the inevitable and irresistible coughing fit.

After a turbulent, feverish night Simon-Arthur awoke for the sixth time with what passed for dawn long past. He could hear Christabel-Sharon, his wife and the children moving around downstairs, coughing their matitudinal coughs.

Then there was another sharp spatter against the window, a repeat of the spattering sound that he now realised had awoken him. He sat up. It was shot, he thought, it has to have been shot. It's too early in the autumn for hail.

He got up, and dressing as hurriedly as he could, he went downstairs. In the dining room his eldest son, Henry, was eating Rice Crispies, taking time out after each mouthful for a few pulls from the mouth-piece of the nebuliser. The crunch-crunch–choof-choof noise was slightly eerie. Simon-Arthur found the rest of the family, and the maid, gathered in the vestibule. The two smaller children were still in their nightclothes.

'Is that the shoot?' asked Simon-Arthur, although he already knew that it was.

'We can't understand why it's so early,' said Jean-Drusilla. The children were looking apprehensive.

'They're shooting d—ed near to the house as well. I'd better go out and have a word.' He took his scarf from the rack by the front door and wound it around his throat.

'Won't you put on a mask, dear?'

'No, no, don't be silly, I'm only popping out for a minute.'

As Simon-Arthur groped his way down the side of the Brown House he berated himself: Why worry about such stupid things? Why need it concern me if Peter-Donald and his cronies see that I can only afford a chemical mask? Such pride is worse than stupidity. But it was the truth – for he was a proud man. And he was right in assuming that the members of the shoot would be fully masked, because the fog was unusually thick this morning, the visibility down to fifteen yards or less.

Once Simon-Arthur had begun to acclimatise he could see the line of huntsmen beyond the low scrub of bushes at the bottom of the garden. He also fancied he could make out a few beaters in among the tangle of sick trees to the rear of the house. He made for the tallest figure in the middle of the former group and was gratified to find, when he got closer, that it was his landlord, Peter-Donald.

'Good morning, Peter-Donald,' he said, on coming up to him. 'You're early today.'

'Ah, Simon-Arthur.' Peter-Donald Hanson rested his Purdey in the crook of his arm and extended his right hand. 'How good to see you, old chap.' The big man's voice issued from a small speaker, just above the knot of his cravat; and was crackly, like a poorly tuned radio.

Simon-Arthur had been right about the mask. Peter-Donald was wearing a full scuba arrangement. The rest of his cronies were all clad in the same, overdone shooting kit: Norfolk jackets and plus-fours, cravats and tweedy hats with grouse feathers in their bands. They looked like the usual mob of city types, members of Peter-Donald's Lloyds syndicate, Simon-Arthur supposed.

'You know, Peter-Donald, the shot is spattering against the windows of the house, I think it's making the children feel a little anxious.'

'Awfully sorry, but the fog's so damn thick today. Wouldn't have come out at all but I got delivery of these yesterday, so we thought we'd give them a try.' He held out his wrist, to which was strapped a miniature radar screen. 'They could make all the difference to the shooting around here.'

Simon-Arthur looked from his landlord's masked face to the black LCD of the mini-radar screen. If there was any trace of irony, or even self-awareness, in Peter-Donald's voice it was effectively destroyed by the throat mike, and his expression was, of course, completely hidden.

A thread of white luminescence circled the screen.

When it sped past a certain region there were splutters of light.

'Are those the birds?' he asked, pointing towards the fading gleams.

'Ya, that's right. Charlie-Bob has rigged them all up with little radar cones. Mind you' – he barked a laugh, which the throat mike transmitted as a howl – 'I don't think you could put 'em on grouse. Poor buggers would be dwarfed by the things!'

There was a scatter of microphonic squawks from the other guns – they were obviously getting restive. 'Well, if you'll excuse me, old boy,' said Peter-Donald, cocking his gun, 'I'll get this drive started and then we'll be off your property, eh?'

Despite the warning painful catch in his throat Simon-Arthur stood his ground, interested to see what would happen. The guns formed up again into a ragged line. Even in the short time he and Peter-Donald had been chatting, the fog had grown denser. Now, not only were the beaters no longer within sight, but the trees themselves were little more than shadows.

Peter-Donald took a wafer-thin cellular phone from the pocket of his jacket and punched one of the buttons on its console. 'I think we're ready now, Charliekins,' he barked, the mouthpiece pressed against his throat mike. 'D'you want to start the drive?'

There was a ragged chorus of shouts and 'Halloos!', together with the sound of stout sticks being smote against the underbrush. Then there was a warbling, almost grunting noise, and ten or fifteen pheasants came staggering out of the bank of fog. They had radar cones tied around their necks. These were silvery-grey rhomboids, at least four times bigger than the birds' heads. The effect was ridiculous and pathetically unnatural: the birds – who Simon-Arthur knew found it hard to fly anyway when the fog was thick – were still further handicapped by this new sporting technology. Only two or three of them could get airborne at all, and then only for a couple of wing beats. The rest just zigzagged in a loose pack across the traverse of the guns, the sharp corners of the radar cones banging first into their eyes and then their soft throats.

There were a few scattered shots – none of which appeared to find a mark. Most of the guns held their fire.

'Not much sport in this, is there?' said Simon-Arthur sarcastically, and then realised with a shock that he had spoken audibly. He had been out in the fog for so long that he had begun to assume that he must be wearing a muffling mask.

But this didn't seem to offend Peter-Donald. He was striding towards the fence, and signalling to the other guns to follow. He turned on his heel for a moment, facing back towards Simon-Arthur, and publicly addressed him. 'It is, if we let them get into the fog bank. D'ye see? Then we've got a shoot entirely on instrumentation' – he indicated the wristscreen – 'now that's real sport!' Then he swivelled round and marched off.

The birds had managed to reach the fence and stagger

over or under it. Then they were enveloped by the fog. The guns followed them, and finally trailing behind came the donkey-jacketed figures of the beaters, who also disappeared, still hallooing. Simon-Arthur noticed that most of them weren't even wearing chemical masks.

Simon-Arthur stood for a moment, and then turned towards the house. But when he reached the front door, and was just about to turn the knob, he saw that one of the pheasants hadn't managed to make it over the fence. It was running about distractedly, crazily even, in the area between the house and the fence. As Simon-Arthur watched it, it charged towards him and then veered away again locking into a spiralling path, like an aeroplane in a flat spin, or a clockwork toy run amok.

The pheasant was producing the most alarming noises, splutterings and gurgles. Simon-Arthur walked towards where its next circumnavigation of the muddy patch of ground ought to take it, arriving just in time for the bird to cough up at his feet an enormous dollop of blood and mucus, and then expire, its radar cone jammed into the ground. 'My God!' exclaimed Simon-Arthur. He leant down to examine the corpse. The pheasant's feathers were matted, greasy and lustreless. It was a male bird, but its plumage was almost entirely dun-coloured. Simon-Arthur felt nauseous upon noticing that there were flecks and dollops of some white matter in the spreading stain of fluid that was still pouring from its beak.

One of the guns must have been lingering behind the group and heard Simon-Arthur's exclamation, because a masked figure carrying a shotgun came striding out of the fog bank, clambered none too nimbly over the fence and walked over to where he was crouched by the dead pheasant. As the figure approached he pulled off his mask. It was, Simon-Arthur realised with an access of warm feeling, Anthony-Anthony Bohm, the local doctor.

'Anthony-Anthony!' Simon-Arthur said, standing up and thrusting out his hand. It was taken and warmly shaken by the doctor, whose rubicund face was registering some concern.

'You really should get inside, Simon-Arthur,' he said. 'This is no kind of a day to be out without a mask, and preferably a scuba.'

'I know, I know, I was just going in when this poor creature expired at my feet. What d'you think of that?'

The doctor crouched down, puffing, and peered at the dead bird. One of his hands went to the ruff of white beard that fringed his pink buttock of a chin, while the other probed the pheasant's neck. It was a gesture so familiar to Simon-Arthur from Anthony-Anthony's consulting room that he smiled to see it in this unusual circumstance. 'Hmm, hmm, hmm-hmm,' the Doctor hmm-ed and then, picking up the bird, opened its beak and looked down it.

'Look at that white matter in the blood – what on earth can it be?'

'Oh that – that's a carcinoma. Nothing particularly mysterious.'

'A carcinoma?'

'Ye-es.'

'So what did it die of?'

'Oh cancer, of course. Yes, definitely cancer – of the throat, and no doubt of the lung as well. The effort of being driven by the beaters like that must have given it a massive haemorrhage.'

'I had no idea the animals were getting cancer in this fashion, Anthony-Anthony.'

'My dear Simon-Arthur, we get cancer, why shouldn't all of God's other creatures, hmm?' The doctor was struggling to his feet again; Simon-Arthur gave him an arm.

'Ooof! Well, that's me for this morning, I think I'll head back to the health centre, I've a surgery this afternoon. Do you mind if I take the pheasant with me, Simon-Arthur?'

'Not at all. Are you going to run some tests on it, Anthony-Anthony, do an autopsy, or whatever it is you call it?'

'Good heavens, no! Oh no, ahaha-no-no-aha-ha-h'ach-eurch-cha-cha – ' The doctor's jolly laughter turned with grim predictability into a coughing fit. Simon-Arthur thumped the tubby man on his broad back, whilst Anthony-Anthony struggled to don his scuba mask again. When he had it on and was breathing easily, he took the dead bird from Simon-Arthur who had picked it up by its sad scruff.

'Thanks very much, old fellow. No, no, I know what

killed the thing so it's of no interest to medical science. I used to be a dab hand with the scalpel, so I'll cut the tumours out and the lady wife and I can have this one for Sunday lunch. Now, do get inside, Simon-Arthur, I don't want to see you at surgery this afternoon.' They bade farewell, and the doctor vanished into the sickly yellow of the boiling fog bank.

The Doctor didn't see Simon-Arthur at his emergency surgery that afternoon, because against Jean-Drusilla and Christabel-Sharon's pleading, he decided to take a walk.

Simon-Arthur had been trying to work in his studio all morning, but the terrible vision from the previous night kept haunting him. He fancied he could still hear every faltering breath and choking cough of the Brown House's inhabitants. And when in the mid-morning he took a break and went down to inhale some steam with Friar's Balsam, the sight of the children sitting in a silent row on one of the sofas in the drawing room, while the maid passed the nebuliser mask from one to the next, brought tears to his eyes.

When they were all seated at the dining-room table, eating off the second-best china because it was a Saturday, Simon-Arthur addressed the table at large, saying, 'I think I'll go out after lunch, just for a breath' – he bit back the figure of speech – 'for a walk.'

'I really feel you oughtn't, Simon-Arthur,' said his wife. 'You were out for far too long this morning, and without a mask. You know what Anthony-Anthony says, even with a chemical mask you shouldn't really be out for more than half an hour at a time.'

'It's just that I feel terribly claustrophobic in the house today. I haven't had a walk for almost a month now. I'll go up to the golf course and then I'll come straight back. I'll be fine. I didn't even have too much of a turn after going out this morning.'

'Please don't, Simon-Arthur,' said Christabel-Sharon. Her freckle-spattered features were tight with concern. 'You know the Patriarch is coming to say a special mass tomorrow. You won't want to miss that. And if you go out for a walk you'll have been out for forty minutes – and you shan't be able to go and get the medicated incense for his censors in Risborough.'

'Please, everyone, don't worry!' Simon-Arthur said this a little louder than he intended to. But he hated having it drawn to his attention just how dependent all of them were on him, right down to the very practice of their religion. 'I'm going out for a walk and that-is-that.'

Simon-Arthur went up the farm track, through the farm and past the manor house where Peter-Donald and his family lived. The fog had lifted ever so slightly and he could see the crenellated chimneys of the house. He wondered whether Peter-Donald had managed to get a good bag, or at any rate a non-cancerous one.

It was uncomfortable walking. The mask he wore was a cheap model. Really only a plastic mouth- and nose-piece, containing a thick wad of cotton wool soaked with Ventalin. The straps chafed the back of his head,

184

and the smell of the chemicals when he inhaled was almost worse than the fog itself.

Simon-Arthur reached the road on the far side of the estate and crossed it. The ground here was completely devoid of grass cover. The land had been bought up by a Japanese syndicate about a year before the fog descended. It was less expensive, then, for Japanese golfers to fly to England to play than to join a club in their own country. The syndicate had landscaped the course, but when the fog came they abandoned the whole project. Now the prospect of bare mud, formed into useless fairways, bunkers and greens that were really browns, looked wholly unearthly and anti-natural, like some section of an alien planet, poorly terraformed.

As he walked, Simon-Arthur dwelt once again – as he had so many times before – on the crippling irony of his bringing his family to live in the country. He had done it because Henry had bad asthma – as he did himself. Their doctor in London was certain that it was pollution-related. About four months after they had taken up residence in the Brown House the fog moved in with them.

'Oh Christ! Oh God, oh Jesus. Please come! Please help us. We are but clay, but dust . . .' Simon-Arthur muttered this through his mask; and then, not quite knowing why, but feeling that if he wanted to pray aloud it was unseemly to do it with this ugly mask on, he took it off.

To his surprise the fog didn't taste that bad, or catch in

his throat. He took a few shallow, experimental breaths to check that he wasn't mistaken. He wasn't: the fog no longer oozed soupily into his constricted chest. He took some deeper breaths, and with a further shock felt his eustachian tubes clear – audibly popping as they did so – for the first time in years. Now he could hear cars moving along the road behind him with great clarity. He took a few more, deeper breaths. It was amazing, the fog must be clearing, he thought; the miasma must be departing from our lives!

Then he started to take in great gouts of air, savouring the cleanness of its taste. 'At last, at last!' he shouted out, and heard his voice reverberate the way it should do, not fall flat. 'Thank you, thank you, thank you, thank you, thank you, thankyou, thangyou, thangyu,' he garbled. The fog was lifting, there was a bright light up ahead of him, beyond the fourth green of the half-constructed course. Simon-Arthur strode towards it, his legs feeling light and springy. He was an intensely religious man, and he crossed himself as he staggered forward; crossed himself and counted out a decade on the rosary in his pocket. He was prepared for Redemption.

They didn't find the icon painter's body until the following day. Jean-Drusilla had alerted the authorities after Simon-Arthur had been gone for forty minutes, but by then it was already getting dark and the fog was too thick for a search party, even with high-powered lights. As for radar, that too was useless, for there was a particularly high magnesium content building up in that evening's opacity.

By chance Peter-Donald and Anthony-Anthony were in the party that found him. He was spread out, smeared even, on the muddy surface, in much the same posture that the cancerous pheasant had expired on the day before. Like the pheasant, a pool of blood and mucus had flowed out from his mouth and stained the ground. And, as before, the doctor knelt down and examined the white flecks in the stain.

'Poor bugger,' he said, 'how strange, he had cancer as well. Never thought to give him an X-ray, because I felt certain that his asthma was going to get him first. He wasn't well at all, you know.'

Peter-Donald was taking his ease on a shooting stick he'd pressed into the mud. 'Well, at least the fellow had the decency not to die on the green, eh?' It wasn't that he was being disrespectful to Simon-Arthur's memory, it was only that the times bred a certain coarseness of manner in some – just as they engendered extreme sensitivity in others.

'Yes, well, he must have had the haemorrhage on the green, and then rolled into this bunker and died.'

'Tidy, what?'

'You could put it that way.' The doctor stood up and indicated to the stretcher bearers who were with them that they should remove the body. 'The peculiar thing is that he and I saw a pheasant die in just this fashion yesterday.'

'What, of cancer?'

'Absolutely.'

'Well, y'know, Anthony-Anthony, I can't say I'm surprised in Simon-Arthur's case. Not only was the fellow asthmatic, but I used to see him all over the shop without a scuba on. Bloody silly – foolhardy even.'

Without bothering further with the corpse, the two men turned and headed off back towards the manor. They were looking forward to a glass of linctus before lunch. Both of them had chronic bronchitis – and neither was as young as he used to be. For a while their conversation could be heard through the clouds of noxious dankness:

'You know, Peter-Donald, I don't believe the Dykeses can afford proper scubas. Hardly anyone in the area can, apart from yourself – I have one because of my job, you know.'

'Really? Oh well, I suppose it stands to reason. Did you say that bird had cancer? D'you think I should get some special masks made for the pheasants? I shouldn't want them all to get it – '

And then they too were swallowed up by the fog.

Grey Area

I WAS STANDING BY the facsimile machine this afternoon, peering through the vertical, textured fabric louvres that cover every window in the Company's offices and which are linked together with what look like lengths of cheap key-chain. I was waiting, because all too often the facsimile machine misfeeds and two sheets run through together. So, when I send a facsimile I always send the sheets through one by one. It's time-consuming, but it leads to fewer mistakes. I have become so adept at this task that I can now perform it by sound rather than sight. When the sheets are feeding through correctly, the machine makes a whirring, chirruping noise, like a large insect feeding. When I push in the leading edge of a new sheet, there is a momentary hesitation, a predatory burr, then I feel the mandibles of nylon-brush clutch and nibble at it. When the entire document has been passed through the body of the facsimile machine, it clicks, then gives off a high-pitched peep.

This afternoon, just as the machine peeped, I sensed a presence behind me. I turned. I had noticed him a couple of times before. I don't know his name, but I have an idea he works in personnel. I noticed him because there is something wrong with his clothing – or the way he wears it, the way it hangs on his body. His suits cling to him, his flies look like an appendicectomy scar, puckered and irregular. We grunted acknowledgements to each other. I tamped the sheets of paper into a neat stack. I moved past him, across the floor, and through the swing doors into the corridor that leads back to the Department.

The Department must always be capitalised when it is referred to by its members, in order to differentiate it from other departments. Of course, other departments must also be capitalised by their members. This makes the paperwork for inter-departmental meetings – for which I often have responsibility – complex to arrange. A different word-processed document is needed for each departmental representative.

The formats and protocols for all the Company's communications were modified by the Head of Department, who's my boss, when he took over about six months ago.

The document that set out these modifications was ring-bound and about seventy pages long. Nevertheless, he asked me to pull apart the plastic knuckles that gripped one of the copies, and attach the sheets in a long row to the bulletin board that runs the entire length of the Department's main corridor. He said that this was so everyone in the Department would be certain to pay attention to them.

It must be as a result of initiatives such as these that my boss has enjoyed such a phenomenally quick rise through the hierarchy of the Company.

I had to walk right along this corridor to get back to my office, which is situated, opposite my boss's, up a dog-leg of stairs at the far end. I can't understand why we don't have a facsimile machine in the Department. Every other department has at least one, and more often than not several. We have a networked computer system, modem links, numerous photocopiers, document-sorters and high-speed laserprinters, but no facsimile machine. I have never asked my boss why this is the case, because it was like this before he became Head of Department, and perhaps he, like me, has come to accept it as an aspect of the status quo.

I turned out of the long corridor that leads to the inter-departmental facsimile machine, and into the corridor that runs the length of the Department. This corridor is wide and low, with a line of strip lights along the ceiling. I usually keep my eyes fixed on these when I'm walking along the corridor, in order to avoid contact with my colleagues. It's not that I don't want to talk to them, it's just that there's always plenty of work to do and I like to keep a rhythm up throughout the day. I have a dread of getting behind.

In my office there is a desk, three filing cabinets, a stationery cupboard, a swivel chair, and a workstation that holds my computer and laserprinter. All of this furniture is a grey-beige colour, very neutral, very gentle on the eye. It helps to offset the rather aggressive carpet tiling, which is chequered in two distinct, but equally electric, shades of blue.

It's a kind of carpet tiling that was advertised a few years ago on television in a gimmicky way. A stretch of tiling was laid down in a kind of test zone, a mocked-up section of an office corridor. Then a live rhinoceros was released from a cage and encouraged to tear up and down the fake corporate environment, snorting and ramping.

It was a startling image: the very embodiment of the rhinoceros, its astonishing combination of bulk and fluidity, imposing itself on the bland anonymity of the set. Then, at the very end of the sequence, the camera angle moved round from the side of the corridor to its end and the rhino charged towards the viewer. The image was so sharp that if you had frozen the frame you could have counted the individual bristles that made up its congealed horn, the wrinkled veins in its vinyl hide.

At the last moment before it came plunging through the screen into your living room, the beast turned tail and dumped a steaming heap of excrement right in the eye of the camera, which tracked down so as to catch it plummeting on to the carpet tiling. The voiceover intoned: 'Rhinotile, tough enough for all the animals in your office!'

I can't get this advert out of my head. The punchline comes to me unbidden whenever I look at, or even think about, the carpet tiling.

I haven't done all that much to personalise my office – the walls are mostly taken up with a noticeboard, a calendar and an organisational chart.

The organisational chart has been done on one of those magnetic whiteboards, to which metallic strips can be affixed, to express lines of command, the skeleton of the hierarchy; and coloured dots or squares, to indicate individuals and their functions.

It's my job to change the shape of the organisational chart as the Department metamorphoses from month to month. The Department doesn't have an exceptionally high turnover of staff, but enough people come and go to make rearranging some strips and dots necessary every few weeks.

I have never asked the Head of Department why it is that, despite my pivotal role in representing the structure of the Department, I have yet to be included in the organisational chart myself.

I stapled the papers I had just faxed and deposited them in a tray for filing. I walked round behind my desk – which faces the door – and sat down. My office is organised so that the working surface is directly in front of me and if I swivel to the right I am sitting at the computer keyboard. This I did.

I had to work on the presentation document for this week's inter-departmental meeting. My boss had made handwritten corrections to the first draft, and these I now set on the document holder that sprouts from a Velcro pad, attached to the side of my monitor.

The corrections were extensive and involved the re-keying of a number of paragraphs. I worked steadily and by five it was done and neatly formated. I hit the keystrokes necessary to activate the laserprinter and then tidied my desk.

Desk tidying is quite an important ritual with me. I like to have every paper clip in its modular plastic container, every pencil, staple, rubber and label in its assigned position. I like my highlighting pens arranged in conformity with the spectrum. I like my blotter located in the exact centre of my desk. I like my mouse mat positioned precisely along the front edge of my work-station.

When I first came to work at the Company I was a lot sloppier about this; my desk was tidy, but it wasn't exact. Now it's exact.

Then I made a list, using the soft 'scherluump-scherluump' that the laserprinter was making as a counterpoint with which to order my thoughts. I always make a list at the end of the working day. They are essential if you want to maintain any kind of ordered working practice. I finished the list just as the presentation document finished printing. The icon came up on the VDU. It shows a smiling and satisfied little laserprinter, with underneath the legend: 'Printing Completed'.

I stacked the papers, punched them, bound them in a ring-binder with a plastic cover, and took the document across the corridor to my boss's office.

He was tipped far back on the rear wheels of his chair,

so that his head was almost hidden between two of the vertical textured-fabric louvres that cover the windows of his office. The posture looked uncomfortable. The black head of the lamp was pulled low over the fan of papers on the wide expanse of his desk. His feet were propped on the desk top and the cuffs of his trousers had ridden up above his socks, exposing two or three inches of quite brown, but hairless ankle. He said, 'Have you re-done the presentation document for the inter-depart-mental meeting?'

I replied, 'Yes, here it is.'

He said, 'Good. Well, I'll see you in the morning then.'

I turned and walked back across the corridor. I shut down my computer and then bent to turn off the laserprinter. Kneeling like this, with my face level with the lower platform of the workstation, I could see right underneath my desk. I could see the flexes of the computer, the laserprinter, the desk lamp and the tele-phone all join together and twist into a spiral stream of mushroom-coloured plastic that disappeared down an oblong cable-routing slot. There was nothing else to see under the desk, no errant rubber bands or propelling pencils gone astray.

The bottom of my workstation is shaped like an upside-down T, with a castor protruding from a rubber bung at either end of the crossbar. I rested my forehead on this bar for a while and let the coolness of the metal seep into me. When I opened my eyes again, I focused not on the distant prospect of the skirting board, but on my immediate vicinity: the beaten path that my varnished nail had cut for the rest of my finger, through the eighth-of-an-inch pile of nylon undergrowth. It was this that caught my attention – a really tiny event.

How small does an event have to be before it ceases to be an event? If you look very closely at the tip of your fingernail as it lies on a clear surface (preferably something white like a sheet of paper), so closely that you can see the tiny cracks in the varnish; and then push it towards some speck of dust, or tweak the end of a withered hair, or flick the corpse of a crumb still further into decay, is that as small as an event can be?

When I stood up I rapped my head on the underside of my workstation. Both it and my skull vibrated. I bit my lip. I stood like that for a few moments, concentrating hard on the angle of one of the flexible fronds in the stack of binders in my stationery cupboard. Then I shut the cupboard doors, snapped the switch that bathed my office in darkness, and left it.

I went down the first flight of stairs, past the plant that lives in the grey granules, down the second flight and along the corridor. The Department was already empty. I knew that, at five on the dot, the entire workforce would have risen up like a swarm, or a flock, and headed for the six big lifts that pinion the Company to the earth.

I also found myself on an empty platform, caught in the hiatus between two westbound trains. The platform's dirty tongue unwound along the side of the tube, which was ribbed like a gullet with receding rings of be-grimed metal. A tired, flat wind, warm with minor ailments, gusted up my nose. The electronic sign above the platform kept on creating the word 'Information' out of an array of little dots of light; as if this in itself was some kind of important message. I listened to the sough and grind of the escalator belt.

Gradually the platform began to fill up with people. The minor-ailment smell was undercut with hamburger and onion, overwhelmed by processed cheese and honey-cured ham, encapsulated by tobacco. They stood in loose groups, bonded together by a mutual desire to try and avoid uniformity. Thus, blacks stood with whites, women with men, gays with the straight, middle class with working class, the ugly with the beautiful, the crippled with the whole, the homeless with the home-owners, the fashionable with the shabby. That so many people could believe themselves different from one another only made them appear more the same.

To my left, clamped against the bilious tiling, was a strange machine. It wasn't clear whether it was mechanical or electronic. It had a curved housing of green plastic. It was eight inches high, and bolted at top and bottom to brackets hammered into the grout. In the middle of the thing was a circular, venetian-blind-slatted plate. Underneath it was a small sign that proclaimed: 'Speak Here'. I pressed my ear against the plate and heard the faint rise and fall of what might have been a recording of outer space, or the depths of the sea.

When the train eventually came, I stood for a moment watching the people get off and get on. The two streams of shoving bodies folded into one another, like the fingers of two hands entwining deep in the lap of the ground.

And that was what my day was like – or at any rate the second half of it. Wherever I start from I will experience the same difficulties, so it might as well be this afternoon, when I sensed the man's presence behind me as I fed the facsimile machine.

One last thing. This morning, as I have for the past fourteen mornings or so, I put a sanitary towel in my underpants. Tonight, when I stood in front of the mirror's oblong and looked at the pouch between my legs, I felt certain that there would be blood absorbed into the quilted paper. Just a few dabs and blotches, together with a brown smear at the edge, denoting earlier bleeding.

But there was nothing. It was virgin territory. No period – period. I haven't had sexual intercourse for over six months – I can't be pregnant. I am normally as regular in my body as I am at work. And over the last two weeks I have felt the swelling feeling, accompanied by an odd sensation of vacuity, that always precedes my coming on; and the dusting of yellow and mauve pimples under the softening, water-retaining line of my jaw has appeared as it should. I've also felt irascible and unaccountably depressed. (Well, normally this depression is accountable, I just can't account for it. Only now is it truly unaccountable.) But still there's been no period. Only the feelings, straining me for day after day.

In the morning the radio woke me at seven-fifteen, as it always does. Outside the sky was limpid, void, without properties of colour or density. Was it light yet? There was no answer to this, it was as light as it was yesterday at this time – and the day before, and the day before that.

I got up and went over to my bureau, where I started flicking through my diary. I looked over the pages of the past six weeks or so. I seldom write anything in the diary but appointments, and there was a scattering of these, like mouse droppings, on the lined paper. I tried to think about those days that had gone, taking with them fading memories of dental appointments and dry-cleaning collection times.

The day my last period was due was marked in red. This is how my life resolves itself: into periods and the periods between periods.

But when I thought about it, summoned up the seven-fifteens of those last forty days, they returned to me decked in the same limpid, void garb as this morning. Could it be true? Could it be that it has been getting light at the same time for over a month now? It made no sense. This is the time of year when the seasons change rapidly, when we become aware of the world turning despite – and not because – of what we do. And yet there was this six-week period during which nothing had changed.

I dressed carefully. I tucked the sanitary towel into the gusset of my underpants, trying hard not to think of it as some magical act, some willing of the jammed wheel of my cycle. I selected a new pair of tights from the drawer, and unsnapped them from their cellophane confines. I put on my bra and a cream-coloured cotton blouse. I took a fawn, two-piece suit from the wardrobe. Stepping into the skirt I caught sight of myself in the mirror on the wardrobe door. It was only momentary, but looking at the slight, sharp-faced young woman I saw reflected there, I realised that while I was by no means indifferent to her, she was moving inexorably towards the periphery of my acquaintance.

When I was fully dressed I sat at my bureau and applied a little eyeliner and a smudge of foundation. I don't wear lipstick as a rule. I knew that my boss would ask me to attend the inter-departmental meeting with him today, so that I could take minutes. Although he would never actually say anything to me about my appearance, I am conscious of the fact that he approves of the way I always make sure I am scrupulously neat, if we are in any context where we are representing the Department to the rest of the Company.

In the kitchen I examined the wash of pale light that fell across the draining board. Was it at precisely the same angle as yesterday? It seemed so. And my bath, gurgling away in a froth of bubbles and white water outside the kitchen window. Was it frothing in exactly the way that it did yesterday? Or was it only my perception of it?

They certainly seemed familiar, those miniature cumuli, sparkling oily greens and blues.

In the middle of the afternoon, I found myself by the facsimile machine again. I was looking out through the vertical textured fabric louvres and trying to decide whether or not the sky was the same colour as at this time yesterday. How would it be possible to do this? I toyed idly with getting a colour chart from the local DIY shop and seeing if I could match the sky's shade to any of its little squares. But the minute I hit upon this idea, I realised that it was absurd, that the sky wasn't like some expanse of silk emulsion on which I could impose my taste.

Then I became aware of his presence again. It was much stronger today. I turned, but he wasn't behind me; all I could see was an ear, poking around the jamb of the door. Its owner must have been talking to someone in the office to the immediate left of the recess where the inter-departmental facsimile machine is housed. I knew it was his ear intuitively. It was a thick, blunt ear, the edges folded over, squaring it off at the top and the side. I began to feel queasy looking at it. It was a typical ear – an ear that revealed what you always have suspected about ears, namely that they don't possess nerves connecting them to any organ capable of apprehending their shape. I couldn't believe that this ear was made from flesh and not some more ductile substance, like wax or putty, that had been moulded and then set.

Involuntarily I clutched at my own ear and kneaded it between my thumb and forefinger. I was jerked out of this nauseating brown study by the insistent peep of the facsimile machine – I had neglected to feed it with the next sheet and the connection was broken. By the time I redialled, fed the oblong maw, then turned to look once more, the ear had gone.

We were hosting the inter-departmental meeting this month. My boss always chooses to hold this in Conference Room 2. I have a suspicion that this is because he wishes to intimidate his fellow heads of department. Conference Room 1 is both more comfortable and more accessible.

Conference Room 2 is at the far end of the Department, further up the flight of stairs, past my office. It is perched on top of a wing of the building that projects out into a medium-sized abyss. Four storeys below the grimy windows of the room, a tangled collection of roofs, aerials, walls and skylights provides no fixed point for the eye to alight on.

Although the horizon is no further than before, the sense of Conference Room 2 being surrounded on three sides by space, and accessible on the fourth only by a dwarf entrance from the main building, makes it cut off and removed. This is heightened by the spectacle of a Portakabin that abuts the Conference Room, the end of which dangles over the edge of the local void.

The short flight of stairs that connects Conference Room 2 to the rest of the building has the ubiquitous corporate trappings: half-conical sconces on the uplights; the feral-animal-strength carpet tiling; the vertical textured-fabric louvres (proportionately tiny – to fit the tiny windows).

I entered Conference Room 2. The heads of department sat around the conference table, a blond wood lozenge. Each one was positioned in front of a representation of the corporate logo attached to the wall: an elephant (Indian), standing on a globe, but so stylised that it's difficult to tell if that's what it really is.

Southam was there, from marketing; Haines from purchasing; Thribble from sourcing; Andersen from accounting; Askey from data processing; Tenniel from personnel, and, of course, my boss, representing the Department.

'Come and sit here.' He clutched a bunch of his black hair in one hand. He was wearing one of those shirts where the collar and cuffs are white, while the rest is striped. This highlighted his brown hands and browner face, making him appear like some executive minstrel. The presentation document was open on the table in front of him, and I could see that he had been making notes in the margin. I got my dictaphone and notebook out and readied myself to take the minutes.

'Gentlemen,' my boss began, leaning forward in his chair, 'as you may recall, last month when it was the turn of my department to host this meeting, I made some proposals regarding the final phase of our corporate restructuring. Since then, as you are all no doubt aware, we have had the Main Board's approval to proceed with their implementation.

'This month I have requested a report from each of you, as to how far you have proceeded with the programme. I'll ask you, Terry, to begin – if you don't mind?'

'Not at all,' said Southam, shifting forward in his seat so that he could pour himself a cup of coffee from the stainless-steel vacuum jug and I could see the puce skin of his tonsure. 'I am happy to be able to report that since last month a further 37 per cent of our allocated spend has been redirected towards internal marketing. This means that as of today a total of' – he consulted his own presentation document – '97 per cent of our budget is now dedicated to the internal market.'

There were a number of nods, and significant grunts, from the other heads of department. Southam went on to explain the new marketing plan his department had developed to cope with the changed situation. I took the minutes diligently, listening to what he was saying, but not troubling to comprehend it.

When he had finished speaking my boss turned to Haines from purchasing. Haines's arms were crossed and with the inside edge of each middle finger he was methodically rubbing the nap of suiting stretched over either elbow. He spoke quietly and expressionlessly, with his eyes fixed on the corporate logo opposite him.

'I think that purchasing can report a success almost exactly congruent with that of marketing. Since last month a further 37 per cent of our purchasing has been reconfigured so as to come from within the Company. This means that 97 per cent of the goods and services we now purchase are sourced from the Company itself.'

In due course, Thribble from sourcing confirmed these figures. The reporting process continued on round the table, in an anti-clockwise direction. I concentrated on the high-pitched 'eek-eek' my fibre-tipped pen made as it steeplechased along the narrow feint. I didn't shut down my automatic dictation pilot until everyone had made their report. Then my boss turned to me and said, 'I think it would be a good idea if, while we discuss the next item on the agenda, you type up the minutes you've taken so far. You can leave the dictaphone running and I'll bring it down when we've finished. I think everyone present would like a copy of the minutes relating to the final phase of the corporate restructuring as quickly as possible.'

There was a scattering of grunted assents to this. I gathered up my pad and, nodding to my boss and the other heads of department, left Conference Room 2.

When I reached the stretch of corridor leading to my office, for no reason that I could think of, I parted two of the vertical textured-fabric louvres that cover the window by the door to my boss's office. From this vantage I could see Conference Room 2 in its entirety, hovering up above me. The heads of the heads of department were outlined by the room's windows. As I stood and watched, someone – I think it may have been Southam –

rose from the table and walked around the room, pulling the lengths of chain that snapped the louvres shut.

I went into my office. I knelt down to switch on my laserprinter. As I had the previous afternoon, I leant my forehead against the crossbar of the workstation.

It was still there. The beaten path that my varnished nail had cut for the rest of my finger, through the eighth-of-an-inch pile of nylon undergrowth. I stared at it for some minutes in disbelief. Then I tried some experiments: I pushed my nails this way and that through the carpet-tile pile; now combing it, now ploughing it. Using one finger, or two, or the whole hand. These actions made streaks of crushed nylon filaments, but they soon sprang back up. Only the path I had created the day before – the really tiny event – remained a reality.

After a short while I grew bored with this. I stood up, turned on my computer, and made ready to type up the minutes of the inter-departmental meeting. I accessed the file with the previous month's minutes in it, and created a new file; I set my pad on the stand and began to type:

The meeting was called to order and the Chairman asked T. Southam, head of marketing, to present the results of the implementation of the last phase of corporate restructuring. T. Southam reported that since last month a further 37 per cent of the marketing department's allocated spend had been redirected towards internal marketing. As of the 5th of this month a total

of 97 per cent of the department's total budget is now
dedicated to the internal market . . .

The pattering of my nails on the keys faltered and died
away. I stared at the paragraph I had just typed. The
cursor blinked at me from the VDU, the complicit eye of
a machine intelligence. Without analysing what I was
doing I saved the file and reentered the file for last
month's minutes. The text scrolled down the green
screen. I read:

The meeting was called to order and the Chairman
asked T. Southam, head of marketing, to present the
results of the implementation of the last phase of corporate restructuring. T. Southam reported that since last
month a further 37 per cent of the marketing department's allocated spend had been redirected towards
internal marketing. As of the 5th of this month a total
of 97 per cent of the department's total budget is now
dedicated to the internal market . . .

I felt sick – sick like vomiting sick. I got up from the
workstation and walked to the window of my office. I
adjusted the vertical textured-fabric louvres slightly, so
that I could open the window and get some fresh air. I
took deep breaths and stared down into the light well my
window looks out on. I counted the paper cups that lay
four storeys down, I counted the pigeons that were
perched on the ledges four storeys up, I counted the

fingers of one hand off on the fingers of the other, and then reversed the process.

I felt the swelling feeling, and the awful, tight vacuity, worse than ever before. I stood there for a long while, my hand lightly brushing the dusting of yellow and mauve pimples under the softening, water-retaining line of my jaw.

Then I went back to the computer, altered the date at the head of the minutes of last month's inter-departmental meeting, and hit the keystrokes necessary to print out the document.

At five I finished up my work for the day. I had transcribed the tape of the latter half of the inter-departmental meeting and left a copy in my boss's in-tray. I now made my list of tasks for the following day and then began to tidy my desk.

But halfway through ordering my pens and papers I had an idea. Instead of aligning everything just so, as usual, I would engage in a little exercise. Using my ruler to calculate the angles – so this would be precise – I shifted the computer keyboard, the desk blotter and the mouse mat out of alignment by two or three degrees. This alteration was so slight as to be barely perceptible to the naked eye, but I knew it was there.

Then I went home.

Tonight, eating a late supper in front of *Newsnight* on the television, it came to me, the expression I really needed to describe the man from personnel. VPL. There used to be an advert on television in which puckered bottom after puckered bottom would float across the screen. Buttock after buttock after buttock, all bobbling away and contained by stretchy cloth beneath the stretchy cloth. VPL – Visible Panty Line. That's what they called it. If you bought their underwear you were free of it, but if you didn't you were condemned to an elastic jail.

That's what he has. Except that it isn't just his bottom – it's his whole body. Every limb and portion of the man from personnel's body is contained in an elasticated pouch, the seams of which show up from under his implausible clothes. What has he got on under there? Some complicated harness that braces his entire body? Some sacred garment enjoined by the Latter Day Saints? Who knows.

The radio woke me at seven-fifteen this morning, and this time there was no doubt in my mind. I got up and stood, looking out of my bedroom window for a long time, marvelling at the limpidity, the utter voidness of the sky.

There was no blood last night and this morning there was no blood in the sleep-warmed sanitary towel either. I stood for quite some time in front of the mirror, scrunging the insides of my thighs; catching up painful bunches of my own flesh and feeling the individual pores between my pincering fingertips. Then I pressed down hard on my belly with both palms and pushed a wave of flesh down to my pudenda, as if I were a giant sponge and I could somehow squeeze the blood out of myself. I repeated this operation a number of times, not really expecting it to work, but thinking it was worth a try.

But I wasn't frightened. Throughout this whole period I haven't felt frightened at all. Perhaps I would feel less disturbed, if only I could get frightened. Perhaps I don't really care that I've stopped menstruating, or that the days are unchanging, or that events tirelessly repeat themselves. Or perhaps I've simply adjusted – as people do.

In the kitchen I examined the wash of pale light that fell across the draining board. It was at precisely the same angle as yesterday. And my bath, gurgling away with a froth of bubbles and white water outside the kitchen window, was frothing in exactly the way that it did yesterday. I greeted the miniature cumuli, sparkling oily greens and blues, like old friends. Childlike, I allowed myself to imagine that I was weightless and miniscule, that I could roam and romp in this pretty, insubstantial gutterscape.

I had an errand to do on the way to work this morning which made me a little late. It was ten to nine before I mounted the wide concrete stairs that lead to the Company's offices. At this hour there was a steady trickle of employees entering the building, but it hadn't yet swelled into the cataract of personnel that flows through the turbine doors between five to and five past.

During those ten minutes at least 90 per cent of the Company's workforce arrive: secretaries, clerks, canteen assistants, data processors, post-room operatives, maintenance men, as well as middle managers of all shapes and sizes; and, of course, executives. They all crowd in, anxious to be seen arriving on time. The subordinates in a hurry to be there before their bosses, and the bosses in a hurry to be there before their subordinates.

But even at ten to, the foot traffic was light enough for people to observe at least nominally the pleasantries of the morning. These consist not in salutations to colleagues, but in the greeting you give to the commissionaire, Cap'n Sidney.

Cap'n Sidney stands in a booth by the security turnstile. He wears a white peaked cap, and a black serge uniform. The epaulettes on his shoulders are blancoed beyond belief. He stands there erect, the awareness that he is the Company's first line of defence written into every line of his face.

Young male employees flirt physically with Cap'n Sidney. They duck and weave as they show him their security passes. They want to give him a little action and so they wave their uncalloused hands in his face, saying things like, 'Howzit going there, Sidders,' and, 'Mind out for the old one-two.' Cap'n Sidney grins benignly and replies, 'Now, Rocky Marciano – there was a boxer.'

Older male employees, perhaps believing that their M & S blazers remind Cap'n Sidney of the officers he served fifty years ago, will touch the tips of their fingers lightly to their foreheads as they pass through the turnstile. It is the merest feint, a tiny gesture towards the communality of the past; and Cap'n Sidney returns it in the same spirit, with a touch of his nicotine-mitted hand to the peak of his cap.

Older female employees always say 'Good morning' to Cap'n Sidney with exaggerated care – as if he were an idiot or an imbecile. And he always says 'Good morning' back to them with exaggerated care – as if they were idiots or imbeciles.

Young female employees say 'Good morning' to Cap'n Sidney, and they touch him with their eyes. Cap'n Sidney is their talisman, their wise old uncle. He understands that, says 'Good morning' in reply and examines their breasts, as if they were security passes.

Cap'n Sidney never says 'Good morning' to me, no matter how early I arrive at work. When it comes to me Cap'n Sidney is oblivious. It's not that he's rude, or insensitive – after all he simply can't salute every single Company employee, there are far too many of us. It's just that we've never really met; and now, over thousands of mornings, a natural reserve has built up between us. It would be all right if some colleague of mine – whether a clerical-weight boxer, officer class, or the Right Breasts – were to introduce us, put us at ease with one another; then I too could become a warm, sincere, ten-second friend of Cap'n Sidney.

This is unlikely to happen.

The strangest of things, though; the last six weeks – which we may call the non-period for the sake of convenience – have marked an apparent shift in my lack-of-a-relationship with Cap'n Sidney. During this non-period, when I have approached his booth, pass held level at the convenient height, by the lobe of my right ear, Cap'n Sidney's eyes have narrowed. And I have thought that, for the split-second my face was turned towards his, as I slid through the turnstile, his expression had a little more openness about it, that something writhed – ever so slightly – beneath his moustache.

The VPL man was in the lift. He smiled at me quite innocently, but as we ascended his presence there became somehow bound up with everything oppressive, everything crammed into the stippled, aluminium booth of my mind. It occurred to me too that the VPL man had only come into my life in the last six weeks or so – at any rate I could dredge up no earlier memory of him.

There is some linkage, some alliance, between my pre-menstrual tension and the VPL man's VPL. He too has something bulging and constrained, yet vacuous, concealed beneath his clothing. These personalised voids, I imagined, were calling to one another, wailing the music of the empty spheres.

Between the third and the fourth floors I shifted tack. It might not be anything quite so nebulous between me and the VPL man. I now entertained the notion that the VPL man had somehow managed to impregnate me, without my knowledge. Perhaps he had crept into the women's toilet midway down the departmental corridor, late one afternoon, when only the cleaners are about, and tossed himself off. There is more plausibility in this image: his puckered form in the formica cubicle, his salty dollop on the mushroom-shaped and mushroom-coloured toilet seat.

But there is someone else about. Me. And he knows that. As he strap-hangs his way home on the tube, he smiles enigmatically, his lips parted – because he knows that mine are parted; and at that very moment are sucking it up, his tadpole, his micro-construction robot, which burrows into me carrying the blueprints for the manufacture of more VPL men and VPL women.

By the time we reached the Department's floor I was convinced of this. I was bearing the VPL man's child, the chopped-ear-man's child, the bastard offspring of he-who-lingers-by-the-facsimile-machine. It could be worse – the child will be a fine, healthy specimen, and grow up to do something undynamic but essential, like becoming a Communications Manager (since my boss took over the Department it has been mandatory for all job titles to be capitalised).

It didn't even occur to me that our child might wish to work in his father's department rather than my own.

I got out before Daddy, who barely looked up from the folded square of newsprint he was reading and re-reading.

A truly annoying morning was entirely dominated by a recurrent system error on my computer. I have a suspicion that we may have a virus in the departmental network. I said as much to my boss, when he poked his head into my office at around eleven. He asked me what was happening – and I explained that every time I exited from the network and tried to import files on to my own hard disc, the machine crashed.

He came round behind my desk to take a look. I pulled back from the workstation, allowing him the room to get at the keyboard. He was wearing one of his newer suits today; and positioned as I was, I found myself confronted by the seat and upper legs of his trousers. The suit is made from soft but durable fabric, and the designer had seen fit to create some miniature chaps of shiny chamois, which stretched a third of the way down my boss's thighs. The chaps were mimicked by the distended epaulettes, which I had already seen flopping from the shoulders of the suit jacket, like the ears of a Basset hound.

'See here?' He flicked his hands over the surface of the keyboard, only occasionally grasping for the mouse, as if he were casting off a stitch. The cursor appeared here and there, in a whirl of shifts between applications and files. Instead of attempting to import the files directly, he went into them where they were stored, as if intent on doing some work on them. He then cut out the entire contents of each file and re-opened it under another application. Finally he imported the new application, and so sneaked around the lurking virus.

'See?' He was heading for the door, while an icon, somewhat like a triumphant Roadrunner, executed a frenzied jig on the VDU, and the tinny speaker cackled, 'Ah-ha-ah-hahahaha!'

The Roadrunner may have known more than I did. At night, the cleaners long departed from the Department, the computer icon could have quit the screen and entered my world of static grey. 'Ah-ha-ah-hahahaha!' Something had been in my office during the night, something fervid but precise – like the Roadrunner icon, because this morning ('Ah-ha-ah-hahahaha!') the computer keyboard, the desk blotter and the mouse mat were all perfectly aligned once more. It wasn't perceptible to the naked eye, but I checked it with my ruler.

At lunchtime I looked hard at the sky for more than five minutes. On the way into work I stopped by the DIY centre and picked up a colour chart. I had been doing comparisons at half-hour intervals all morning. Initially I was certain the shade the sky corresponded to was 'pearl grey', but latterly I made up my mind that it was really 'mid-grey'. It was mid-grey for the rest of the morning.

In fact it grew more convincingly mid-grey the more I checked it, until at lunchtime it was no comparison at all; it was rather that the tiny rectangle on the chart was a miniature window, looking out on to another quadrant of the grey heavens. All it needed was its own vertical textured fabric louvres, to complete the marriage between sample and sky.

I went down to the café and bought my sandwiches, a can of Diet Coke and one of those giant, crumbly cookies.

In the park I sat with other office workers in a circle of

benches that surrounds a sagging rotunda. This feature is built from red London bricks. It's damp and destitute, long since re-pointed. The pillars resemble a demented loggia, which instead of moving forward has turned in on itself, forming a defensive corral. The pools of rusty water at the base of each pillar seem evidence of incontinence, a suitable indignity for wayward park furniture.

The office workers sat canted sideways on the benches. An occasional pigeon hopped up to one of these sandwich eaters, clearly shamed by its capacity to fly and doing its best to hide tattered wings. These exchanges between people and birds were embarrassing to watch. That's the truth. We have now advanced so far into a zone of the genetically furtive, that office workers, contemplating these flying vermin, feel their own humanity compromised in some way. So they roll up bread pills, and averting their eyes, proffer them to the un-stuck craws.

All afternoon I sat in my office and worked. The straining in my belly grew, swelled, became even more pregnant. I was certain that I was on the verge of getting my period. My nipples were so sensitive that I could feel every bump and nodule on their aureoles, snagging against the cotton of my bra. The afternoon was also punctuated by a series of quite sharp abdominal pains. After every one of them I was convinced I would feel the familiar ultimate lancing. I was poised, ready to head for the toilet – the venue for my imagined impregnation by the VPL man – but no blood came.

Instead I occupied myself with the collation and binding of a series of management briefings that the Department was publishing for the greater edification of the Company as a whole.

Five o'clock found me bending the flexible prongs back on the clean sheets, to house them securely in their plastic covers. My boss hung his face around the door-jamb and grunted approval. I couldn't see his ear – and this troubled me. I wanted to ask him to take a step into the room, so that I could check on his ear, check that it was still there and still his. But the idea of it was silly, a nitrous oxide thought that giggled in my head. To stop myself from smirking I concentrated on the odd, phallic intervention, made at waist-height, by the black-taped handle of his squash racket.

Then he left. I ordered my desk, and soon afterwards went home.

At home I ate and then had a bath, hoping that it would ease the pre-menstrual tension. It didn't. I put on a dressing gown and wandered about my flat. Never before had it seemed so claustrophobic. The neat, space-saving arrangement of double-seater sofa and twin arm-chairs was a cell within a cell. The coffee table, with its stack of magazines and dish of pot-pourri, was part of a set for a chat show that never made it past the development stage. The images on the walls were tired, static, self-referential, each one a repository of forgotten insights, now incapable of arousing fresh interest.

I turned on the television, but couldn't concentrate. I

must have slept, squelched down amongst the foam-filled, polyester-covered cushions. Slid into sleep, the surfaces of my eyes grounding quickly on the salty, silty bottom of unconsciousness. There I floated, twisting slowly in the deceptive currents.

Assembled backwards. Quickly. Scherlupppp! The elements of my dream: I arrive for work and see that the organisational chart has been rearranged overnight. The strips, dots and squares have been manipulated so as to form a new configuration, which places a dot I haven't seen before at the very apex of the Department's hierarchy. I consult the legend, a small ring-binder dangling from the rail at the bottom of the board by a length of twine, only to discover that the dot is me.

I realise that I will have to move across the corridor into my ex-boss's office. I am relieved to see him coming through my door; cradled in his arms is his desk blotter and giant mouse mat. On top of these surfaces is a miscellany of objects he has culled from his desk: a Rotadex, a date-a-day diary, a dictaphone, and a collection of plastic beakers, joined at the root, brimming with pens, pencils and paper clips.

He finds it difficult to meet my eye, but I'm wholly unembarrassed. I gesture to the collation and binding exercise that I was undertaking the previous evening, and which is still spread out on my desk. I say, 'Finish this off, will you?' He nods, dumbly.

I cross the corridor to my new office. I go behind the broad, black slab of desk and sit down. My former boss has left one object behind on his desk top, an executive toy of some kind, saved from the era when these mini constructions of stainless steel and black plastic had a vogue.

This one takes the form of a Newton's cradle. But in the place of ball bearings, there are tiny, humanoid figures hanging from the threads by their shiny aluminium hands. The figures are naked, and when I set the cradle in motion, they engage in dangerously athletic congress. There is silence, except for the sound of miniature, metal, intercrural activity.

Piled under the vertical textured-fabric louvres; tucked up against the vents under the storage heaters; squidged sideways to lie along the top of the cable-tracking conduit, which circles the office at knee height; stacked in loose bundles on every flat surface, bar the desk itself, are many many panty liners, tampons and sanitary towels. Staunchers, stemmers, cotton-wool barriers. There is so much plastic-backed absorbent material in my new office that, taken together with the fabric-covered walls and carpet-tiled floor, the effect is of a recording studio. The clicking of the Newton's cradle has amazing clarity. The shadows of the figurines banging into one another are thrown into sharp relief against the whiteboard on the far wall. A cord of pain, running like a zipper up through the flesh from my vagina to my throat, threatens to undo me, to spill out my interior, like so much offal, or rhino shit, on the carpet tiles.

★   ★   ★

When I awake *Newsnight* is on the television. Peter Snow is running the world from his modular grey bunker of a studio. He's sitting in front of oversized venetian-blind slat panels, and ignoring the micro-computer that has sunk at an oblique angle into the vinyl-veined console he's sitting behind.

He is speaking with undue emphasis. It's this undue emphasis that impinges on me first – but it occurs to me immediately afterwards that perhaps everything I have ever heard anyone say has been subjected to undue emphasis.

Snow is talking to two pop academics. I can tell this with some certainty, because one of them is too well dressed for a politician, and the other too badly. Like a dentist with mass appeal, Snow is getting down to extracting the truth from this duo. He cants himself towards the badly dressed, froggy-looking one.

'Now, Dr Busner, haven't we been hearing for years now – from you and others – about the possible effects of such a bottoming-out?'

'Quite so,' says the man called Busner, 'although I'm not sure that "bottoming-out" is the right expression. What we have here is a condition of stasis. I'm not prepared to hazard any long-term predictions about its duration on the basis of the sanity quotient figures we currently have; but what I can say is that the Government's response has been woefully inadequate – a case of too little, too late.'

He falls to rolling and unrolling the ragged strip of mohair tie that flows down over the soft folds of his belly. He does this extremely well, with one hand, the way a card sharp runs a coin through his fingers. Snow now cants himself towards the other man, a virile sixty year old, with intact and ungreying hair, wearing a sharp Italian suit with the narrowest of chalk stripes. 'Professor Stein, a case of too little, too late?'

'I think not.' Stein steeples his fingers on top of the console. 'Like Dr Busner, I would reserve the right to comment at some later date. The evidence we have at the moment is sketchy, incomplete. But that being noted, even if the conditions today's report draws our attention to are fully realised, it only points towards the non-event I am certain will not occur.'

'So, contrary to what you have said in the past, you now think something may well happen?' Snow is delighted that he has caught Stein's double-negative.

'That's not what I said,' Stein fires right back at the lanky television presenter. 'I appreciate the implications of this data. It is bizarre – to say the least – to have so many people apparently experiencing a lengthy period of climatic and seasonal stasis; but we must bear in mind that, as yet, this is a localised phenomenon, confined to a discrete area. It has only been this way for some six weeks – '

'More like two months!' Busner cuts in.

This gives Peter Snow the opportunity to try and

knock the discussion down, so he can drag it somewhere else. 'How-can-you-Doc-tor-Busner' – he is in profile, Struwwelpeter-like, fingers splayed, elongated, nose sharp, rapping out the words in a dot-dash fashion, letting his pentameters beat up on each other – 'be-so-o-certain-about-the-ex-act-time-the-stasis-began?'

'Well, I admit' – Busner, far from being cowed, is invigorated by Snow's tongue-tapping – 'it can be difficult to ascertain when nothing begins to happen.' His plump lips twitch, he is sucking on the boiled irony, 'But not, I think, impossible.

'Take events – for example. How small does an event have to be before it ceases to be an event?'

'Yes, yes, that is a very interesting question.' This from Stein. The three of them are now all canted towards one another, forming a boyish huddle. 'I myself am intrigued by small events, matters of the merest degree. Perhaps I might give an example?'

'Please do.' Peter Snow's tone has softened, it's clear that the idea interests him.

'Can we have the camera in very tight on the surface of the console, please?'

'Pull right in, please, camera 2.' Snow makes a come-on-down gesture.

The camera zooms right down until the veins in the grey vinyl of the console are rift valleys. What must be the very tip of Stein's fingernail comes into view. I can see the grain of it. It pokes a little at the vinyl, dislodging a speck of something. It could be dust or a fragment of skin, or mica. But the speck is both very small – less than a tenth of the width of Stein's fingernail – and very grey; as grey as the console itself.

The camera zooms back out in. The three middle-aged men are beaming. 'So there we have,' says Peter Snow, addressing a portion of the nation, 'a very small event. Thank you, Professor Stein, and you, Dr Busner.' The two pop academics incline their heads, slightly.

The camera moves back in until Snow fills the screen. There are some fresh newspapers, interleaved by his elbow. 'Well-that's-about-it-for-tonight-except-for-a-quick-look-at-tomorrow's-papers.' His hands pull them out, one at a time, while he recites the headlines, '*The-Times*: "No-New-Developments-in-Stasis-Situation". The *Guardian*: "Government-Ministers-Knew-that-Nothing-Had-Happened". And-*Today*-with-the-rather-racier: "We're-in-a-Grey-Area!".

'Jeremy-Paxman-will-be-here-tomorrow-night. But-for-now-this-is-Peter-Snow-wishing-you-good-night.' The grey man on the screen smiles, picks up the pile of papers from the grey console in front of him, and shuffles them together, while the camera pulls up and away.

I pull up and away, and go next door to the bedroom. I take off my dressing gown and hang it on a hook behind the door. I take my nightie from beneath my pillow and put it on. I get a fresh pair of underpants from the chest of drawers and wriggle into them. I set the alarm clock for seven-fifteen. And I get a new sanitary towel and place it in the gusset of my underpants.

My period might start during the night.

Inclusion®

Y OU ARE HOLDING in your hands a folder. The hands cannot be described by me, because they are yours, but the folder can. A shiny, white thing, the standard A4 size, it has sparse, expensively embossed, blue lettering on the cover, together with a corporate logo. The first line of the lettering reads: 'Cryborg Pharmaceutical Industries' and underneath it says: 'Inclusion, a Revolutionary Approach to Anti-Depressant Medication'. Beneath that there is the corporate logo, an odd thing that looks somewhat like a pineapple with wavy lines radiating all around it. Whether or not it expresses some attribute of Cryborg Pharmaceutical Industries is moot, or merely obscure, depending on how interested you are. Depending on how far you are prepared to include the marketing brochures of pharmaceutical companies in your life. Give them headroom.

If you open the Inclusion folder you'll find what you expect to find. Namely, that the marketing budget didn't quite reach to laminating overleaf, and further, that the two sides of the folder are equipped with diagonal pockets – pockets that house on the right the Inclusion marketing brochure and on the left a miscellany of order forms, sheets covered with corporate information, information on other Cryborg products etc., etc.

So, you ease out the marketing brochure from its pocket and start to flip through. The paper is creamy and textured, the type is artful and elegant, the photographs and illustrations are composed, if a little arid. Of course, initially, it's amusing to see that anti-depressant drugs are marketed in exactly the same way as lingerie, or cars. But it's an amusement that soon fades to a faint wryness and then winks out altogether.

On page two a photo shows a young couple with a toddler. The man is laughing and holding the child – who's also laughing – up in the air. The woman is looking at him with milch cow eyes, slopping over with admiration – there will be no crying over this spillage. The photo caption reads: 'Once a patient is being treated with Inclusion, he can be maintained indefinitely at a constant, regular dosage. A lifetime of positive engagement lies ahead.'

Turning back a page we discover why it is that this should be the case. See here: the same couple, but now his brown model face is crammed with agony against a rain-speckled windowpane. And her lighter-brown model hand, sketching a gesture of tenderness across his knotted back, will soon – it's absolutely clear – be shrugged off. He may even belt her one. The neglected toddler sits on the floor at their feet, looking up at them with tiny, dull eyes.

This is a man who needs Inclusion, that's the conclusion you have to draw. This man is crying out for Inclusion, or at any rate he would be if he knew what it was.

A flip-through the rest of the brochure is all that's needed for you to clock the pastel, shaded drawings of dissected brains. If you tilt the brochure this way and that you will see that the portion of the brain that contains the receptors to which these benign Inclusion molecules attach themselves has been coated with a lozenge of varnish, so that it shines.

The accompanying text is, however, unilluminating – an unholy mish-mash of medicalese and promotional claptrap that combines together to produce repellent patois like the following:

> Inclusion has fewer contra-indications than the tricyclics and the SSRIs.★ Better still, the attractive, easy-to-swallow spanules come in a variety of quality-enhanced patternings: paisley, Stuart tartan, heliotrope . . . etc., etc.

If there is anything to be learnt from the Inclusion folder it isn't contained in the brochure. The brochure is quite clearly not for the general reader. But what's this? Poking out from among the order forms in the opposite pocket there is a thick wadge of typescript. Funny to think that it

★ Selective Seratonin Re-Uptake Inhibitors, i.e. Prozac®, and other brand-name anti-depressants such as Sustral®, Faverin® and Sebcocat®. Author's note.

could be hiding there, in this folder which seemed so flimsy, so insubstantial, when first you hefted it. Pull it out now:

What is it? We-ell, it looks like a report of some sort. It's word-processed rather than printed, but it's been done on a good machine with an attractive typeface, a Palatino or Bodoni. It isn't bound – the corners of the fifteen or so pages are mashed together with a single paper clip, yet somehow the report is instantly alluring. Right at the top is written:

Ref. Inc/957 [and underneath] Report from R.P.H. to Main Board [and beneath that] Strictly for Board Eyes Only. Confidential.

God, how exciting! Not at all like the Inclusion brochure. You have a prickly little thrill, don't you? You have the thrill of reading someone's private correspondence in a silent house, on a Sunday afternoon. Somewhere in the mid-distance a dog barks. You read on:

Report of the Incident at the Worminghall Research Facility
From: R.P. Hawke
To: All Main Board Directors

Attached to this report are two relevant documents which I suggest are read and then destroyed. They are: Dr Zack Busner's journal of the events surrounding the aborted Inclusion trial and a diary kept by one of his guinea-pigs (the painter Simon Dykes). I have appended them to my report because I feel they may be of some interest to Board members. However, little of what either Busner or Dykes has to say is of any significance when it comes to understanding, or even attempting to explain, the events at Worminghall over the past four months.

That task is my responsibility. As the Company's senior public relations manager I was asked to conduct the appropriate damage limitation exercise after the incident. The results of this are as follows:

1. The Worminghall Facility itself has been cleared. All evidence of the cyclotron explosion has been disposed of. Our operatives have conducted an exhaustive cleansing operation using the most sophisticated reagents available. All stocks of Inclusion held at the Facility have been destroyed; and I am confident that any residual traces of Inclusion that may have permeated the facility following the explosion will be soon neutralised.

2. As you are all no doubt aware, the explosion was reported by a local resident to the desk sergeant at Thame Police Station before anyone at Cryborg Head Office knew what had transpired. Fortunately, the fact of the explosion did not gain any wider currency. The police sergeant and the local resident (a Mrs Freeling) have been made extensive, *ex gratia* payments.

3. As far as local and national bureacracy is concerned

i.e., planning committees, health and safety committees, licensing bodies etc., as you all know, the Worminghall Facility was never licensed for pharmaceutical research of any kind. Indeed, as far as the local authorities were aware, the Facility was merely a 'rest home' in the Chilterns for Cryborg employees who had collapsed due to work-related stress disorders. No medical treatments were to be carried out there and Dr Busner himself was listed in the original planning application for the Facility as a non-medical director-cum-manager. All medical care for employees residing at the Facility was to be contracted out, on a private basis, to a GP at the local practice.

4. This brings me to the issue of Dr Anthony Bohm. As Board members are aware, Bohm was Busner's conduit for the secret testing of Inclusion. Bohm was paid to prescribe Inclusion to his patients, and to provide Busner with an adequate control. Unfortunately Busner did not confine himself to bribing Bohm. Indeed, despite the handsome sums paid to him, the threat of personal ruin and professional disgrace which that money represented does not seem to have been Bohm's main motivation. Judging from Busner's journal, Bohm was an ideological convert to Inclusion, as was MacLachlan, the local pharmacist who distributed the Inclusion prescriptions.

Busner persuaded them all that the illegal prescription of an unlicensed, untested psychoactive drug was a positively humanitarian gesture. How he managed this I cannot say. The account of his relationship with these parties that his own journal gives is fantastic and almost certainly false.

After arriving at Worminghall, assessing the damage and immediate potential for toxicological fall-out, my next thought was to secure Bohm. However, when I got to the health centre I found that he was away, allegedly on holiday in France for two weeks. At the pharmacy I got the same story. I need hardly emphasise to the Board how important it is for the containment of the Inclusion incident that Bohm – and MacLachlan – are apprehended on their return to the UK. Until we have interviewed them there can be no guarantee that the prescription of Inclusion to ordinary NHS patients in the Worminghall locality can be effectively covered up.

5. Busner's disappearance and Dykes's ongoing condition are, of course, the most worrying aspects of the whole Inclusion débâcle. If we could be certain that Busner was dead it would be possible for us to abandon the complex subterfuge required to convince his family that he is still attending a neuro-pharmacological conference in the USA. On the other hand, were he to reappear it would open the way to attaching the culpability to Busner himself.

The Dykes problem is bound up with Busner. Dykes has had a complete mental breakdown. Psychiatrists who owe no loyalty to the company are convinced that his ravings about having 'included' Dr Zack Busner into himself, are just that: ravings.

Nevertheless, having spoken to both Dykes and his

wife myself, I am now convinced that he is suffering from an Inclusion-induced psychosis of some kind. Should he recover and be discharged from the Warneford Hospital in Oxford, the company may have some awkward questions to answer. And if we wish to pronounce Busner dead, we will have to come up with a body.

In conclusion: the Inclusion trials are far from over. If you examine Busner's journal and Dykes's diary I think you will gain some idea of just how potent and dangerous a drug Inclusion is.

It does not come within my remit to criticise company policy. However – as some of you will no doubt recall – I joined Cryborg eight years ago, specifically to deal with the bad press the company was receiving in the wake of the Rutger breakout. Given that I was able to persuade an overwhelmingly hostile media that there were sound medical reasons for surgically bifurcating the feet of African tribesmen in order to provide them with two giant prehensile toes, any aspersions cast on my loyalty to Cryborg are unwarranted.

Be that as it may – I am appalled by what transpired at Worminghall. On the day of the incident, arriving at the Facility after a breakneck drive from London, I found the buildings inside the compound deserted.

I ran from one to the next. Their floors were scattered – not with the debris I expected – but with piles of things, objects of all kinds, and intact. There were antique victrolas and pharmacological reference works;

laboratory equipment and cuddly toys; pill boxes and plastic pachyderms; fruit and electronic components; curling equipment and ancient votive statuary; stuffed animals and exercise equipment; sporting trophies and antiquarian books; model trains and silverware; samovars and sousaphones; clothes and carpet off-cuts.

There was no obvious explanation. It was a remarkably diverse assemblage of stuff. There wasn't even enough room in the Research Facility to house it all. The buildings were overflowing; things bulged from windows and spilled out through doors.

I worked my way across the compound towards the farthest building, the one housing Busner's laboratory, his office and the Inclusion cyclotron. As I drew closer I began to see a pattern in these drifts of impedimenta. The car batteries and Eskis; tin cans and slipper socks; VCRs and fondue forks, formed a series of concentric circles, covering the entire area of the Research Facility. Busner's laboratory was the epicentre.

Entering the building I found evidence that gave me a partial explanation. The cyclotron had exploded. Busner's laboratory and office were wrecked. Equipment and papers had been hopelessly mangled together. The concentric rings of objects that covered the rest of the Facility were some kind of embroidery, an elaboration of the shock waves of the explosion.

These waves or rings were present in the laboratory as well. As they diminished in size, so did the objects that composed them. At the outer edge of the laboratory the rings comprised Rotadexes and file holders; typewriter ribbons and plastic beakers; Bunsen burners and test-tube racks. Whilst the smaller rings were made up of paper clips and drawing pins; biros and match books; fragments of glass and fragments of mica. The smallest rings were just dust.

The rings were disconcerting. Their utter regularity, the way they retained circularity by running up and over the buildings – or even traversing them altogether – implied both conscious agency and blind force. I was bewildered. Even more unsettling were the two bound notebooks that sat in the middle of the smallest ring. They were so at odds with the evidence of destruction that they must have been placed there after the explosion . . .

You look once more into the pocket of the shiny folder – purely out of idle curiosity. You certainly don't expect to find either of these mysterious notebooks – how could their bulk be contained within its two shiny dimensions? When you hefted the folder earlier on it just wasn't sufficiently weighty – yet there they both are, wedged down tight, behind a sheaf of order forms. Hawke had included both of them – as he said he would. He also wrote a further rider, on a Post-It Note attached to the first notebook:

Please note: the term 'log' is slightly misleading. For while what follows does present some calibrated information on the course of the Inclusion trial, the document by no means displays the dispassionate, observational approach one would expect from a psychiatrist and a clinician of Busner's standing. It is more accurate to describe the notebook as Busner's personal journal. R.P.H.

First Extract from Dr Zack Busner's Log

5th October
Anthony Valuam waylaid me in the corridor this morning and suggested that I lunch with him and one of the research directors of Cryborg Pharmaceuticals next week. I surprised myself by agreeing. On balance I think that, whatever they propose, it can hardly be less ethical than the work I am currently doing at Heath Hospital.

12th October
Lunch was far better than I expected. Gainsford, the research director, took us to Grindley's Upstairs. I enjoyed my rack of lamb, but perhaps disgraced myself by setting fire to rolled-up Amaretti papers and watching them float up to the ceiling.

Gainsford wants me to resign my consultancy and come and work for him at Cryborg. He was rather coy about the project he has in mind. He made a big pitch, saying Cryborg would pay me four times what I'm currently earning. If this is really the case I will be making far more than I ever have – even during my heyday as a TV pundit in the early seventies.

I told Gainsford that nothing could be more anti-thetical – even now – to my concept of mental health treatment, than working for a multinational drug company. He simply laughed. He's a little man, his round face decorated with one of those mini goatee-and-moustache combinations. While he spoke it twitched, registering his circumspection.

22nd October

Through Valuam I have intimated to Gainsford that I might be interested in leaving Heath Hospital to work for Cryborg. Gainsford phoned me today and told me that he could only fill me in on the project if I was prepared to sign some sort of corporate secrets waiver. I agreed to this readily enough – I love secrets. We arranged to meet at the Cryborg head office in Victoria next Thursday.

30th October

It's a drug trial, how droll. But what a drug. I understand now why Gainsford was so insistent on secrecy. The range of applications and the potential market for the drug is absolutely staggering. From the evidence Gainsford presented to me it is clear that Cryborg are on the verge of a really major advance in neuro-pharmacology.

The drug has been tentatively given the name 'Inclusion'. It is relatively easy to produce, being derived entirely from the cadaverous and faecal matter of an obscure insect parasite. Once the psychoactive ingredient is isolated it can be stabilised using a specially devised cyclotron. Gainsford demonstrated the whole procedure for me in a laboratory adjoining the main Cryborg boardroom.

Gainsford wants me to test the drug for him. The catch is that the trial has to be conducted in secret – and on the general population. This is obviously why Cryborg approached me. Even though my conduct as a professional has been impeccable over the past fifteen years I am still known as an unorthodox practitioner; a whacko shrink who is prepared to undertake courses of research well outside the mainstream.

Nevertheless, were money the sole consideration I would have given Gainsford short shrift. However, my curiosity had been awakened – and once that's happened there is little that can stop me. The evidence that Gainsford presented on Inclusion was remarkable. This clearly showed that astonishing results had already been achieved using Inclusion for the following broad range of reactive depressive symptoms: anxiety, insomnia, stress, impotence etc. There is no known toxic dose for the drug either.

Could this be the panacea we have been searching for for so long? I no longer have any faith in the talking cures, nor do I find it easy to prescribe drugs like the tricyclics, which I know will only help a very small number of the patients who are referred to me. That the refined crap of a bee mite might prove to be the salvation of our growing legions of misery is fantastic enough and ironic enough to be believable!

5th November

A sad day for me. I handed in my notice to Archer, the senior administrator at the Health Authority. He insisted on having a long chat with me about my future – I was evasive. Under instructions from Gainsford I have not admitted to anyone – even my family – what the precise nature of my employment at Cryborg will be. Archer wouldn't let it lie. He kept on bleating about what a loss it was, how he'd thought I would stay at Heath until my retirement, how they needed me to fight the depredations of the Government. Whenever the conversation flagged, he would crank it up again like some Klaxon, until he was wailing away again, saying we should keep in touch, how he thought of me as family etc. He's the sort of person who gives gregariousness a bad name.

13th November

I'm winding down my work on the wards. My replacement is yet to be decided on, in the meantime Jane Bowen will cover Ward 8 and Anthony Valuam Ward 9. I feel far more emotional about leaving Heath Hospital than I thought I would. Particularly as Misha Gurney – one of my patients and the son of my old friend Simon Gurney, the sculptor – committed suicide last night. They found him early this morning in one of the abandoned radiography suites in the hospital basement. He had hung himself. Poor, sad boy. Perhaps Inclusion might have helped him. Now we'll never know.

24th November
Gainsford drove me up to Worminghall in the Chilterns today, and we toured the new Research Facility. He had been given a very large Toyota saloon by the Cryborg car pool, which was unfortunate as he is almost too small to reach the pedals. Driving out of London we had a number of near misses, but once we got on to the M40 Gainsford put on the cruise control and knelt on the driving seat. We both relaxed and he began telling me about Inclusion in far greater detail.

Apparently Cryborg have for a number of years employed a young research chemist called Sumner, to explore the Amazonian rainforest. Sumner's job is to get as close as possible to the various Amerindian tribes and discover the secrets of their medicinal plants. Naturally Cryborg are not alone in this – the drug rush has been going on for at least a decade now. Apparently, in some remote parts of South America, the research chemists outnumber the tribespeople.

Of course, most pharmacologists have treated the toughened roots, waxy leaves and gungy pastes brought back from these expeditions with the utmost scepticism. And really, most of the 'discoveries' have proved to be nothing but the chemical equivalent of the raffia tat and facial mud sold by pseudo-ecological shops.

But Sumner had more luck. He was far more adventurous and determined than his rivals, and journeyed long into the rainforest on trips that lasted for months. Trips during which he moved entirely within the ambit of tribal groups of hunter-gatherers that had never seen a European before.

According to Gainsford, on one such trip Sumner encountered the most bizarre group of indigenes imaginable. These people – who called themselves the Maeterlincki – had a life-cycle (metaphysic, socio-cultural form, collective psychopathology) entirely bound up with the harvesting of honey. Honey produced by terrifying swarms of cliff-dwelling bees.

The Maeterlincki's knowledge of these valuable domestic animals is comprehensive, pragmatic and highly sophisticated. Despite the fact that they maintain a view of the cosmos that is entirely apiacentric. For, according to the Maeterlincki, each of their individual consciousnesses is merely the slumbering reverie of a single bee. A death in the tribe coincides with a bee awakening.

Needless to say, this rather baroque belief system gave rise to incredibly complicated explanations by the tribal elders, when they were asked by Sumner how it was that they presided over the establishment and then decay of entire bee colonies, whilst their own life-spans were no longer than a few hours.

Sumner became intrigued by the Maeterlincki's skill as apiarists and went with them to witness the honey harvest. He watched, while they climbed up the granite outcrops where the bees built their hives, and extracted the vast, dripping golden combs. The comb-extraction teams were made up of three tribesmen. (The actual harvesting of the honey is taboo for women.) One of the men would perform a mime of a bee – intended to distract the swarm; the second would remove the combs from the hive; the third would stand by as a decoy and allow himself to be stung – usually to death. Sumner said he had never witnessed such indifference to pain as that displayed by the sacrificial member of the team.

Sumner stayed with the Maeterlincki for six months. Long enough for him to gain their trust, and for the tribal elders to allow him to become an initiate. The initiation involved the ingestion – in its raw form – of the substance that Gainsford has since named 'Inclusion'.

I am able to include here some of Sumner's own description of the initiation rite. When we reached Beaconsfield (Junction 2), Gainsford suddenly announced that he had a friend he wanted to visit who lives in the precincts of the Bekonscot Model Village. He left me in the Toyota, together with a copy of Sumner's field report to Cryborg. I popped out of the car a few minutes later and ran across the road to Pronta-Print, where I photo-copied the following:

Extract from Dr Clive Sumner's Field Report to the Cryborg Research Division

On the morning appointed for my initiation I went, together with Colin and Paul, the other two members of my cell (marginal note: Remember, the Maeterlincki's social organisation is entirely apian.Z.B.), to the base of the granite outcrop.

Colin cut and trimmed a long, hollow bamboo tube, whilst Paul prepared the sacred dust for ingestion. He broke open one of the desiccated hives, which had been abandoned by its colony.

The hive was a great, tattered bundle of dried and flaking material with the texture of papyrus. It was roughly ovoid, but with a flat back, where the bees' mucilage had cemented it to the rock. Paul split it open and invited me to examine the hive's internal structure. This was unusual – to say the least – and it was at this point that I began to suspect that I was on the verge of an exciting and unusual discovery.

The interior of the hive had the familiar structure of serried ranks of hexiform chambers, connected by minute passageways radiating from the central chamber of the hive, where the queen once resided. But within the hive a secondary structure had been constructed: a hive inside a hive.

This subsidiary hive had the same hexiform chambers and minute passageways, but they were far smaller. These chambers were delicately positioned in the very interstices of the apian chambers. I asked Paul what had caused this. He directed me to look closely at one of these small chambers, which was no bigger than a quarter of a pinhead. Entombed within it was the perfectly preserved cadaver of a mite.

Wringing the explanation for this phenomenon out of Paul and Colin was a tiresome business. As I have written above, the Maeterlincki lack much of the conceptual equipment that we take for granted and their language is devoid of certain key terms necessary for the description of social forms. But here is a paraphrase of my cell-fellows' 'Song of the Bee Mite':

These parasitic mites are quite unlike ordinary bee mites. Rather than infesting the actual body of the bee, they attack the structure of the hive, creating, as I had observed, a secondary hive. The Maeterlincki explained that this invasion was accompanied by a gradual shift in the hive's social organisation. The normal and successful ratio between workers (sexually undeveloped females) and drones (sexually productive males) was reversed, so as to favour the development of more drones and fewer workers.

Very gradually the hive began to succumb to parasitically induced decadence. Unless the queen and her remaining workers managed to summon the energy to abandon the hive and swarm, the hive's economy became moribund. Eventually, all that was left was a dying queen surrounded by starving drones. It was as if the collective consciousness of the hive – if such an entity can be posited – had given in to a form of apian anomie.

The Maeterlincki regard this process as a necessary part of their relationship with the bees. They couldn't tell me for how long they had been harvesting the defunct hives, nor how they discovered the psycho-active properties of the dust made from the mites' crushed corpses and sub-hives. Legend had it that in some previous dark age, the Maeterlincki had been beset by an abiding and terrible collective depression, a truly pathological boredom and lack of interest. Remnants of this pre-bee mite era remained embedded in their language (they have, for example, over twenty different words to express the concept of eyes 'glazing over').

My cell-mates then made much of my own frequent bouts of apathy and tedium vitae. They urged me to cast aside my reservations and embrace the great spirit of the beehive.

The bamboo tube was primed with the dust. One end was rammed into my nostril and Colin blew hard from the other. My other nostril received the same treatment, with Paul as the blower this time. We then did the same for Colin and Paul, rotating roles and nostrils. When we were done we returned to the Maeterlincki's longhouse and life went on as before. Thereafter, for the duration of my stay, I was expected to ingest more of the mite powder on a daily basis.

And what was the effect of this peculiar dust? To begin with I noticed nothing at all. Perhaps this was because I had been expecting something really radical, like the psychotropic drugs used by other Amerindian tribes: ayahuasca, yopo, yage and datura. But the bee-mite powder wasn't painful as it was absorbed into the mucous membranes, nor did it produce nausea. There were no hallucinations, no sensations of a paradigm shift in either body- or ego-awareness.

But over the next few days I began to feel more firmly bound into the culture of the Maeterlincki than before. Little things that they did, such as basket weaving, pottery decoration and cicratisation, began to interest me in a way that they hadn't formerly. I wouldn't go so far as to say that I became like the Maeterlincki, but the idea that my mind was the dream of an individual bee did acquire a comforting sort of plausibility, in so far as spiritual beliefs go.

During this period I conducted a number of tests on the mite powder, but I was unable, using my field-test kit, to analyse the active ingredient. It belonged to none of the major classes of psychoactive drug: narcotic, analgesic, hypnotic, sedative, stimulant or hallucinogen.

That's the end of the photocopied extract from Sumner's report. The A4 sheets were folded twice before being pasted into Busner's notebook. When you unfolded the sheet a drift of grey powder was caught in the paper cranny. Some of it got on your fingertips, and idly, as one might taste anything, you dabbed your lips.

There's also an old Worminghall Co-operative Dairy bill caught in the folds of the photocopy, which reads as follows:

30th December

Milk (40 pints)	£12.64
Yoghurt (30 pots, assorted)	£15.84
Single cream (5 pots)	£7.25
Total	£35.73

Busner must have tucked the thing inside the photocopy and forgotten it. Either that, or he is/was an unusually anally retentive man – even for a psychiatrist.

You turn back to Busner's log and glance at the next few entries. They are unilluminating. During his first few weeks at the Worminghall Facility Busner was pre-occupied with the routine work of getting any institution going: arranging catering, interviewing auxiliary staff, ensuring the buildings and laboratory were fully equipped.

Although there is some of Busner in all of this, it is hardly self-revelatory stuff. On occasion he complains about the grind of having to commute from London on a weekly basis, the tediousness of the M40 motorway, and the lack of a decent service centre between Junction 1 (the M25) and Junction 5 (Stokenchurch). But for the most part he gives a flat account of events.

By the middle of December most of this work had been completed. Busner's staff was in place (both those required to keep up the pretence that the Worminghall Facility was a rest home, and his own assistants), and the trial was ready to begin:

17th December

I have made contact with a Dr Anthony Bohm at the
Thame Health Centre. He's a rather Chekhovian figure,
white-haired, with a great pink bum of a chin. He's been
out to the Facility several times to play chess with me.
He's not a bad player, although I find his habit of
neighing whenever he moves his knights intensely
irritating.

This evening I broached the question of Inclusion
with him for the first time. I was highly circumspect,
saying merely that I had been reading in an American
journal about a new anti-depressant that seemed to be
having phenomenal success with both exogenous and
endogenous depressions.

He rose to the bait effortlessly, saying that he would
positively murder for such a drug – if it worked. The
numbers of patients he saw with depressive symptoms
have been steadily increasing over the last few years, and
hardly any of them are responsive to treatment.

Often these people appear psychologically blameless,
but for all that they lapse into states of almost catatonic
despair, neglecting themselves, their families, their jobs
and careers. I put it to him that this was quite a
reasonable response to living in the Thame area. We
both laughed heartily at this.

23rd December

Anthony Bohm was up again last night for chess. He's
added to his repertoire of irritation. He now says,

'Forgive me, Father, for I have sinned,' every time he moves a bishop. I steered the subject back gradually to the issue of medical ethics and what a general practitioner should be allowed to prescribe to his patients. I wasn't disappointed.

Of course, I knew already that Bohm had susceptibilities in this area. The Cryborg people's decision to locate the Facility here was partly due to their having positively vetted a number of GPs in the Oxfordshire region who might be prepared – for various reasons – to engage in the illegal Inclusion trial. I'm glad that I approached Bohm first, though; my other options included a doctor in Abingdon who Cryborg discovered was an illegal abortionist and one in High Wycombe, who has more than a passing affection for diamorphine. But Bohm's motivation, if I can activate it, will be altogether purer.

Bohm told me that he thought it was a physician's prerogative and duty to cast his net as wide as possible for the right treatment. He is quite a libertarian. He even intimated that the whole notion of medical licensing seemed to him an infringement of personal rights. He then began to speak of what I knew already – namely his involvement in the use of MDMA as a 'marital aid' in the early seventies.

Bohm was then a psychiatric intern at a hospital in the Midlands. He took to using MDMA with a vengeance – and achieved impressive results. The problem was he himself also took to using MDMA with a vengeance –

and achieved an impressive number of patient seductions. He missed being struck off by a whisker. Only the fact that none of his patients would tesify against him saved his neck. He left psychiatry and retrained as a GP.

Of course, he didn't admit all of this to me. He gave a sanitised version. But the fact that he was prepared to own up to prescribing MDMA at all shows that he is beginning to trust me.

9th January

The cyclotron is now fully installed at Worminghall and today some technicians came up with Gainsford to give me a demonstration.

I cannot claim to understand much of the physical chemistry involved in isolating pure Inclusion from the cadaverous and faecal matter of the bee mites. Indeed, I don't think I've ever heard of a cyclotron being used in any similar process before. Gainsford told me that it was a method he, together with the other research chemists at Cryborg, had hit upon by trial and error. Although the bee-mite powder is effective in its raw state, the quantities needed are large and the correct dosage difficult to determine. Gainsford also implied that they had had some problems with side-effects, but when I pressed him he wouldn't elaborate.

I watched as Gainsford used a micron scale to measure the correct quantity of mite powder to be placed in the cyclotron. Obviously, this was far too small to be seen by the naked eye. When the process was complete and

Gainsford's technicians were working with mine to make the fresh Inclusion up into a batch of pills, he told me that less than four hundred thousandths of a milligram was required to synthesise a thousand doses.

11th January
I can't help being fascinated by the Inclusion. The pills Gainsford made are sitting in the lab looking utterly innocent. Looking, in fact, just like Amytriptaline, which is what most of the potential Inclusion guinea-pigs will be taking already.

Every few hours I find myself drawn to the locked cabinet in the laboratory. I open it – and scrutinise the Inclusion – as if it could tell me something. The technical staff look at me curiously, but they know better than to ask me what I am doing.

16th January
What if Inclusion really does work? The results Gainsford has shown me from animal experimentation are remarkable. Rats learning to conga; gerbils apparently meditating after taking Inclusion; beagles that have been blinded with detergents as part of product testing completely rehabilitated by the drug, seemingly more engaged with the world than when they were sighted.

The human data is equally impressive, but as yet Gainsford has only tested the drug on a few isolated individuals, catatonics and severe autistics at a London teaching hospital where Cryborg have some insidious pull. He hasn't done a proper trial on either a non-depressive, or anyone with an orthodox clinical depression.

I have a great inclination to take Inclusion myself. It's not that I wish to claim some part in its discovery – should it prove to be an effective palliative. It's more that I feel that the only way to justify the unethical character of the trial is for me to break down some of the traditional – and, I believe, artificial – distinctions between the scientist and the supposed objects of his study. Why not think of my brain as a sort of culture, and Inclusion as a bacterium growing within it. I would become another Alexander Fleming – but a Fleming of the psyche!

20th January
I have taken Inclusion. If I was expecting an experience like that of Hofmann, when he accidentally took LSD-25 and unleashed the psychedelic revolution, then I would have been disappointed. But, of course, I wasn't, and was delighted.

I took two Inclusion tablets at about five yesterday evening and then retired to my quarters to see what would happen. At first I sat, straining with all my mental apparatus to try and discern some effect. Nothing happened. After an hour I grew listless and distracted. I tidied up the place a bit – it was in a fearful mess. Another hour passed, still no effect.

Eventually I grew tired, and quite frankly, bored. I

turned on the television and slumped in front of it. For some reason there was nothing on but sport, which has never interested me. I found myself staring blankly at a Senior League Curling Championship, being broadcast from Peebles.

If most sport leaves me cold – curling positively curdles my mind. I can see nothing more asinine than hefting the 'stones', which look like outsize doorstops, down an ice rink so that they get as close as possible to a fixed point. If bowls is boring, how much more boring can frozen bowls be! A bowls that tends towards absolute zero.

Yet, after about ten minutes of staring sightlessly at the set, I found that I was actually beginning to become absorbed by the curling. I started noting the names of individual players and how well they were doing. I listened to what the commentator was saying about overall averages and positioning. My attention was focused on questions of technique: how much sweeping of the rink is necessary to ensure a good run for the stones; what the best wrist action is for releasing the stone cleanly; what the regulations are concerning equipment and appropriate clothing.

When the programme eventually finished I was quite disconsolate. But my spirits rose when the announcer said that the next programme would be a film dramatisation of Betjeman's 'Summoned by Bells'. Then I pulled myself up short. Betjeman? It's not that I exactly dislike his poetry, it's just that I'm pretty well indifferent to it.

It's like that for so many things as far as I'm concerned. The idea of them interests me, and if my interest becomes positively engaged then I will take up with just about anything for a while, from car-boot sales to Kant. But I'm not one of these people who has 'interests', a real passion for model trains, or moutaineering. I have often thought that a suitable epitaph for me – given the gad-fly nature of my enthusiasms – would be 'He had no interests but interest'. And yet here I was, looking forward to a film dramatisation of 'Summoned by Bells'.

It was the Inclusion. I realised this tremulously – if the drug was powerful enough to get me interested in curling and Betjeman, there was no telling what other properties it might have. I decided to run some simple psychodiagnostic tests on myself, perceptual, relational and conceptual, to check that I wasn't becoming disoriented.

I became so absorbed by the tests that I missed most of *Summoned by Bells*. But no matter – they told me what I already knew intuitively; that the only true effect of Inclusion was to make me feel more positively engaged with whatever I directed my attention to. I was experiencing no hallucinations, no distortions of space or time, no kinaesthesia or synaesthesia. My reality-testing was perfect and my intelligence quotient unaffected.

Nor were there any perceptible toxic side-effects, or hangover. When I awoke the following morning I was quite clearly back to normal. When the alarm rang at 8 a.m. the thought of another working day was just as excruciatingly dull as ever.

22nd January

Bohm was up this evening. We played a few speed games. It helps if we play speed chess, because he doesn't feel he has time to neigh, or say, 'Forgive me, Father, for I have sinned.' However, when he check mates, he picks up the piece of his that has mated my king and simulates intercourse between the two of them. He really is a most juvenile individual – if indispensable.

As I anticipated I had no difficulty in encouraging him to try some Inclusion. I told him the effect the drug had had on me, and how completely localised and harmless it appeared to be, with no contra-indications. He took two pills and we went on playing.

After about an hour Bohm went to the toilet. When he hadn't returned after twenty minutes or so, I grew concerned. I went out into the corridor and found him standing there, rapt. Apparently, what had happened was that when he was in the toilet he became fascinated by the particulate structure of the fire-resistant tiles on the ceiling. He told me there was nothing disturbing about this, he merely found that the whole subject of fire-resistant tiles began to interest him. He admitted that he was one of those people who are normally fairly oblivious of their immediate environment, and that Mrs Bohm often complains when he doesn't register some alteration she has made to the decoration of their home.

He wanted to get back to the chess game, but felt that he really ought to undertake some sort of comparative study of the fire-resistant tiles in the Facility. He had visited the other buildings and spent some time studying their fire-resistant tiles, and then begun to work his way back towards my rooms. When I found him he was nearly finished. However, it's an indication of just how benign and localised the effects of Inclusion are that when I suggested he cut this exercise short, he happily acceded.

30th January

Bohm has come up with the names of twenty of his patients who he anticipates having to prescribe anti-depressants to within the next month. In place of the tricyclics or SSRIs he will, of course, prescribe Inclusion. Another group of twenty patients who are currently on tricyclics or SSRIs will be put on to Inclusion; and a third group of 'new depressives' will be given a placebo.

I will give the batches of prepared Inclusion to MacLachlan, the pharmacist. He will then make up the prescriptions in conformity with this schema. Bohm will, of course, have no idea which of his patients will be in receipt of Inclusion. His task is merely to record data as and when they present themselves to him. This is as reasonable a conformity to the principles of the double blind as we can manage under the circumstances.

I did suggest to Gainsford that I introduce another level of blind to the trial, as Ford and I did for our now infamous double-double blind trial at my Concept House in the seventies. But Gainsford is too much of a plodder to recognise its brilliance and knocked me back.

Gainsford is, needless to say, absolutely delighted with my progress on the trial. And he relayed a special message to me from the Cryborg Main Board, which said: 'We are absolutely delighted.' Gainsford hadn't thought I would get to this stage for at least six months. In part this is fortuitous. If Bohm was an enthusiastic convert to the potential of Inclusion, MacLachlan is positively messianic about the stuff.

He himself has been treated for depression on and off for a number of years. Although it's a far from empirically sound assessment of the drug's potential, its effect on MacLachlan was heartwarming. He came out to Worminghall with Bohm one night for a few hands of bridge. MacLachlan's play was so diffident and unresponsive that he was hardly more proactive than the dummy.

Bohm and I persuaded him to come out for two more sessions; and on the third we broached the issue of Inclusion. Initially, MacLachlan was sceptical – not suspicous, just sceptical. However, when Bohm and I reported our own experiences of the drug to him, he was eager to try it.

When we resumed play an hour after MacLachlan had ingested some Inclusion, he was a different man. Witty, engaged, eloquent, both on the game in hand

and the whole history and practice of bridge; there was little Bohm and I could do to contain him. His countenance – which is mousey in the extreme, hidden behind a water-rat beard of terrible lankness – brightened and brightened. His impressions of Omar Sharif became hard to deal with, but overall I can say that MacLachlan's Inclusion-based rehabilitation was one of the most humane things I have witnessed in almost thirty years as a medical practitioner.

Bohm and I have restricted MacLachlan to a nugatory dosage of Inclusion. He himself admits that if he takes too much he becomes overly absorbed in the little pictures that adorn the labels of the shampoo he sells at the pharmacy, or some such irrelevance. However, on a mild dose he just feels that loose sense of positive engagement that we are looking for.

9th February

The trial has been underway for a week now and everything is going smoothly. There is actually remarkably little for me to do now, except wait for Bohm to begin relaying the data.

I have been in the habit of commuting to Worminghall on a weekly basis. Really it is a tedious place. On a good day there is something affecting about the view from the Chiltern escarpment where the Facility is, down on to the rolling country of Oxfordshire. Walking along the Ridgeway path, where it dives under the M40, I am often reminded of early Renaissance paintings depicting enclosed landscapes like this; and can half imagine that the cooling towers of Didcot Power Station are some Tuscan fortification.

On a good day, that is. On a bad day it's dreary beyond belief. Often thick fogs roll in from the north, and the whole countryside is rendered both tatty and claustrophobic. On my walks I pass chicken-wired pheasant runs and abandoned piggeries. They give a disagreeable impression of *urb in rus*. The fog distorts my sense of scale, and I toy with the notion that I am wandering over a giant, derelict tennis court, or a still vaster cat's litter tray that no one has bothered to empty for a while.

It's mordant fantasising such as this that has driven me to what might be termed 'recreational' use of Inclusion. I am very rigorous about this, though, I have no desire to experience an Inclusion dependency – if such a thing turns out to be possible. So I only take Inclusion when playing ping-pong with one or other of the auxiliary staff. I can't say that the Inclusion makes my game any better, but it does make me considerably more interested. I now really appreciate ping-pong and am extremely glad that I've decided to make it a part of my life.

4th March

The trial has now been going for over a month and the results are very encouraging. Bohm's reports clearly demonstrate that the depressive patients treated with

Inclusion are responding far better than those on tri-cyclics or SSRIs, and far, far better than the control group. If things carry on this way for another month I shall have to recommend that Cryborg find a way of legitimating the discovery and the trial findings. To allow things to go much further, would, I feel, cast into doubt the ethics of what we have been doing. I shall relay this conviction of mine to Gainsford in my next report.

11th March

I had a worrying phone call from Bohm this afternoon. What he had to tell me has unsettled me and cast into doubt some of my faith in Inclusion. One of Bohm's patients, a painter called Simon Dykes who lives on the Tiddington side of Thame, has been saying some very strange things to him.

I am fairly certain that Dykes must be on Inclusion. There is no other explanation for his behaviour, if Bohm's report of it is to be believed.

Bohm has been prescribing 'anti-depressants' to Dykes for almost six weeks now. Dykes came to see him complaining of a sense of futility, emotional aliena-tion, impotence etc., etc. He made light of his depres-sion, but his wife – who attended with him – told Bohm, in confidence, that he had been a nightmare since last year and had to be hospitalised, briefly, over Christmas.

Initially the Inclusion seemed to be having a beneficial

effect on Dykes. He reported to Bohm just the sense of positive engagement that we look for from the drug. Dykes said that he was sorting out his problems with his wife, he was enjoying the company of his children and had begun to paint again after a block lasting some six months.

However, last week when Dykes went to see Bohm for his check-up, he told him that he was having doubts about his sanity again. He now felt that he was 'going the other way'. When Bohm asked Dykes to elaborate, the painter said that he was having difficulty in controlling his capacity for being involved with things. That when he turned his attention to something – whether it be a person, an object, a whole area of knowledge, or merely some abstract notion – he couldn't prevent himself from being sucked deep into its contemplation. Furthermore, the painter claimed that he began to feel as if he knew more about whatever it was than he possibly could.

Bohm asked him for an example and Dykes came up with the Boxer Rising. He said he was looking through an old edition of the *Britannica* when he came across the entry on the Boxer Rising. Accompanying it was a picture of the Chinese Boxers attacking the British Embassy. Dykes swears he didn't read the entry at first. Instead he merely stared at the old engraving (apparently he leafs through such old books looking for graphic material for his work), and found himself being 'sucked into it'. While in this reverie he became acquainted with a vast amount of information on the Boxer Rising, including the names of the ring-leaders, and even elements of their motivation.

When he was sufficiently recovered, he read the accompanying entry. All of the facts that had come to him in the reverie turned out to be true! He even knew some things that weren't in the entry, but when he did some further research at the Bodleian in Oxford, they panned out as well!

If all of this wasn't bad enough, the horrific clincher came this week. Dykes arrived for his appointment as usual, at about eleven. Bohm said that the painter was haggard and unkempt. His eyes darted this way and that around Bohm's consulting room, lighting on object after object, as if he were seeing not the things themselves, but looking deep into their anatomy.

Bohm asked him how he was feeling and Dykes said that he knew he wasn't taking an anti-depressant, but some experimental drug. When Bohm challenged him and asked how could he be so sure, Dykes replied that he knew the man who was behind it. His name was Busner and he was operating out of a compound in the Chilterns near Worminghall.

Dykes had seen me – he claimed – in the Three Pigeons Inn by Junction 7 of the M40. He hadn't paid any particular attention to me when he went into the pub, but after he grew tired of contemplating the history and evolution of the towelling bar mat, he turned his attention to the 'froggy-looking man in the corner wearing the mohair tie'. He said that I wasn't as easy to read as the bar mat, or the engraving of the Boxer Rising, but that merely by looking at me he could include elements of my mental terrain into his own. So it was that he discovered that I was doing some sort of drug trial, and that it involved anti-depressant medication.

The bugger is that I do have a drink in the Three Pigeons from time to time, and there's every possibility that Dykes has seen me in there. Although I cannot recall noticing anyone paying undue attention to me. On the contrary, it's often extremely difficult to get served in there, despite a bar staff to drinker ratio of about 1:1.

After this encounter Dykes formed the conviction that his current predicament had something to do with me. He then challenged Bohm with this information. Bohm told me that he was as circumspect as possible. He advised Dykes to stop taking the Inclusion immediately and switch to a tranquilliser. Dykes refused, and as he already has a repeat prescription for Inclusion, Bohm realised that he would be unable to force the issue. Especially as Dykes then said he wanted Bohm to arrange a meeting with me, and that if he didn't, or if I refused to see him, he would get in touch with the press.

Bohm displayed as much sang-froid as he could under the circumstances. He told Dykes to go home and try to relax, and that he would 'see what he could do'. As soon as Dykes left the health centre he called me.

I have been put into such a state by this news that I've been unable to come up with a definitive analysis of the situation. Can it be that this is some kind of Inclusion-induced psychosis? And if so, will it occur in all of the patients who have been prescribed the drug? I shudder to think. An alternative possibility is that Dykes is going into a psychotic or schizoid interlude despite, rather than because of, the Inclusion, and that the facts he has adduced about the Inclusion trial and myself are lurid supposition, hit upon by chance.

Whatever the case, I cannot at this stage bear to inform Gainsford. I know that he would overreact and jeopardise what we have achieved so far. If we can contain the situation with Dykes then there is no reason to abort the trial. So, I told Bohm that he was to bring Dykes up to Worminghall as soon as possible. He called back an hour or so later and said that they would be coming up tomorrow night. Until then I will see if I can't discover some more about the drug's effects. Obviously, the best way to do this is for me to take an extra-large dose of Inclusion myself.

This may appear foolhardy, but the whole thing intrigues me so much that I am determined to get to the bottom of it. I am passionately interested in Inclusion, and wish it at all costs to remain a large part of my life.

And that's it. That's the last entry in Busner's journal. Or at any rate the last that you're able to read. There are a few pages after this entry that have obviously been torn out by someone – just a ragged fringe of paper remains, close to the binding; the rest of the notebook is empty.

That doesn't immediately concern you. What's far more intriguing is the other notebook, the one you know already is Simon Dykes's own diary. How did it come to be at the Worminghall Facility? Did Dykes take it up there himself on the climactic night of the 12th of March? And is the fact that it's exactly the same kind of notebook as Busner's purely coincidental? Or is it yet another ramification of the Inclusion trial?

You don't hesitate. You pick it up and give it a heft. Well, that won't tell you anything. Open it up and have a read:

12th October
Why fucking bother? Why fucking bother at all? Why fuck and why bother? I would be angry – if I had the energy. I would hate myself more, if I didn't feel dead already. I hate doing this. I hate writing these things. Write down your feelings. It's the sort of shit that that dickhead psychotherapist at the Warneford told me to do, when I made the profound mistake of going to see him on Tony Bohm's recommendation.

If I find myself writing this stuff down, it's only because I have to make something external, something that's tangible, just to keep alive in me the idea that I'm alive at all.

I haven't painted now for over four months. I feel as

remote from my art as I do from Tierra del Fuego. You might as well ask a man to stretch his cock to the moon, as ask me to pick up a brush again, or even prime a canvas.

I can't see things the way I used to. I used to see form spontaneously. Just looking at a miscellany of objects would intrude the idea of a composition. A quality of light, or a particular texture, would impinge on me with amazing force. Colour, chiaroscuro, the very sense of the volume of an object, a portion of the sky, or the geometry of a human face – all came to me unbidden. I never knew how fucking lucky I was, how blessed really, blessed with a gift. A gift that's gone as if it was never there to begin with.

Of course, as my charming wife sees fit to remind me, I have had these 'episodes' before. That's nice, isn't it – 'episode', like an episode of some tawdry soap. 'Here it is, folks,' the announcer says cheerily, 'this week's episode of Simon Dykes's chronic fucking depression. Sit back and enjoy.'

I can't stand the anger I feel towards Jean – she really isn't to blame for all this. But all right, I've always been a bit unstable, had my ups and downs. I don't subscribe to the notion that the depressive and the creative mentality go hand in hand – only a fucking shrink would – but I can admit that about myself.

But I've never felt as bad as this, as futile, as purposeless. I experience the love I thought I had for Jean as an irritation, a niggling under my skin. And as for the kids, when I look at them, particularly Henry, a sharp pain comes into me. A pain that's a sort of probing finger coming into my grey area of depression and titillating it with the possibility of feeling love once more. It's disgusting, almost as if I don't want it. It's like Jean reaching for my flaccid cock – which she does nowadays as if she were a weary bell-ringer – and giving it an uncalled-for tug.

22nd October
I didn't think things could get worse – but they have. Even Magnus and Henry are a burden to me now. I look at them from the studio window, playing on the lawn, wrapped up in autumnal scarves and mittens, and it occurs to me that they aren't the right size for children of their age. Rather, that they're like some fucking emotional decoys. Decoy ducks are made twice the size of ordinary ducks, so that the poor fuckers flying over will misjudge the distance to the ground and crash into it when they dive down to join what they imagine are their fellows.

That's what's happening to me with those kids. My love for them is a suicidal plunge. It isn't until I get close to them that I see how chronically I have misjudged everything in my life, exaggerated my own precious obsession with my art, at the cost of everything else.

Jean says I should go and see Tony Bohm, and of course, like another member of the plainting chorus, Christabel says the same. But I won't go. What would he do anyway, save for put me on some fucking drug, that would act like a governor on my brain? I hate that. I've been on those anti-depressants before, and they make me feel madder than I feel now. The sensation of those drugs coming on is just as I imagine the feel of a surgeon's knife, probing into your grey matter, seeking out the right place to sever your fucking hemispheres.

30th October

The longer I'm sunk in this mire, the worse things get. Shrinks divide up depressions, don't they? They say this one's 'chemical', or somesuch; and that one's down to all the crap you've got in your life. But with me the crap inside and the crap outside merge into one great ocean of shit, flowing into and of me.

No work means no money. No money means I can't face the idea of work because I've got so far to go just to pay off the bills this lay-off has ranked up. George called today and I couldn't even speak to him. I just told Jean to say to him, 'You haven't got a client any more, you've just got a piece of shit. And unless you want to put on an exhibition of turds, there's little point in calling me.'

I wonder if she relayed this message? She hardly talks to me at all now. I guess she's worried. No, actually she's past being worried – or concerned, she's just fed up. I only sit in the studio now – the rest of the house seems threatening to me. I don't want to go there.

Even sitting up here for hours on end, I'm hardly

comfortable in my depression. There's nothing cosy in this unremitting greyness, this corporate gothic, with its grinding, emotional bureaucracy.

5th November
My mind is like a fly, it buzzes around in a fucking febrile fashion, and when it alights on some crumb, or fragment of an idea, it's off again before I can apprehend it.

I'm getting paranoid. I look out over the garden and across the fence and across the farm track, and I'm convinced that I can see figures moving there. I joke about it to Jean, I suppose to stop her from becoming frightened. I say, I think our creditors have built a hide over there, in the shape of a giant dunning letter. They've elected one of their number to sit in it and observe the Brown House all day, in case I try and leave.

Jean doesn't think it's funny. I hear her praying a lot nowadays. She wanders around the house muttering under her breath. She knows I despise religion as a fucking opiate.

I wish I had some fucking opiate myself. Something that would take away this pain that is indifference to everything. I hate it when I'm reminded of the pain of others. If I see some item on the television, showing kids starving, or women raped in the war, I hate them. I hate them because the reality, the fucking substantial nature of their pain, seems to mock the nebulousness of my own. It says, you think you're in pain, you're not in pain, you're faking it. And then I think of killing myself, believe me, I really do.

Oh Jesus! (Ha–fucking–ha!) the effort of staying interested in anything. It's like trying to clench a paralysed fist. If I try and take a drink to numb the awful sensation out, I just feel sick and woozy. I can't get drunk anymore, no matter how much I pour down my fucking neck.

13th November

Images of suicide all the time now. Every day. I've got them now as I write: Simon dead in a bath, blood flowing from his slashed wrists in gentle, billowing clouds; Simon dead from a shotgun blast in the mouth, the mess of grey, white and red on the wall behind his deflated head at last forming an interesting composition; Simon dead from a drug overdose, the blue tones of his skin reminiscent of a Renoir. The thoughts are scampering across my shoulders. I can feel their wing-beats around my ears.

24th November

I've had what I believe is called 'an intervention'. This afternoon I was sitting in my studio, as usual, mulling over the Hiroshima of my life, the razed buildings of my hopes, the charred corpses of my former loves, when they all fucking came down on me, the whole bunch of the wankers. There was Jean, of course, and Christabel. George had driven up from the gallery. They'd even dug my brother up from somewhere. They all stood around me and told me how my being so unhappy was upsetting the children (Jean was in tears by this point), and that it would be better for everyone if I considered going into hospital for a while.

I tried to remain calm – although I felt like screaming – because I knew that if I let on just how bad things were they'd send for the men in the white coats, and then they'd take me away and put a hot wire through my brain; and then I'd be gone, there'd just be this shell left behind, with Simon's head painted on it.

So I stayed calm, but told them in no uncertain terms that I'd rather be dead than go into one of those grotesque NHS bedlams, where the 'patients' wander around making Hogarth look understated. This raised a bit of a laugh from George – but the rest of them stayed grim, stony-jawed.

George then said that he was prepared to put up the dosh for me to go to some private place that he knows about in Wiltshire. He claims that it's OK there and they won't necessarily put me on drugs. They won't even make me talk about things if I don't want to. They'll also let me have as many visitors as and when I want.

I said I was very grateful to George (even though I know he's only doing it to protect his fucking asset, the mercenary cunt). And I said I would go – if that's what they wanted. But that if I did George had to promise to come and see me every week, and if I wasn't happy he had to get me discharged. He agreed to this. So, I'm off tomorrow. I suppose I have to admit that I'm a bit relieved, the suicide shit is beginning to get to me badly. I wouldn't want the kids to find Daddy strung up from the light socket.

There's then a gap of about two months until the next entry.

22nd January

Dear Fuck-wit Diary

Well, I managed to get myself out of that joint at long last. What a pile of wank! To think that people get paid for administering that so-called therapy, and other people are prepared to pay for it. The blind pissing on the blind – that's what it is. The best thing I can say about my stay at the funny farm is that it cut the costs at home – thanks to George's largesse. And I managed to miss out on Christmas, which has to be the most depressing time of the year.

George was right about one thing, though, the cunts didn't make me talk about myself, or take anything I didn't want to. They did however insist on my sitting in on group therapy sessions. What an absurd idea! As if forcing a lot of unhappy people to sit in a circle, prating on about their private miseries, could possibly make any of us feel any better.

30th January

It's not as if I ever really felt any better – so I suppose I can't be feeling substantially worse. The house has been wreathed in thick fog for the past week or so. Every morning when I get up, I look out of the window and see it hanging like a cloud of gas at the end of the garden. I can almost imagine that soldiers are about to emerge from it wearing puttees and carrying Lee Enfields with bayonets fixed. They are advancing towards me, determined to capture the trench of my mind.

I like to move very carefully now. To cross a room, or even pick up some small object, I affect an undulant motion, like someone with Parkinson's disease who's just taken some L-Dopa. I have to get the right rhythm into my actions in order for them to happen at all. Often I'll be halfway towards doing something when I'll realise that I don't have the correct rhythm, and then I'll just collapse back into despair.

9th February

I went to see Tony Bohm yesterday. Not because of my mental health, but because of a cyst in one of my nipples. I joked with him, saying perhaps he should inject a little collagen into the other nipple, to even things up.

He gave me a peculiar look, and said in that nannyish way that doctors have, 'You're not at all well, Simon, are you?' I confessed that I didn't feel my stay with the other sads had done me a great deal of good, but so what? He suggested – in a roundabout sort of a way – that I try going on anti-depressants again. According to him, these drugs are far better designed than they used to be. They can now target exactly the receptors in the brain responsible for depression, like some smart misery-seeking bomb, dropped down the ventilation shaft of the mind.

I started waving my hands about when he began this eulogy, saying All right, all right, I'll take the bloody pills! I don't know why. Perhaps I'm just exhausted, tired of fighting this thing day in and day out. I want some respite from my head, and I dread the suicidal urges coming back. I read last week in the *Bulletin of Suicidology* that the suicide rate for male painters in their early forties is 700 per cent higher than the national average. No wonder I want to do a Rothko.

I left Bohm's surgery with a prescription and went across to get it at MacLachlan's. For some reason the pharmacist in there – a drowned rat of a man, who is normally sulky and silent – gave me a broad grin, together with my pot of head-governors.

I came home and took a couple. I'm waiting for the mushy feeling that comes before I've adjusted to the dosage. Waiting for it with something that could be anticipation – but isn't. Rather it's something that stands in the same relation to anticipation as a whore does to a lover.

11th February
No mushy feeling yesterday, and none today either. Instead a peculiar lightening in my mood. It's not that I exactly want to do anything, or that I don't feel the depression still gnawing at me, it's just that I can almost – almost, mind – imagine what it might be like to feel

interested in something again, to want to include some of its essence within myself.

Sat in my studio all day and listened to the sounds of the house around and below me. Jean's shoes clacking across the wooden floors; the children's crashing entries and slamming exits; the occasional waft of music; the chirrup and trill of the phone. I smiled, thinking about how I constantly complain that this rumpus upsets my work, when the truth is I haven't done any work now for so long.

12th February
On some odd impulse I bought an antique victrola today. It was sitting in the window of the noncey little antique shop in Thame, together with the usual cataract of tat. I had noticed the thing a number of times before, but on this occasion I found myself intrigued by it. With primitive music machines like this, the analog of the sound they make is so visible, so tangible. I only had to touch the thing to imagine that Chaliapin was creaking and groaning the 'Song of the Volga Boatmen'. It will make a great object to place at the centre of a canvas.

13th February
Started work on the victrola painting today. I thought I'd do some charcoal sketches of it just to get my hand in, and then it struck me: I was working! I had the yen to work for the first time in months. I had the impulse to shout, hoot, do a little jig, rush down and tell Jean and

Christabel . . . but I restrained myself. What if it was just an illusion, some function of the happy pills Bohm has given me?

So, this afternoon I drove into Oxford and went to the Science Library. I had intended to look up all the anti-depressants commonly prescribed, and see if I could account for my creative rebirth. But when I got down among the stacks and was leafing through the pharma-cological reference works, I lost interest in this mundane task. The juxtapositions of carpet tiling, strip lighting and blond wood in the library fired my imagination. The library – and the way it acts as an analog of the information contained in its rank upon rank of volumes – struck me as a counterpart to the victrola I bought yesterday in Thame.

Why not amalgamate the two into one canvas? I could see exactly what it should look like: the victrola, hunched and black, with chunks of pharmacological gobbledygook radiating from its flaring horn. It will look Dadaist, and be a suitable memento of my voyage back across the psychic Styx.

14th February
I stayed up late last night and drew Jean a Valentine's card. She seemed shocked when she saw it among the breakfast things – and then burst into tears and ran out of the room. I ran after her and caught her in the drawing room, where she hugged me and sobbed for a while. She said she had despaired of my ever improving and had

made arrangements to take the children away, if I wouldn't agree to go back into hospital.

I was shaken by this. It's peculiar how from the vantage point of even a partial recovery the idea of my former negativity, my rejection of the world and all its works, seems so remote.

Worked on the victrola painting all morning. I've got hold of some second-hand pharmacological reference works back from Oxford, and I spent the morning cutting them up into the appropriately sized chunks. I've given up on doing the charcoal sketches and have decided to work directly on to canvas. I feel that confident.

16th February

I went into the health centre this morning to see Bohm. I told him, with some humility, that he was right and the new anti-depressants did seem to be having a remarkable effect on me. I now find that more or less anything I direct my attention to appears interesting to me, and worthy of some place in my life. Bohm asked me if I would describe this as 'positive engagement'. I replied that this was a bit technical, but that I did feel a general enthusiasm for life and all it offers.

The truth is that the posters Bohm has put up in his consulting room, which show cuddly toys – teddies and suchlike – inhabiting their own parallel realm, had begun to intrigue me, and I wasn't directing much of my attention to him. He's obviously put them up for the children, but perhaps, in a way, they represent an idea of a better world that adults also find seductive. It would be interesting to do a series of paintings, in a photoreal style and employing the same colour scheme, but showing the cuddly toys working in laboratories, or industrial plants.

20th February

Jean is a bit concerned about the way the house is filling up with laboratory equipment and cuddly toys. I've explained that they're essential for the new painting *World of Bears*; and that I simply haven't room for them all in the studio, where I am busily posing a scene that comprises four near life-size stuffed bears in white coats, working at a chemical experiment.

It isn't that I've lost interest in the victrola painting, but right now this project grabs me more. Possibly it needs to be a triptych?

22nd February

I went for a walk with Jean and the boys today. What a joy it is to see one's children growing up and taking an interest in the world they inhabit. I think Magnus will be the more scientifically minded of the two. Even at the age of six he looks at everything in structural and normative terms; while the older Henry is so plainly responding to the imagistic and the emotional in everything he does.

We walked all the way to the golf course and back, the four of us chattering away. I felt nothing but interested in everything that they said; none of my former sense of irritation with the family seems to remain. On the way back Jean and I walked arm in arm, and last night she came to me.

26th February

Perhaps a falling out always comes after a reunification. I don't know. But yesterday Jean and I had a bit of a spat. It started like this: she was telling me about some work she was doing for the local church, collecting for a famine relief charity, when I conceived an overpowering interest in everything she was saying. I wanted to know all about the charity: everything that it did; where its projects were sited, what they hoped to achieve; how they stood in relation to the rest of the charitable sector; the relationship between that sector and the foreign aid budget; the history of foreign aid.

All of these questions came surging up in me, together with the realisation that Jean didn't know enough to satisfy me. It was rude and peremptory of me, but I couldn't help it. I threw up my hands and said, 'There's no point in your going any further with this, you haven't got enough information,' and turned away from her.

I don't blame her for being upset, but she must appreciate the overwhelming need I have to incorporate and assimilate things at the moment. I feel that this faculty has been in abeyance for so long now that I must give it as free a rein as I can.

28th February

I've started on a 'found object' sculpture, using pill boxes and plastic pachyderms. The pill boxes are glued to the elephants' backs like miniature howdahs.

29th February

Sat in my studio all morning experiencing a surge of motiveless and directionless interest in everything. I found this quite disturbing. Any line of thought that I tried to pursue came up against some thing, idea, or individual, and all infinitely worthy of a lifetime's devotion.

For hours my thoughts were like aeroplanes, stacked overhead for landings on my consciousness that were always being aborted. Not that dissimilar to states of mind I remember from my depression days.

In the afternoon I rallied a bit. All the surfaces of the studio appeared unnecessarily bare to me, so I began to decorate them with a pattern loosely based on *The Marriage of the Arnolfini*.

3rd March

It has to be those pills. I don't think it can reasonably be anything else. What little objectivity I still retain tells me that it isn't normal to feel this way, so tirelessly interested. I can't sleep because I have to count all the little black and red diamonds that constitute my retinal after-image. I can sense that the barrier between my consciousness and the world is becoming fuzzy and indeterminate — so much of it have I become prepared to include within myself.

If I sit in the studio I can no longer differentiate between the many Post-It Notes I have stuck up on the walls to remind me of errands, ideas, images and facts, and the thoughts that gave rise to them in the first place. Perhaps the studio is an extension of my own mind? And if I start to combine and recombine these original thoughts, I will witness the telekinesis of their representation?

I must remember to phone Ivor Saluki, the engraver. About ten years ago he borrowed a biography of Cézanne from me, and I really do need it back.

Jean is furious about the boxes of fruit that have been turning up at the house. I need that fruit! I need it for my work. I have in mind a great mound of rotting fruit studded with electronic components. Such an installation will present a fantastic satirical vision of mind, as the fruit rots and the components rust! Despite my anxieties over the medication, I know that I'm still coming up with creative solutions of the first order.

5th March
Walking up to the Three Pigeons at lunchtime today I found myself absorbing the very topography of the land surrounding the Brown House. The fields were as much in me as I was in them. The landscape seethed as I allowed myself to think through it and annex it to the territory of my own psyche.

Then in the pub I became transfixed by the towelling bar mat. It was the same as with the print of the Boxer Revolt I looked at the other day. Through the individual bar mat, I felt myself being sucked into a durable history of other bar mats. I romped down the evolutionary pathways of this mundane object, turned into temporal byways, and then returned to the present.

There was a man sitting in the corner. An ageing hippy dressed in a crumpled poplin jacket and a yanked-tight snake of woollen tie. I knew he had a connection with the pills Bohm has been prescribing me the minute I saw him. I can't explain this in a commonsensical way; such things are not like a species of prescience, or any kind of ESP, they're rather like remembering that you already knew something that you'd forgotten for a while. It's a reacquaintance with the facts of the matter.

I knew this man was called Busner. I knew that he was involved in secretly (and illegally) testing a new psychoactive drug in the Thame area. I knew that he knew Anthony Bohm. I knew that he thought Glen Gould a vulgar pianist. I knew that he once caught his foreskin in the fly of his trousers, whilst holidaying in Positano in Italy, and had to be hospitalised for a day. I knew that he was interested in curling.

I was intrigued and frightened in equal measure by the revelation of Busner and his impact on my life. I didn't announce myself to him, because I couldn't think of any way of doing it that wouldn't be melodramatic.

287

7th March

Busner is the Hierophant. He oversees the auguries, decocts potions, presides over rituals that piddle the everyday into a tea-strainer reality. I can sense him moving around there up in Worminghall, his shit-kicker shoes squeaking on the linoleum floor as he struggles to return that loop shot from one of his technicians. The way he has surreptitiously tinkered with the architecture of my mind is an obscenity. I must confront him with it, but at the moment I am too taken with the idea of some art work that expresses his attributes to be seriously bothered.

I've ordered some curling equipment through a sports mail-order catalogue. It's only a tentative idea so far (although I feel strong enthusiasm for it), but some melding together of both curling equipment and ancient votive statuary into a purely figurative sculpture of Busner would do the man justice.

8th March

More stuffed animals and exercise equipment arrived at the Brown House today. Jean is beside herself. She says there isn't enough room for all this in the house. I shouted at her. After all, if I can include it in my mind, why can't she have it in the house? People are so lazy nowadays. They confine themselves to some one role or other, and with it comes a narrowing and specialisation of what their minds allow.

Take sporting trophies, for example. I think they've

been unjustifiably ignored. Sure, there are a few pocket guides to them, but no truly informative and exhaustive history. I intend to remedy this situation as soon as I can find the time off from cataloguing my antiquarian library; electroplating my model trains; completing the construction of my combination sousaphone-and-samovar; and launching my collection of designer clothing made entirely from carpet off-cuts.

9th March

I will see Bohm tomorrow and arrange to meet with the Magus of Worminghall. I have no idea what will transpire, but it may prove illuminating. I can sense a growing concentricity in my manner of thinking, a desire to circle back on my own thoughts, to tergiversate, to animadvert, to extemporise. When I am too distracted even to formulate this in language, I am driven to express it in an odd kind of dance or jig.

I choreograph these spontaneously, hopping from one leg to another in a symmetrical pattern, which seems to have a semiotics of its own. The dances are saying, 'Here are interesting ideas, over there are more things worthy of inclusion in your life.'

What to do with the car batteries and Eskis that were delivered today? A sculpture is out of the question. I may just leave them as they are, boxed up and so splendidly replete.

10th March

A tedious encounter with Bohm today. I told him what I knew and he had the temerity to look shocked, like a little boy who's been caught cheating. I know that he himself has taken Inclusion, so why was he nonplussed by my gift of some tin cans, a pair of slipper socks, and a transcript of a lecture delivered by I.A. Braithwaite to the British Ephemeral Society on 'In-Flight Magazines for People in Temporarily Grounded Aircraft'?

The fool tried to persuade me to come off Inclusion. I told him I would blow the whole incident wide open if he didn't arrange for me to meet Busner. I spoke to him later in the afternoon and Busner has acceded to my demand. I would feel some trepidation about going to Worminghall tomorrow evening, but I don't find it nearly as interesting as trying to divine how many fondue forks I can shove into a VCR before it stops working.

This is the final entry in Simon Dykes's increasingly spikey and manic scrawl. You turn a few pages on and there is nothing. You turn a few pages more and you find two final entries, dated 11th March and 19th March. They aren't in Dykes's hand, but Busner's:

11th March

I have been included within the psyche of Simon Dykes in a most perverse fashion. I would be horrified by this eruption in the very skin of reality, were it not so very interesting.

He and Bohm arrived at the Facility some hours ago. It may have been foolish of me to take some Inclusion shortly before they turned up, but I did it in a spirit of scientific enquiry.

Under the influence of the Inclusion, Dykes appeared to me as an ever-mutating thing. The very composition of his head and body was of found objects, and constantly transmogrifying.

The Rotadexes and file holders; typewriter ribbons and plastic beakers; Bunsen burners and test-tube racks that fill my office and laboratory were snaffled up by this protean being. When our eyes met there was a great humming and crackling in the atmosphere. Bohm, and MacLachlan, who had come with him, turned tail and fled. Paper clips and drawing pins bulged from the surface of his eyeballs. Biros and match books ruckled beneath his skin.

The cyclotron in the corner began to hum and pulse, even though I knew it wasn't activated. Then there was an appalling explosion, but instead of feeling myself blown apart, expanded, I had the sensation of being sucked in: a plume of genie being drawn into a bottle. Fragments of glass and fragments of mica, bigger than boulders, plummeted past the screen of my vision like some cheap special effect.

19th March

I am still in here. Dykes's mind is a cluttered place, as you have no doubt gathered. He leaves me pretty much to myself. During one of his rare lapses in physical activity, he allows me the indulgence of employing his motor abilities to jot down notes such as these. For the rest of the time I am free to roam the museum of grotesque ideas, images and objects that the drug has driven him to acquire willy-nilly. I am pure intention, a secondary and immaterial will operating inside the Dykes psyche.

Dykes naturally thinks he is psychotic – and in a way I suppose he is. But it's comfortable enough here in the Warneford: a choice of meals, and at least one chat a day with a jejune shrink.

It has occurred to me that the only way to understand the Inclusion incident is to view it at a metaphoric level. The drug was originally made from the corpses of the bee mites that infested the hives, much in the way that I now infest Dykes's mind. I have become – as it were – Inclusion.

Mind you – it's just a thought.

And that is that. Or at least it would be if the Inclusion folder wasn't bulging and flexing in a sinister way between your hands. Didn't anyone ever tell you not to read things that don't belong to you, not to interfere with private correspondence? The thoughts are scampering across your shoulders now; now, as the first of the leaflets on Blaenau Ffestiniog Slate Quarry falls out of the Inclusion brochure, followed by the 1984–5 Eastbourne and District Phone Directory, followed by the *Atlas of Cancer Incidence in England and Wales 1968–1985*.

There's more to this Inclusion brochure than first met your eye. You should stay interested in it and not allow your thoughts to stray to unanswered letters, unreturned phone calls, unpaid bills, unfulfilled ambitions, wasted opportunities and people unloved and unmissed.

The End of the Relationship

'WHY THE HELL don't you leave him if he's such a monster?' said Grace. We were sitting in the Café Delancey in Camden Town, eating *croques m'sieurs* and slurping down *cappuccino*. I was dabbing the sore skin under my eyes with a scratchy piece of toilet paper – trying to stop the persistent leaking. When I'd finished dabbing I deposited the wad of salty stuff in my bag, took another slurp and looked across at Grace.

'I don't know,' I said. 'I don't know why I don't leave him.'

'You can't go back there – not after this morning. I don't know why you didn't leave him immediately after it happened . . .'

That morning I'd woken to find him already up. He was standing at the window, naked. One hand held the struts of the venetian blind apart, while he squinted down on to the Pentonville Road. Lying in bed I could feel the judder and hear the squeal of the traffic as it built up to the rush hour.

In the half-light of dawn his body seemed monolithic: his limbs columnar and white, his head and shoulders solid capitals. I stirred in the bed and he sensed that I was awake. He came back to the side of the bed and stood looking down at me. 'You're like a little animal in there. A little rabbit, snuggled down in its burrow.'

I squirmed down further into the duvet and looked up at him, puckering my lip so that I had goofy, rabbity teeth. He got back into bed and curled himself around me. He tucked his legs under mine. He lay on his side – I on my back. The front of his thighs pressed against my haunch and buttock. I felt his penis stiffen against me as his fingers made slight, brushing passes over my breasts, up to my throat and face and then slowly down. His mouth nuzzled against my neck, his tongue licked my flesh, his fingers poised over my nipples, twirling them into erection. My body teetered, a heavy rock on the edge of a precipice.

The rasp of his cheek against mine; the too peremptory prodding of his cock against my mons; the sense of something casual and offhand about the way he was caressing me. Whatever – it was all wrong. There was no true feeling in the way he was touching me; he was manipulating me like some giant dolly. I tensed up – which he sensed; he persisted for a short while, for two more rotations of palm on breast, and then he rolled over on his back with a heavy sigh.

'I'm sorry – '

'It's OK.'

'It's just that sometimes I feel that – '

It's OK, really, please don't.'

'Don't what?'

'Don't talk about it.'

'But if we don't talk about it we're never going to deal with it. We're never going to sort it all out.'

'Look, I've got feelings too. Right now I feel like shit. If you don't want to, don't start. That's what I can't stand, starting and then stopping – it makes me sick to the stomach.'

'Well, if that's what you want.' I reached down to touch his penis; the chill from his voice hadn't reached it yet. I gripped it as tightly as I could and began to pull up and down, feeling the skin un- and re-peel over the shaft. Suddenly he recoiled.

'Not like that, ferchrissakes!' He slapped my hand away. 'Anyway I don't want that. I don't want . . . I don't want . . . I don't want some bloody hand relief!'

I could feel the tears pricking at my eyes. 'I thought you said – '

'What does it matter what I said? What does it matter what I do . . . I can't convince you, now can I?'

'I want to, I really do. It's just that I don't feel I can trust you any more . . . not at the moment. You have to give me more time.'

'Trust! Trust! I'm not a fucking building society, you know. You're not setting an account up with me. Oh fuck it! Fuck the whole fucking thing!'

He rolled away from me and pivoted himself upright. Pulling a pair of trousers from the chair where he'd chucked them the night before, he dragged his legs into them. I dug deeper into the bed and looked out at him through eyes fringed by hair and tears.

'Coffee?' His voice was icily polite.

'Yes please.' He left the room. I could hear him moving around downstairs. Pained love made me picture his actions: unscrewing the percolator, sluicing it out with cold water, tamping the coffee grains down in the metal basket, screwing it back together again and setting it on the lighted stove.

When he reappeared ten minutes later, with two cups of coffee, I was still dug into the bed. He sat down sideways and waited while I struggled upwards and crammed a pillow behind my head. I pulled a limp corner of the duvet cover over my breasts. I took the cup from him and sipped. He'd gone to the trouble of heating milk for my coffee. He always took his black.

'I'm going out now. I've got to get down to Kensington and see Steve about those castings.' He'd mooched a cigarette from somewhere and the smoking of it, and the cocking of his elbow, went with his tone: officer speaking to other ranks. I hated him for it.

But hated myself more for asking, 'When will you be back?'

'Later . . . not for quite a while.' The studied ambiguity was another put-down. 'What're you doing today?'

'N–nothing . . . meeting Grace, I s'pose.'

'Well, that's good, the two of you can have a really trusting talk – that's obviously what you need.' His chocolate drop of sarcasm was thinly candy-coated with sincerity.

'Maybe it is . . . look . . .'

'Don't say anything, don't get started again. We've talked and talked about this. There's nothing I can do, is there? There's no way I can convince you – and I think I'm about ready to give up trying.'

'You shouldn't have done it.'

'Don't you think I know that? Don't you think I fucking know that?! Look, do you think I enjoyed it? Do you think that? 'Cause if you do, you are fucking mad. More mad than I thought you were.'

'You can't love me . . .' A wail was starting up in me; the saucer chattered against the base of my cup. 'You can't, whatever you say.'

'I don't know about that. All I do know is that this is torturing me. I hate myself – that's true enough. Look at this. Look at how much I hate myself!'

He set his coffee cup down on the varnished floor-boards and began to give himself enormous open-handed clouts around the head. 'You think I love myself? Look at this!' (clout) 'All you think about is your-own-fucking-self, your own fucking feelings.' (clout) 'Don't come back here tonight!' (clout) 'Just don't come back, because I don't think I can take much more.'

As he was saying the last of this he was pirouetting around the room, scooping up small change and keys from the table, pulling on his shirt and shoes. It wasn't until he got to the door that I became convinced that he actually was going to walk out on me. Sometimes these scenes could run to several entrances and exits. I leapt from the bed, snatched up a towel, and caught him at the head of the stairs.

'Don't walk out on me! Don't walk out, don't do that, not that.' I was hiccupping, mucus and tears were mixing on my lips and chin. He twisted away from me and clattered down a few stairs, then he paused and turning said, 'You talk to me about trust, but I think the reality of it is that you don't really care about me at all, or else none of this would have happened in the first place.' He was doing his best to sound furious, but I could tell that the real anger was dying down. I sniffed up my tears and snot and descended towards him.

'Don't run off, I do care, come back to bed – it's still early.' I touched his forearm with my hand. He looked so anguished, his face all twisted and reddened with anger and pain.

'Oh, fuck it. Fuck it. Just fuck it.' He swore flatly. The flap of towel that I was holding against my breast fell away, and I pushed the nipple, which dumbly re-erected itself, against his hand. He didn't seem to notice, and instead stared fixedly over my shoulder, up the stairs and into the bedroom. I pushed against him a little more firmly. Then he took my nipple between the knuckles of his index and forefinger and pinched it, quite hard, muttering, 'Fuck it, just fucking fuck it.'

He turned on his heels and left. I doubled over on the

stairs. The sobs that racked me had a sickening component. I staggered to the bathroom and as I clutched the
toilet bowl the mixture of coffee and mucus streamed
from my mouth and nose. Then I heard the front door
slam.

'I don't know why.'

'Then leave. You can stay at your own place – '

'You know I hate it there. I can't stand the people I
have to share with – '

'Be that as it may, the point is that you don't need
him, you just think you do. It's like you're caught in
some trap. You think you love him, but it's just your
insecurity talking. Remember,' and here Grace's voice
took on an extra depth, a special sonority of caring, 'your
insecurity is like a clever actor, it can mimic any emotion
it chooses to and still be utterly convincing. But whether
it pretends to be love or hate, the truth is that at bottom
it's just the fear of being alone.'

'Well why should I be alone? You're not alone, are
you?'

'No, that's true, but it's not easy for me either. Any
relationship is an enormous sacrifice . . . I don't
know . . . Anyway, you know that I was alone for
two years before I met John, perhaps you should give
it a try?'

'I spend most of my time alone anyway. I'm perfectly
capable of being by myself. But I also need to see
him . . .'

As my voice died away I became conscious of the voice of another woman two tables away. I couldn't hear what she was saying to her set-faced male companion, but the tone was the same as my own, the exact same plangent composite of need and recrimination. I stared at them. Their faces said it all: his awful detachment, her hideous yearning. And as I looked around the café at couple after couple, each confronting one another over the marble table tops, I had the beginnings of an intimation.

Perhaps all this awful mismatching, this emotional grating, these Mexican stand-offs of trust and commitment, were somehow in the air. It wasn't down to individuals: me and him, Grace and John, those two over there . . . It was a contagion that was getting to all of us; a germ of insecurity that had lodged in all our breasts and was now fissioning frantically, creating a domino effect as relationship after relationship collapsed in a rubble of mistrust and acrimony.

After he had left that morning I went back to his bed and lay there, gagged and bound by the smell of him in the duvet. I didn't get up until eleven. I listened to Radio Four, imagining that the deep-timbred, wholesome voices of each successive presenter were those of ideal parents. There was a discussion programme, a gardening panel discussion, a discussion about books, a short story about an elderly woman and her relationship with her son, followed by a discussion about it. It all sounded so cultured, so eminently reasonable. I tried to construct a new view of myself on the basis of being the kind of young woman who would consume such hearty radiophonic fare, but it didn't work. Instead I felt quite weightless and blown out, a husk of a person.

The light quality in the attic bedroom didn't change all morning. The only way I could measure the passage of time was by the radio, and the position of the watery shadows that his metal sculptures made on the magnolia paint.

Eventually I managed to rouse myself. I dressed and washed my face. I pulled my hair back tightly and fixed it in place with a loop of elastic. I sat down at his work table. It was blanketed with loose sheets of paper, all of which were covered with the meticulous plans he did for his sculptures. Elevations and perspectives, all neatly shaded and the dimensions written in using the lightest of pencils. There was a mess of other stuff on the table as well: sticks of flux, a broken soldering iron, bits of acrylic and angled steel brackets. I cleared a space amidst the evidence of his industry and taking out my notebook and biro, added my own patch of emotion to the collage:

I do understand how you feel. I know the pressure that you're under at the moment, but you must realise that it's pressure that *you* put on *yourself*. It's not me that's doing it to you. I do love you and I want to be with you, but it takes time to forgive. And what you did to me was almost unforgivable. I've been hurt before and I don't want to be hurt again. If you can't understand that, if you can't understand how I feel about it, then it's probably best if we don't see one another again. I'll be at the flat this evening, perhaps you'll call?

Out in the street the sky was spitting at the pavement. There was no wind to speak of, but despite that each gob seemed to have an added impetus. With every corner that I rounded on my way to King's Cross I encountered another little cyclone of rain and grit. I walked past shops full of mouldering stock that were boarded up, and empty, derelict ones that were still open.

On the corner of the Caledonian Road I almost collided with a dosser wearing a long, dirty overcoat. He was clutching a bottle of VP in a hand that was blue with impacted filth, filth that seemed to have been worked deliberately into the open sores on his knuckles. He turned his face to me and I recoiled instinctively. It was the face of a myxomatosic rabbit ('You're like a little animal in there. A little rabbit, snuggled down in its burrow'), the eyes swollen up and exploding in a series of burst ramparts and lesions of diseased flesh. His nose was no longer nose-shaped.

But on the tube the people were comforting and workaday enough. I paid at the barrier when I reached Camden Town and walked off quickly down the High Street. Perhaps it was the encounter with the dying drunk that had cleansed me, jerked me out of my self-pity, because for a short while I felt more lucid, better able to look honestly at my relationship. While it was true that he did have problems, emotional problems, and was prepared to admit to them, it was still the case that nothing could forgive his conduct while I was away visiting my parents.

I knew that the woman he had slept with lived here in Camden Town. As I walked down the High Street I began – at first almost unconsciously, then with growing intensity – to examine the faces of any youngish women that passed me. They came in all shapes and sizes, these suspect lovers. There were tall women in floor-length linen coats; plump women in stretchy slacks; petite women in neat, two-piece suits; raddled women in unravelling pullovers; and painfully smart women, Sindy dolls: press a pleasure-button in the small of their backs and their hair would grow.

The trouble was that they all looked perfectly plausible candidates for the job as the metal worker's anvil. Outside Woolworth's I was gripped by a sharp attack of nausea. An old swallow of milky coffee reentered my mouth as I thought of him, on top of this woman, on top of that woman, hammering himself into them, bash after bash after bash, flattening their bodies, making them ductile with pleasure.

I went into Marks & Sparks to buy some clean underwear and paused to look at myself in a full-length mirror. My skirt was bunched up around my hips, my hair was lank and flecked with dandruff, my tights bagged at the knees, my sleeve-ends bulged with snot-clogged Kleenex. I looked like shit. It was no wonder that he didn't fancy me any more, that he'd gone looking for some retouched vision.

'Come on,' said Grace, 'let's go. The longer we stay here, the more weight we put on.' On our way out of the café I took a mint from the cut-glass bowl by the cash register and recklessly crunched it between my molars. The sweet pain of sugar-in-cavity spread through my mouth as I fumbled in my bag for my purse. 'Well, what are you going to do now?' It was only three-thirty in the afternoon but already the sky over London was turning the shocking bilious colour it only ever aspires to when winter is fast encroaching.

'Can I come back with you, Grace?'

'Of course you can, silly, why do you think I asked the question?' She put her arm about my shoulder and twirled me round until we were facing in the direction of the tube. Then she marched me off, like the young emotional offender that I was. Feeling her warm body against mine I almost choked, about to cry again at this display of caring from Grace. But I needed her too much, so I restrained myself.

'You come back with me, love,' she clucked. 'We can watch telly, or eat, or you can do some work. I've got some pattern cutting I've got to finish by tomorrow. John won't be back for ages yet . . . or I tell you what, if you like we can go and meet him in Soho after he's finished work and have something to eat there – would you like that?' She turned to me, flicking back the ledge of her thick blonde fringe with her index finger – a characteristic gesture.

'Well, yes,' I murmured, 'whatever.'

'OK.' Her eyes, turned towards mine, were blue, frank. 'I can see you want to take it easy.'

When we left the tube at Chalk Farm and started up the hill towards where Grace lived, she started up again, wittering on about her and John and me; about what we might do and what fun it would be to have me stay for a couple of nights; and about what a pity it was that I couldn't live with them for a while, because what I really needed was a good sense of security. There was something edgy and brittle about her enthusiasm. I began to feel that she was overstating her case.

I stopped listening to the words she was saying and began to hear them merely as sounds, as some ambient tape of reassurance. Her arm was linked in mine, but from this slight contact I could gain a whole sense of her small body. The precise slope and jut of her full breasts, the soft brush of her round stomach against the drape of her dress, the infinitesimal gratings of knee against nylon, against nylon against knee.

And as I built up this sense of Grace-as-body, I began also to consider how her bush would look as you went down on her. Would the lips gape wetly, or would they tidily recede? Would the cellulite on her hips crinkle as she parted her legs? How would she smell to you, of sex or cinnamon? But, of course, it wasn't any impersonal 'you' I was thinking of – it was a highly personal *him*. I joined their bodies together in my mind and tormented myself with the hideous tableau of betrayal. After all, if he was prepared to screw some nameless bitch, what would have prevented him from shitting where I ate? I shuddered. Grace sensed this, and disengaging her arm from mine returned it to my shoulders, which she gave a squeeze.

John and Grace lived in a thirties council block half-way up Haverstock Hill. Their flat was just like all the others. You stepped through the front door and directly into a long corridor, off which were a number of small rooms. They may have been small, but Grace had done everything possible to make them seem spacious. Furniture and pictures were kept to an artful minimum, and the wooden blocks on the floor had been sanded and polished until they shone.

Grace snapped on floor lamps and put a Mozart concerto on the CD. I tried to write my neglected journal, timing my flourishes of supposed insight to the ascending and descending scales. Grace set up the ironing board and began to do something complicated, involving sheets of paper, pins, and round, worn fragments of chalk.

When the music finished, neither of us made any move to put something else on, or to draw the curtains. Instead we sat in the off-white noise of the speakers, under the opaque stare of the dark windows. To me there was something intensely evocative about the scene:

two young women sitting in a pool of yellow light on a winter's afternoon. Images of my childhood came to me; for the first time in days I felt secure.

When John got back from work, Grace put food-in-a-foil-tray in the oven, and tossed some varieties of leaves. John plonked himself down on one of the low chairs in the sitting room and propped the *Standard* on his knees. Occasionally he would give a snide laugh and read out an item, his intent being always to emphasise the utter consistency of its editorial stupidity.

We ate with our plates balanced on our knees, and when we had finished, turned on the television to watch a play. I noticed that John didn't move over to the sofa to sit with Grace. Instead, he remained slumped in his chair. As the drama unfolded I began to find these seating positions quite wrong and disquieting. John really should have sat with Grace.

The play was about a family riven by domestic violence. It was well acted and the jerky camerawork made it grittily real, almost like documentary. But still I felt that the basic premise was overstated. It wasn't that I didn't believe a family with such horrors boiling within it could maintain a closed face to the outside world, it was just that these horrors were so relentless.

The husband beat up the wife, beat up the kids, got drunk, sexually abused the kids, raped the wife, assaulted social workers, assaulted police, assaulted probation officers, and all within the space of a week or so. It should have been laughable – this chronically dysfunctional family – but it wasn't. How could it be remotely entertaining while we all sat in our separate padded places? Each fresh on-screen outrage increased the distance between the three of us, pushing us still further apart. I hunched down in my chair and felt the waistband of my skirt burn across my bloated stomach. I shouldn't have eaten all that salad – and the underdone garlic bread smelt flat and sour on my own tongue. So flat and sour that the idea even of kissing myself was repulsive, let alone allowing him to taste me.

The on-screen husband, his shirt open, the knot of his tie dragged halfway down his chest, was beating his adolescent daughter with short, powerful clouts around the head. They were standing in her bedroom doorway, and the camera stared fixedly over her shoulder, up the stairs and into the bedroom, where it picked up the corner of a pop poster, pinned to the flowered wallpaper. Each clout was audible as a loud 'crack!' in the room where we sat. I felt so remote, from Grace, from John, from the play . . . from him.

I stood up and walked unsteadily to the toilet at the end of the corridor. Inside I slid the flimsy bolt into its loop and pushed the loosely stacked pile of magazines away from the toilet bowl. My stomach felt as if it were swelling by the second. My fingers when I put them in my mouth were large and alien. My nails scraped against the sides of my throat. As I leant forward I was aware of myself as a vessel, my curdled contents ready to pour. I looked down into the toilet world and there – as my oatmeal stream splashed down – saw that someone had already done the same. Cut out the nutritional middle-woman, that is.

After I'd finished I wiped around the rim of the toilet with hard scraps of paper. I flushed and then splashed my cheeks with cold water. Walking back down the corridor towards the sitting room, I was conscious only of the ultra-sonic whine of the television; until, that is, I reached the door:

'Don't bother.' (A sob.)

'*Mr Evans . . . are you in there?*'

'You don't want me to touch you?'

'*Go away. Just go away . . .*'

'It's just that I feel a bit wound up. I get all stressed out during the day – you know that. I need a long time to wind down.'

'*Mr Evans, we have a court order that empowers us to take these children away.*'

'It's not that – I know it's not just that. You don't fancy me any more, you don't want to have sex any more. You've been like this for weeks.'

'*I don't care if you've got the bloody Home Secretary out there. If you come in that door, I swear she gets it!*'

'How do you expect me to feel like sex? Everything around here is so bloody claustrophobic. I can't stand these little fireside evenings. You sit there all hunched up and fidgety. You bite your nails and smoke away with little puffs. Puff, puff, puff. It's a total turn-off.'

(*Smash!*) '*Oh my God. For Christ's sake! Oh Jesus . . .*'

'I bite my nails and smoke because I don't feel loved, because I feel all alone. I can't trust you, John, not when you're like this – you don't seem to have any feeling for me.'

'Yeah, maybe you're right. Maybe I don't. I'm certainly fed up with all of this shit . . .'

I left my bag in the room. I could come back for it tomorrow when John had gone to work. I couldn't stand to listen – and I didn't want to go back into the room and sit down with them again, crouch with them, like another vulture in the mouldering carcass of their relationship. I couldn't bear to see them reassemble the uncommunicative blocks of that static silence. And I didn't want to sleep in the narrow spare bed, under the child-sized duvet.

I wanted to be back with him. Wanted it the way a junky wants a hit. I yearned to be in that tippy, creaky boat of a bed, full of crumbs and sex and fag ash. I wanted to be framed by the basketry of angular shadows the naked bulb threw on the walls, and contained by the soft basketry of his limbs. At least we felt something for each other. He got right inside me – he really did. All my other relationships were as superficial as a salutation – this evening proved it. It was only with him that I became a real person.

Outside in the street the proportions were all wrong. The block of flats should have been taller than it was long – but it wasn't. Damp leaves blew against, and clung to my ankles. I'd been sitting in front of the gas fire in the flat and my right-hand side had become numb with the heat. Now this wore off – like a pain – leaving my clammy clothes sticking to my clammy flesh.

I walked for a couple of hundred yards down the hill, then a stitch stabbed into me and I felt little pockets of gas beading my stomach. I was level with a tiny parade of shops which included a cab company. Suddenly I couldn't face the walk to the tube, the tube itself, the walk back from the tube to his house. If I was going to go back to him I had to be there right away. If I went by tube it would take too long and this marvellous recon-ciliatory feeling might have soured by the time I arrived. And more to the point there might not be a relationship there for me to go back to. He was a feckless and promiscuous man, insecure and given to the grossest and most evil abuses of trust.

The jealous agony came over me again, covering my flesh like some awful hive. I leant up against a shopfront. The sick image of him entering some other. I could feel it so vividly that it was as if I was him: my penis snagging frustratingly against something . . . my blood beating in my temples . . . my sweat dripping on to her upturned face . . . and then the release of entry . . .

I pushed open the door of the minicab office and lurched in. Two squat men stood like bookends on either side of the counter. They were both reading the racing form. The man nearest to me was encased in a tube of caramel leather. He twisted his neckless head as far round as he could. Was it my imagination, or did his eyes probe and pluck at me, run up my thighs and attempt an imaginative penetration, rapid, rigid and metallic. The creak of his leather and the cold fug of damp, dead filter tips, assaulted me together.

'D'jew want a cab, love?' The other bookend, the one behind the counter, looked at me with dim-sum eyes, morsels of pupil packaged in fat.

'Err . . . yes, I want to go up to Islington, Barnsbury.'

'George'll take yer – woncha, George?' George was still eyeing me around the midriff. I noticed – quite inconsequentially – that he was wearing very clean, blue trousers, with razor-sharp creases. Also that he had no buttocks – the legs of the trousers zoomed straight up into his jacket.

'Yerallright. C'mon, love.' George rattled shut his paper and scooped a packet of Dunhill International and a big bunch of keys off the counter. He opened the door for me and as I passed through I could sense his fat black heart, encased in leather, beating behind me.

He was at the back door of the car before me and ushered me inside. I squidged halfway across the seat before collapsing in a nerveless torpor. But I knew that I wouldn't make it back to him unless I held myself in a state of no expectancy, no hope. If I dared to picture the two of us together again, then when I arrived at the house he would be out. Out fucking.

We woozed away from the kerb and jounced around the corner. An air freshener shaped like a fir tree dingled and dangled as we took the bends down to Chalk Farm

Road. The car was, I noticed, scrupulously clean and poisonous with smoke. George lit another Dunhill and offered me one, which I accepted. In the moulded divider between the two front seats there sat a tin of travel sweets. I could hear them schussing round on their caster-sugar slope as we cornered and cornered and cornered again.

I sucked on the fag and thought determinedly of other things: figure skating; Christmas sales; the way small children have their mittens threaded through the arms of their winter coats on lengths of elastic; Grace . . . which was a mistake, because this train of thought was bad magic. Grace's relationship with John was clearly at an end. It was perverse to realise this, particularly after her display in the café, when she was so secure and self-possessed in the face of my tears and distress. But I could imagine the truth: that the huge crevices in their under-standing of each other had been only temporarily papered over by the thrill of having someone in the flat who was in more emotional distress than they. No, there was no doubt about it now, Grace belonged to the league of the self-deceived.

George had put on a tape. The Crusaders – or at any rate some kind of jazz funk, music for glove compart-ments. I looked at the tightly bunched flesh at the back of his neck. It was malevolent flesh. I was alone in the world really. People tried to understand me, but they completely missed the mark. It was as if they were always looking at me from entirely the wrong angle and mistaking a knee for a bald pate, or an elbow for a breast.

And then I knew that I'd been a fool to get into the cab, the rapistmobile. I looked at George's hands, where they had pounced on the steering wheel. They were flexing more than they should have been, flexing in anticipation. When he looked at me in the office he had taken me for jailbait, thought I was younger than I am. He just looked at my skirt – not at my sweater; and anyway, my sweater hides my breasts, which are small. He could do it, right enough, because he knew exactly where to go and the other man, the man in the office, would laughingly concoct an alibi for him. And who would believe me anyway? He'd be careful not to leave anything inside me . . . and no marks.

We were driving down a long street with warehouses on either side. I didn't recognise it. The distances between the street lamps were increasing. The car thwacked over some shallow depressions in the road, depressions that offered no resistance. I felt everything sliding towards the inevitable. He used to cuddle me and call me 'little animal', 'little rabbit'. It should happen again, not end like this, in terror, in violation.

Then the sequence of events went awry. I subsided sideways, sobbing, choking. The seat was wide enough for me to curl up on it, which is what I did. The car slid to a halt. 'Whassermatter, love?' Oh Jesus, I thought, don't let him touch me, please don't let him touch me, he can't be human. But I knew that he was. 'C'mon, love, whassermatter?' My back in its suede jacket was like a carapace. When he penetrated me I'd rather he did it from behind, anything not to have him touch and pry at the soft parts of my front.

The car pulls away once more. Perhaps this place isn't right for his purposes, he needs somewhere more remote. I'm already under the earth, under the soft earth . . . The wet earth will cling to my putrid face when the police find me . . . when they put up the loops of yellow tape around my uncovered grave . . . and the WPC used to play me when they reconstruct the crime will look nothing like me . . . She'll have coarser features, but bigger breasts and hips . . . something not lost on the grieving boyfriend . . . Later he'll take her back to the flat, and fuck her standing up, pushing her ample, smooth bum into the third shelf of books in his main room (some Penguin classics, a couple of old economics text books, my copy of *The House of Mirth*), with each turgid stroke . . .

I hear the door catch through these layers of soft earth. I lunge up, painfully slow, he has me . . . and come face to face with a woman. A handsome woman, heavily built, in her late thirties. I relapse back into the car and regard her at crotch level. It's clear immediately – from the creases in her jeans – that she's George's wife.

'C'mon love, whassermatter?' I crawl from the car and stagger against her, still choking. I can't speak, but gesture vaguely towards George, who's kicking the front wheel of the car, with a steady 'chok-chok-chok'.

'What'd 'e do then? Eh? Did he frighten you or something? You're a bloody fool, George!' She slaps him, a roundhouse slap – her arm, travelling ninety degrees level with her shoulder. George still stands, even glummer now, rubbing his cheek.

In terrorist-siege-survivor-mode (me clutching her round the waist with wasted arms) we turn and head across the parking area to the exterior staircase of a block of flats exactly the same as the one I recently left. Behind us comes a Dunhill International, and behind that comes George. On the third floor we pass a woman fumbling for her key in her handbag – she's small enough to eyeball the lock. My saviour pushes open the door of the next flat along and pulls me in. Still holding me by the shoulder she escorts me along the corridor and into an overheated room.

'Park yerself there, love.' She turns, exposing the high, prominent hips of a steer and disappears into another room, from where I hear the clang of aluminium kettle on iron prong. I'm left behind on a great scoop of upholstery – an armchair wide enough for three of me – facing a similarly outsize television screen. The armchair still has on the thick plastic dress of its first commercial communion.

George comes in, dangling his keys, and without looking at me crosses the room purposively. He picks up a doll in Dutch national costume and begins to fiddle under its skirt. 'Git out of there!' This from the kitchen. He puts the doll down and exits without looking at me.

'C'mon, love, stick that in your laugh hole.' She sets the tea cup and saucer down on a side table. She sits alongside me in a similar elephantine armchair. We might be a couple testing out a new suite in some furniture warehouse. She settles herself, yanking hard at the exposed pink webbing of her bra, where it cuts into her. 'It's not the first time this has happened, you know,' she slurps.' Not that George would do anything, mind, leastways not in his cab. But he does have this way of . . . well, frightening people, I s'pose. He sits there twirling his bloody wheel, not saying anything and somehow girls like you get terrified. Are you feeling better now?'

'Yes, thanks, really it wasn't his fault. I've been rather upset all day. I had a row with my boyfriend this morning and I had been going to stay at a friend's, but suddenly I wanted to get home. And I was in the car when it all sort of came down on top of me . . .'

'Where do you live, love?'

'I've got a room in a flat in Kensal Rise, but my boyfriend lives in Barnsbury.'

'That's just around the corner from here. When you've 'ad your tea I'll walk you back.'

'But what about George — I haven't even paid him.'

'Don't worry about that. He's gone off now, anyway he could see that you aren't exactly loaded . . . He thinks a lot about money, does George. Wants us to have our own place an' that. It's an obsession with him. And he has to get back on call as quickly as he can or he'll miss a job, and if he misses a job he's in for a bad night. And if he has a bad night, then it's me that's on the receiving end the next day. Not that I hardly ever see him, mind. He works two shifts at the moment. Gets in at three-thirty in the afternoon, has a kip, and goes back out again at eight. On his day off he sleeps. He never sees the kids, doesn't seem to care about 'em . . .'

She trails off. In the next room I hear the high aspiration of a child turning in its sleep.

'D'jew think 'e's got some bint somewhere? D'jew think that's what these double shifts are really about?'

'Really, I don't know – '

' 'E's a dark one. Now, I am a bit too fat to frolic, but I make sure he gets milked every so often. Yerknowha-tImean? Men are like bulls really, aren't they? They need to have some of that spunk taken out of them. But I dunno . . . Perhaps it's not enough. He's out and about, seeing all these skinny little bints, picking them up . . . I dunno, what's the use?' She lights a cigarette and deposits the match in a free-standing ashtray. Then she starts yanking at the webbing again, where it encases her beneath her pullover. 'I'd swear there are bloody fleas in this flat. I keep powdering the mutt, but it doesn't make no difference, does it, yer great ball of dough.'

She pushes a slippered foot against the heaving stomach of a mouldering Alsatian. I haven't even noticed the dog before now – its fur merges so seamlessly with the shaggy carpet. 'They say dog fleas can't live on a human, yer know, but these ones are making a real effort. P'raps they aren't fleas at all . . . P'raps that bastard has given me a dose of the crabs. Got them off some fucking brass, I expect, whad'jew think?'

'I've no idea really – '

'I know it's the crabs. I've even seen one of the fuckers crawling up me pubes. Oh gawd, dunnit make you sick. I'm going to leave the bastard – I am. I'll go to Berkhamsted to my Mum's. I'll go tonight. I'll wake the kids and go tonight . . .'

I need to reach out to her, I suppose, I need to make some sort of contact. After all she has helped me – so really I ought to reciprocate. But I'm all inhibited. There's no point in offering help to anyone if you don't follow through. There's no point in implying to anyone the possibility of some fount of unconditional love if you aren't prepared to follow through . . . To do so would be worse than to do nothing. And anyway . . . I'm on my way back to sort out *my* relationship. That has to take priority.

These justifications are running through my mind, each one accompanied by a counter argument, like a sub-title at the opera, or a stock market quotation running along the base of a television screen. Again there's the soft aspiration from the next room, this time matched, shudderingly, by the vast shelf of tit alongside me. She subsides. Twisted face, foundation cracking, folded into cracking hands. For some reason I think of Atrixo.

She didn't hear me set down my cup and saucer. She

didn't hear my footfalls. She didn't hear the door. She just sobbed. And now I'm clear, I'm in the street and I'm walking with confident strides towards his flat. Nothing can touch me now. I've survived the cab ride with George – that's good karma, good magic. It means that I'll make it back to him and his heartfelt, contrite embrace.

Sometimes – I remember as a child remembers Christmas – we used to drink a bottle of champagne together. Drink half the bottle and then make love, then drink the other half and make love again. It was one of the rituals I remember from the beginning of our relationship, from the springtime of our love. And as I pace on up the hill, more recollections hustle alongside. Funny how when a relationship is starting up you always praise the qualities of your lover to any third party there is to hand, saying, 'Oh yes, he's absolutely brilliant at X,Y and Z . . .' and sad how that tendency dies so quickly. Dies at about the same time that disrobing in front of one another ceases to be embarrassing . . . and perhaps for that reason ceases to be quite so sexy.

Surely it doesn't have to be this way? Stretching up the hill ahead of me, I begin to see all of my future relationships, bearing me on and up like some escalator of the fleshly. Each step is a man, a man who will penetrate me with his penis and his language, a man who will make a little private place with me, secure from the world, for a month, or a week, or a couple of years.

How much more lonely and driven is the serial

monogamist than the serial killer? I won't be the same person when I come to lie with that man there, the one with the ginger fuzz on his white stomach; or that one further up there – almost level with the junction of Barnsbury Road – the one with the round head and skull cap of thick, black hair. I'll be his 'little rabbit', or his 'baby-doll', or his 'sex goddess', but I won't be me. I can only be me . . . with him.

Maybe it isn't too late? Maybe we can recapture some of what we once had.

I'm passing an off-licence. It's on the point of closing – I can see a man in a cardigan doing something with some crates towards the back of the shop. I'll get some champagne. I'll turn up at his flat with the bottle of champagne, and we'll do it like we did it before.

I push open the door and venture inside. The atmosphere of the place is acridly reminiscent of George's minicab office. I cast an eye along the shelves – they are pitifully stocked, just a few cans of lager and some bottles of cheap wine. There's a cooler in the corner, but all I can see behind the misted glass are a couple of isolated bottles of Asti spumante. It doesn't look like they'll have any champagne in this place. It doesn't look like my magic is going to hold up. I feel the tears welling up in me again, welling up as the offie proprietor treads wearily back along the lino.

'Yes, can I help you?'

'I . . . oh, well, I . . . oh, really . . . it doesn't matter . . .'

'Ay-up, love, are you all right?'

'Yes . . . I'm sorry . . . it's just . . .'

He's a kindly, round ball of a little man, with an implausibly straight toothbrush moustache. Impossible to imagine him as a threat. I'm crying as much with relief – that the offie proprietor is not some cro-magnon – as I am from knowing that I can't get the champagne now, and that things will be over between me and him.

The offie proprietor has pulled a handkerchief out of his cardigan pocket, but it's obviously not suitable, so he shoves it back in and picking up a handi-pack of tissues from the rack on the counter, he tears it open and hands one to me, saying, 'Now there you go, love, give your nose a good blow like, and you'll feel better.'

'Thanks.' I mop myself up for what seems like the nth time today. Who would have thought the old girl had so much salt in her?

'Now, how can I help you?'

'Oh, well . . . I don't suppose you have a bottle of champagne?' It sounds stupid, saying that rich word in this zone of poor business opportunity.

'Champagne? I don't get much of a call for that round here.' His voice is still kindly, he isn't offended. 'My customers tend to prefer their wine fortified – if you know what I mean. Still, I remember I did have a bottle out in the store room a while back. I'll go and see if it's still there.'

He turns and heads off down the lino again. I stand and look out at the dark street and the swishing cars and the shuddering lorries. He's gone for quite a while. He must

326

trust me – I think to myself. He's left me here in the shop with the till and all the booze on the shelves. How ironic that I should find trust here, in this slightest of contexts, and find so little of it in my intimate relationships.

Then I hear footsteps coming from up above, and I am conscious of earnest voices:

'Haven't you shut up the shop yet?'

'I'm just doing it, my love. There's a young woman down there wanting a bottle of champagne, I just came up to get it.'

'Champagne! Pshaw! What the bloody hell does she want it for at this time of night?'

'I dunno. Probably to drink with her boyfriend.'

'Well, you take her bottle of champagne down to her and then get yourself back up here. I'm not finished talking to you yet.'

'Yes, my love.'

When he comes back in I do my best to look as if I haven't overheard anything. He puts the bi-focals that hang from the cord round his neck on to his nose and scrutinises the label on the bottle: 'Chambertin demi-sec. Looks all right to me – good stuff as I recall.'

'It looks fine to me.'

'Good,' he smiles – a nice smile. 'I'll wrap it up for you . . . Oh, hang on a minute, there's no price on it, I'll have to go and check the stock list.'

'Brian!' This comes from upstairs, a great bellow full of imperiousness.

'Just a minute, my love.' He tilts his head back and

calls up to the ceiling, as if addressing some vengeful goddess, hidden behind the fire-resistant tiles.

'Now, Brian!' He gives me a pained smile, takes off his bi-focals and rubs his eyes redder.

'It's my wife,' he says in a stage whisper, 'she's a bit poorly. I'll check on her quickly and get that price for you. I shan't be a moment.'

He's gone again. More footsteps, and then Brian's wife says, 'I'm not going to wait all night to tell you this, Brian, I'm going to bloody well tell you now – '

'But I've a customer – '

'I couldn't give a monkey's. I couldn't care less about your bloody customer. I've had it with you, Brian – you make me sick with your stupid little cardigan and your glasses. You're like some fucking relic – '

'Can't this wait a minute – '

'No, it bloody can't. I want you out of here, Brian. It's my lease and my fucking business. You can sleep in the spare room tonight, but I want you out of here in the morning.'

'We've discussed this before – '

'I know we have. But now I've made my decision.'

I take the crumpled bills from my purse. Twenty quid has to be enough for the bottle of Chambertin. I wrap it in a piece of paper and write on it 'Thanks for the champagne'. Then I pick up the bottle and leave the shop as quietly as I can. They're still at it upstairs: her voice big and angry; his, small and placatory.

★   ★   ★

328

I can see the light in the bedroom when I'm still two hundred yards away from the house. It's the Anglepoise on the windowsill. He's put it on so that it will appear like a beacon, drawing me back into his arms.

I let myself in with my key, and go on up the stairs. He's standing at the top, wearing a black sweater that I gave him and blue jeans. There's a cigarette trailing from one hand, and a smear of cigarette ash by his nose, which I want to kiss away the minute I see it. He says, 'What are you doing here, I thought you were going to stay at your place tonight?'

I don't say anything, but pull the bottle of champagne out from under my jacket, because I know that'll explain everything and make it all all right.

He advances towards me, down a couple of stairs, and I half-close my eyes, waiting for him to take me in his arms, but instead he holds me by my elbows and looking me in the face says, 'I think it really would be best if you stayed at your place tonight, I need some time to think things over – '

'But I want to stay with you. I want to be with you. Look, I brought this for us to drink . . . for us to drink while we make love.'

'That's really sweet of you, but I think after this morning it would be best if we didn't see one another for a while.'

'You don't want me any more – do you? This is the end of our relationship, isn't it? Isn't that what you're saying?'

'No, I'm not saying that, I just think it would be a good idea if we cooled things down for a while.'

I can't stand the tone of his voice. He's talking to me as if I were a child or a crazy person. And he's looking at me like that as well – as if I might do something mad, like bash his fucking brains out with my bottle of Chambertin demi-sec. 'I don't want to cool things down, I want to be with you. I need to be with you. We're meant to be together – you said that. You said it yourself!'

'Look, I really feel it would be better if you went now. I'll call you a cab –'

'I don't want a cab!'

'I'll call you a cab and we can talk about it in the morning –'

'I don't want to talk about it in the morning, I want to talk about it now. Why won't you let me stay, why are you trying to get rid of me?'

And then he sort of cracks. He cracks and out of the gaps in his face come these horrible words, these sick, slanderous, revolting words, he isn't him anymore, because he could never have said such things. He must be possessed.

'I don't want you here!' He begins to shout and pound the wall. 'Because you're like some fucking emotional Typhoid Mary. That's why I don't want you here. Don't you understand, it's not just me and you, it's everywhere you go, everyone you come into contact with. You've got some kind of bacillus inside you, a contagion –

everything you touch you turn to neurotic ashes with your pick-pick-picking away at the fabric of people's relationships. That's why I don't want you here. Tonight – or any other night!'

Out in the street again – I don't know how. I don't know if he said more of these things, or if we fought, or if we fucked. I must have blacked out, blacked out with sheer anguish of it. You think you know someone, you imagine that you are close to them, and then they reveal this slimy pit at their core . . . this pit they've kept concreted over. Sex is a profound language, all right, and so easy to lie in.

I don't need him – that's what I have to tell myself: I don't need him. But I'm bucking with the sobs and the needing of him is all I can think of. I'm standing in the dark street, rain starting to fall, and every little thing: every gleam of chromium, serration of brick edge, mush of waste paper, thrusts its material integrity in the face of my lost soul.

I'll go to my therapist. It occurs to me – and tagged behind it is the admonition: why didn't you think of this earlier, much earlier, it could have saved you a whole day of distress?

Yes, I'll go to Jill's house. She always says I should come to her place if I'm in real trouble. She knows how sensitive I am. She knows how much love I need. She's not like a conventional therapist – all dispassionate and uncaring. She believes in getting involved in her clients' lives. I'll go to her now. I need her now more than I ever have.

When I go to see her she doesn't put me in some garage of a consulting room, some annex of feeling. She lets me into her warm house, the domicile lined with caring. It isn't so much therapy that Jill gives me, as acceptance. I need to be there now, with all the evidence of her three small children spread about me: the red plastic crates full of soft toys, the finger paintings sell-otaped to the fridge, the diminutive coats and jackets hanging from hip-height hooks.

I need to be close to her and also to her husband, Paul. I've never met him – of course, but I'm always aware of his after-presence in the house when I attend my sessions. I know that he's an architect, that he and Jill have been together for fourteen years, and that they too have had their vicissitudes, their comings-together and fallings-apart. How else could Jill have such total sympathy when it comes to the wreckage of my own emotions? Now I need to be within the precincts of their happy cathedral of a relationship again. Jill and Paul's probity, their mutual relinquishment, their acceptance of one another's foibles – all of this towers above my desolate plain of abandonment.

It's OK, I'm going to Jill's now. I'm going to Jill's and we're going to drink hot chocolate and sit up late, talking it all over. And then she'll let me stay the night at her place – I know she will. And in the morning I'll start to sort myself out.

Another cab ride, but I'm not concentrating on anything, not noticing anything. I'm intent on the vision I have of Jill opening the front door to her cosy house. Intent on the homely vision of sports equipment loosely stacked in the hall, and the expression of heartfelt concern that suffuses Jill's face when she sees the state I'm in.

The cab stops and I pay off the driver. I open the front gate and walk up to the house. The door opens and there's Jill: 'Oh . . . hi . . . it's you.'

'I'm sorry . . . perhaps I should have called?' This isn't at all as I imagined it would be – there's something lurking in her face, something I haven't seen there before.

'It's rather late – '

'I know, it's just, just that . . .' My voice dies away. I don't know what to say to her, I expect her to do the talking to lead me in and then lead me on, tease out the awful narrative of my day. But she's still standing in the doorway, not moving, not asking me in.

'It's not altogether convenient . . .' And I start to cry – I can't help it, I know I shouldn't, I know she'll think I'm being manipulative (and where does this thought come from, I've never imagined such a thing before), but I can't stop myself.

And then there is the comforting arm around my shoulder and she does invite me in, saying, 'Oh, all right, come into the kitchen and have a cup of chocolate, but you can't stay for long. I'll have to order you another mini cab in ten minutes or so.'

'What's the matter then? Why are you in such a state?'

The kitchen has a proper grown-up kitchen smell, of wholesome ingredients, well-stocked larders and fully employed wine racks. The lighting is good as well: a bell-bottomed shade pulled well down on to the wooden table, creating an island in the hundred-watt sun.

'He's ending our relationship – he didn't say as much, but I know that that's what he meant. He called me "an emotional Typhoid Mary", and all sorts of other stuff. Vile things.'

'Was this this evening?'

'Yeah, half an hour ago. I came straight here afterwards, but it's been going on all day, we had a dreadful fight this morning.'

'Well,' she snorts, 'isn't that a nice coincidence?' Her tone isn't nice at all. There's a hardness in it, a flat bitterness I've never heard before.

'I'm sorry?' Her fingers are white against the dark brown of the drinking-chocolate tin, her face is all drawn out of shape. She looks her age – and I've never even thought what this might be before now. For me she's either been a sister or a mother or a friend. Free-floatingly female, not buckled into a strait-jacket of biology.

'My husband saw fit to inform me that our marriage was over this evening . . . oh, about fifteen minutes before you arrived, approximately . . .' Her voice dies away. It doesn't sound malicious – her tone, that is, but what she's said is clearly directed at me. But before I can reply she goes on. 'I suppose there are all sorts of reasons for it. Above and beyond all the normal shit that happens in relationships: the arguments, the Death of Sex, the conflicting priorities, there are other supervening factors.' She's regaining her stride now, beginning to talk to me the way she normally does.

'It seems impossible for men and women to work out their fundamental differences nowadays. Perhaps it's because of the uncertainty about gender roles, or the sheer stress of modern living, or maybe there's some still deeper malaise of which we're not aware.'

'What do you think it is? I mean – between you and Paul.' I've adopted her tone – and perhaps even her posture. I imagine that if I can coax some of this out of her then things will get back to the way they should be, roles will re-reverse.

'I'll tell you what I think it is' – she looks directly at me for the first time since I arrived – 'since you ask. I think he could handle the kids, the lack of sleep, the constant money problems, my moods, his moods, the dog shit in the streets and the beggars on the Tube. Oh yes, he was mature enough to cope with all of that. But in the final analysis what he couldn't bear was the constant stream of neurotics flowing through this house. I think he called it "a babbling brook of self-pity". Yes, that's right, that's what he said. Always good with a turn of phrase is Paul.'

'And what do you think?' I asked – not wanting an answer, but not wanting her to stop speaking, for the silence to interpose.

'I'll tell you what I think, young lady.' She gets up

and, placing the empty mugs on the draining board, turns to the telephone. She lifts the receiver and says as she dials, 'I think that the so-called "talking cure" has turned into a talking disease, that's what I think. Furthermore, I think that given the way things stand this is a fortuitous moment for us to end our relationship too. After all, we may as well make a clean sweep of it . . . Oh, hello. I'd like a cab, please. From 27 Argyll Road . . . Going to . . . Hold on a sec – ' She turns to me and asks with peculiar emphasis, 'Do you know where you're going to?'

ALSO AVAILABLE BY WILL SELF

THE QUANTITY THEORY OF INSANITY

'He writes like a devil'
MAIL ON SUNDAY

This is the sparkling debut with which Will Self burst onto the literary scene. In it, we discover a superhumanly dull tribe of Amazonians, the terrible, seductive secret of Ward 9 and why you are right to think that London is full of dead people. Full of his trademark jagged-edge satire and dark wit, this short-story collection is acerbic, hilarious and, most of all, utterly unique in its imaginative vision.

'Very funny and very good, with that unmistakable sign of the genuine comic writer's absurdity that unfurls logically from absurdity, but always as a mirror of what we are living in – and wish we didn't'
DORIS LESSING

THE BUTT

'Self writes here with an adroit impersonation of coarse exuberance that makes *The Butt* as readable as a blokeish airport novel ... Ingenious'
SUNDAY TELEGRAPH

When Tom Brodzinski finally decides to give up smoking during a family holiday in a weird, unnamed land, a moment's inattention becomes his undoing. Flipping the butt of his last cigarette off the balcony of the holiday apartment, it lands on the head of the elderly Reggie Lincoln, and burns him. Despite Brodzinski's liberal attitudes and good intentions, the local authorities treat his action as an assault. Soon the full weight of the courts and tribal custom is brought to bear. What follows is a journey through a fantastically distorted world, a country that is part Australia, part Iraq and entirely the heart of distinctively modern darkness.

'*The Butt* is Self's most gripping and disturbing novel in years'
HARPER'S BAZAAR

B L O O M S B U R Y

MY IDEA OF FUN

'This is a brilliant first novel, obscene, funny, opulently written, and, of course, agonisingly moral'
OBSERVER

Ian Wharton is having devilish and murderous thoughts, courtesy of the influence of Mr Broadhurst – companion, confidant and the manifestation of Ian's mental illness – who is now apparently being carried around in his wife's womb. How he got there isn't important (though Dr Gyggle, Ian's psychiatrist, might disagree), but what he wants from Ian certainly is...

'No one else I can think of writes about contemporary Britain with such élan, energy and witty intelligence. Rejoice'
NICHOLAS LEZARD, GUARDIAN

WALKING TO HOLLYWOOD

'Apocalyptic humour and fizzing contempt'
Guardian

Obsessive, satirical and elegiac, in *Walking to Hollywood* Will Self burrows through the intersections of time, place and psyche to explore some of our deepest fears and anxieties with characteristic fearlessness and jagged humour, pushing memoir to the limits of invention.

'Extremely funny ... quintessentially Selfish – dazzling'
Times Literary Supplement

BLOOMSBURY

GREAT APES

'A brick dropped into the stagnant pond of contemporary English prose'
NEW STATESMAN

When Simon Dykes wakes one morning, he discovers that his girlfriend has turned into a chimpanzee. And, to his horror, so has the rest of humanity. His bizarre delusion that he is 'human' brings Simon to the attention of eminent psychologist (and chimp), Dr Zack Busner. For, with this fascinating case, Busner thinks he may finally make his reputation as a truly great ape.

'Exultantly hallucinogenic ... achieves the rare feat of temporarily altering the reader's perspective'
GUARDIAN

COCK & BULL

'Imagine a film of Kafka's *Metamorphosis* scripted by William Burroughs and shot by David Cronenberg ... pure delight to verbal perverts everywhere'
SUNDAY TIMES

In *Cock: A Novelette*, Carol is dissatisfied with her sex life, and her effete husband's drinking problem is not helping. Then, one evening while he is out, Carol discovers something unexpected about herself. Then there is *Bull: A Farce*. John Bull is a man's man: A sports writer, a rugby player, a drinker. But he's about to wake up to something of an anatomical surprise...

'Mordant, acute ... exquisitely cunning ... the funniest book about late onset hermaphroditism you'll read all year'
INDEPENDENT

B L O O M S B U R Y

THE SWEET SMELL OF PSYCHOSIS

'A tour de force'
TIME OUT

Thrust into the seedy underworld of hack reporters and Soho drinking dens, young Richard Hermes is skidding down a cocaine slope of self-destruction in pursuit of the impossibly beautiful socialite-cum-columnist Ursula Bentley. But between Richard and his object of desire stands his omnipresent nemesis, the lubricious Bell, doyen of late night radio shows, provider of drugs and gossip, and ringmaster of the Sealink Club. Erudite and witty as ever, this hilarious novella is vintage Self at his acerbic, incisive best, brilliantly illustrated by Martin Rowson's sharp, dark, satirical pen.

'Self is the master of the art of a telling sentence'
OBSERVER

JUNK MAIL

'An explosive collection'
J.G. BALLARD, GUARDIAN

Martin Amis, William Burroughs and Damien Hirst; East End crack dens, cocaine and hallucinogens; English culture, satanic abuse and severed heads in liquid nitrogen. Punctuated by his other-worldly cartoons, *Junk Mail* is a Self-selection of his most brilliant essays; an innovative and irreverent trawl through a landscape of drugs, literature, politics, art and motorways.

'Locking antlers with his personal gods of British fiction, we finally get the undivided Self in all his maddening brilliance'
SPECTATOR
